SKADI'S TIME: ANSUZ

John Samuel MacKay

BOOK ONE

First paperback edition November 2022

Book design by Thea Magerand
Map by Thea Magerand

ISBN 978-1-7782-9910-0 (paperback)
ISBN 978-1-7782-9911-7 (ebook)

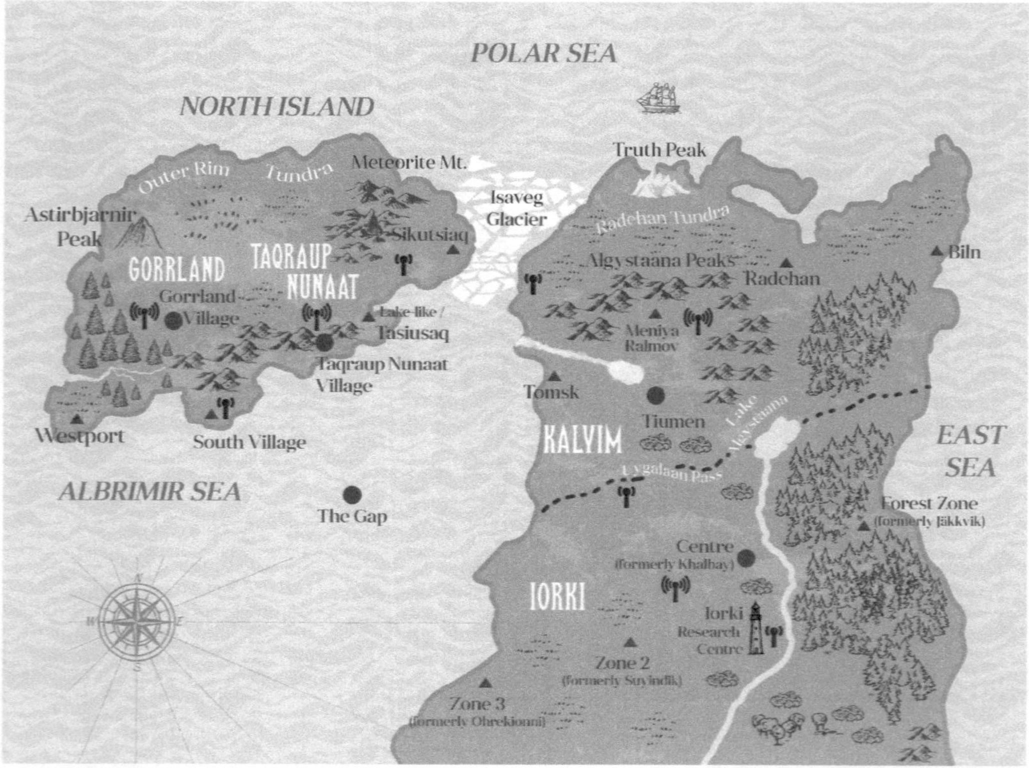

POLAR SEA
NORTH ISLAND
Truth Peak
Meteorite Mt.
Outer Rim
Tundra
Isaveg Glacier
Astirbjarnir Peak
Radehan Tundra
Sikutsiaq
Algystaana Peaks
Biln
GORRLAND
TAQRAUP NUNAAT
Radchan
Gorrland Village
Lake-like /
Meniya Ralmov
Tasiusaq
Taqraup Nunaat Village
Tomsk
Tiumen
Lake Alaystaana
KALVIM
EAST SEA
Westport
South Village
Uygalaan Pass
ALBRIMIR SEA
The Gap
Forest Zone (formerly Jäkkvik)
Centre (formerly Khalhay)
IORKI
Iorki Research Centre
Zone 2 (formerly Suyindik)
Zone 3 (formerly Ohrekioani)
N
E
S
W

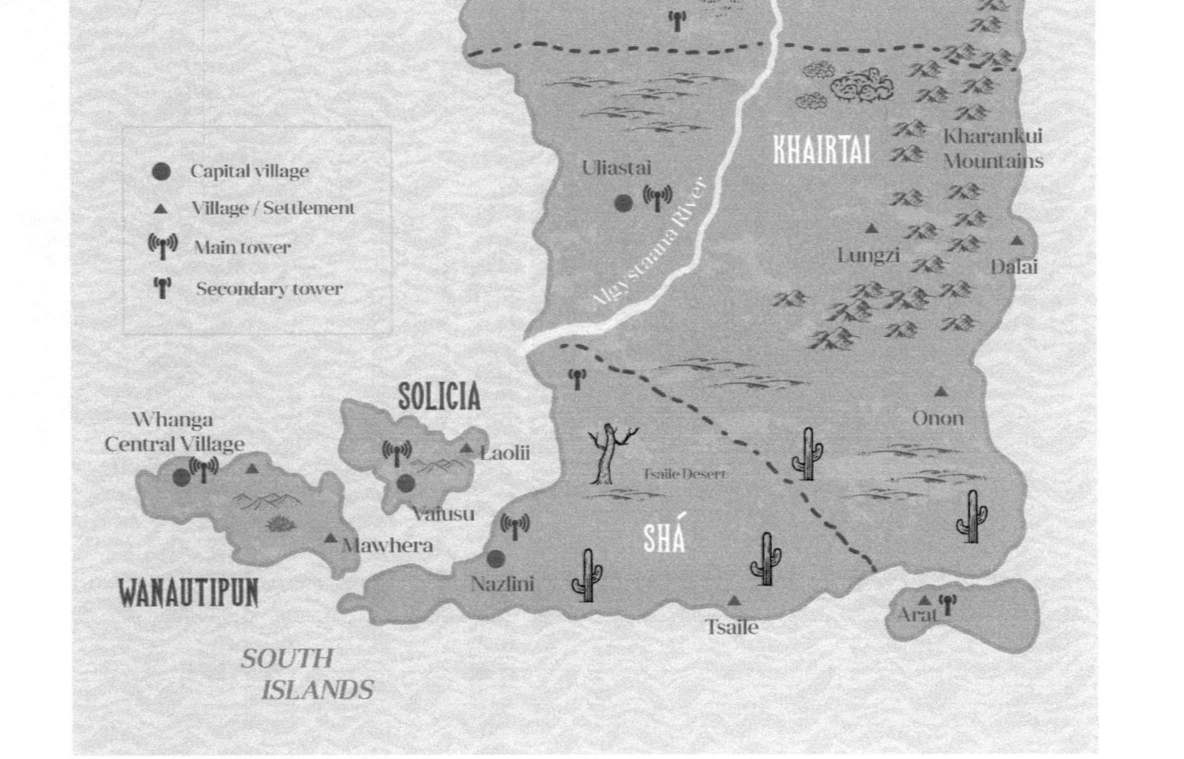

Capital village
Village / Settlement
Main tower
Secondary tower
KHAIRTAI
Kharankui Mountains
Uliastai
Algystaana River
Lungzi
Dalai
Onon
SOLICIA
Whanga Central Village
Laolii
Tsaile Desert
Vaiusu
SHÁ
Mawhera
Nazlini
Tsaile
Arat
WANAUTIPUN
SOUTH ISLANDS

Author's Note

First of all, I thank you for trusting me enough to purchase this book. I will share a few words, here and now, before your reading experience begins, in the hopes that they will make it (at least slightly) clearer...

I am currently a graduate student of anthropology. As such, I am accustomed to observing, describing and presenting aspects of cultures, and the subtle and not-so-subtle differences between them. While it is true that these observations, descriptions and presentations are usually located in the real world rather than a fantasy world, it is also true that they require a great deal of representation. Representation is no stranger to the imagination. In the pursuit of studies of real-world cultures, in my experience at least, more imaginary representations have been activated than many would like to admit. Anthropological work has given me many an idea for potential stories, each one needing and producing a representation of the world in which it is to take place. Such a representation may be closer to, or farther from, the reality of the lived-in "real" world. Yet regardless of the proximity to the latter, a story always involves a representation, making use of an individual "imaginary" world, located in the consciousness of the represanter, though conditioned by many things all-too real.

Ansuz is the first instalment in a three-book series, *Skadi's Time*. The series takes place on the fictional planet of Albrimir. It will, however, be clear to many readers that the worlds in this book are greatly inspired by real cultures and societies on planet Earth. Two of these societies' interactions are particularly central to *Ansuz*. While the identity of these real-world cultures will be rather clear due to certain names, language, lore, and landscapes, their interactions take place in a world that is indeed an imaginary reality. It is rather far removed from the real world, though by no means as far as it could be. Real lore is included amid elements that emerge purely from my imagination. The fantastical elements of the story will be enough for the reader to brush aside any creeping thoughts about similar interactions taking place now, or having at one point taken place somewhere in "real world" planet Earth. But perhaps they are not enough to stop the thoughts-that-need-brushing-off from creeping in altogether.

Such is fine. Actually, if such happens, that will have meant *Skadi's Time* has succeeded in a modest goal: placing an imaginary representation somewhere out there (anywhere!) within the conceivable reaches and corners of the shared "real" world. *Ansuz* and its themes may yet be happening in my head and also in the real world (somewhere!), past, present, or future. It is a potential worth considering...

John Samuel MacKay

Prologue
The Order of the Communicators

The blasts from the Gap destroyed all of Meniyan civilization, from the City to the Temple. The Eight Shishilms of the Council, still inside the Temple, resisted bravely but were forced to flee when the force was too strong. They scattered, each one bringing their own crystal to receive and transmit the Cosmic Dust.

Unbeknownst to the Shishilms, however, the reason for the intense Dust blasts in the first place was because the High One, Master of the Flares, was calling out to the Exiled Woman, the ninth Shishilm, who had been removed from the Council several years prior by the other Eight. The Flares needed her to usher in a new level of consciousness. With her now gone, the remaining Eight could not resist the blasts, and so the Temple fell. Each of the Eight buried their crystal in a spot on the planet and perished. The Exiled Woman, however, never died but wandered the planet, making periodic use of her crystal.

A little more than 350 years after the Fall of Meniya, a man on North Island discovered a buried crystal. He played with it but soon noticed that its weight changed, depending on how he held it. He seemed to be able to push energy out of it at times and, at other times, to receive energy in it, which made the boulder-sized crystal extra heavy.

The man was obsessed with the crystal, and he never put it down. One day, he discovered that a push with a particular rotation not only made the crystal lose nearly all of its weight, but that the removed weight could also be felt and seen as an energy field drifting away. This energy field could carry audio and visual perceptions from where it was emitted.

The man kept the crystal in his tent and snow house, never tiring of playing with it. One day, though, something remarkable happened. He received a return energy signal. It carried the voice of *a woman who spoke a language he didn't understand. He replied as best he could, and a "conversation" went on for a week. Then, a third signal replied! After one month had passed, eight clear signals were in contact with each other via energy field, generating clear messages that were both visual and audio. Of course, with no one understanding each others' language, communication was complicated. So, the eight people transmitting and receiving spent two years developing their own language, whereby they could understand each other. They learned the location of one another, and they gave names to each Land of the known planet. They called themselves the Communicators of Albrimir.*

The Eight Communicators were from different Folks, and they shared information about their cultures and learned a great deal. But knowledge of Great Meniya was lost, save for occasional images that were sent from a source external to the Eight. At times, they saw fiery destruction. At times, they saw the Flares engulf the throne room. Then one day, there came the image of a woman walking away, abandoned and alone, forsaken. Once this image was seen, there was a period in which all signals stopped. The crystals' power was diminished. It only came back once the Communicator from the Land known as Kalyim, unknowingly the closest to Ancient Meniya, brought the crystal to a high peak. There, this man spoke to all seven other Lands. He accidentally received a signal from a woman. She was very old but of timeless beauty. She roamed the worlds, unable to set herself down again among gods or men…

Kalyim's Communicator shared this image to the others, and it was convened that they would try to contact the wandering woman. All at once, they would direct their energies towards where they had previously received her signal. Their attempt was successful, and they saw this untamed female trudging over differing terrains wearing animal pelts. They saw that she had left an ancient temple, and that soon after she'd left, the Temple was besieged by the blasts of the Dust, destroying the old world, and burying its secrets in distant corners. They saw that she, the exiled, lived on, while the Eight who had exiled her, had all perished. Her departure and the Temple's destruction were inextricably linked. The Temple had been the product of a great civilization that was lost. This vision would be compared to oral narratives in all Eight Lands, which all involved mighty blasts of blinding Dust-light that were spewed by a force to which they gave the name "The Flares" in their new Albrimese language.

The Wandering Woman, however, was not pleased that the Council of Eight Communicators had contacted her, for the previous Eight Shishilms of Meniya had wantonly expelled her in times before destruction. So, she showed herself to them all, revealing her beautiful face and her naked body, and speaking to them directly in their new language.

"This is how they once saw me, and then their view of me changed. As such, you will see me now as they came to think I was!"

And with that, she transformed into a hideous monster before their eyes, then took her own crystal in her hands and shattered it against the mountain.

From that point on, all vision in communication was removed. People could only hear each other through the thinnest voice mixed with fuzz. Towers were built so as to increase the strength of the crystals by giving them altitude. No visions returned. In destroying her crystal, the Exiled Woman severed her last link with the Crystals of Meniya. No one would again speak with clarity and vision because no one had seen her or her visions. But the shards of crystals that were smashed on the mountain drifted in many locations, still retaining some of their unique abilities. The gifts they held were there, though not exerting as strong a pull in the world as when the crystal was intact. Still, as Communicators' practices generalized and were centralized in Towers, signals of varying degrees came in from outside the known world. For several decades talk remained of a Ninth Tower, but this disappeared by the year 450, with figures of a type of wandering female limited to various local mythologies.

The Communicators put their efforts to technology. They learned to split crystals to make smaller communicating devices that responded to the large ones. These devices changed over the years to become the radios they are today. The Communicators also discovered that the crystals could use Dust as energy for light and power. Mechanical divisions of Communicators were created to develop these properties. This progress took place gradually over five hundred years, but really took off in the last sixty, while modern radios have been in existence for the past century. Crystal-augmenting techniques could be used to add Dust strength to existing tools like swords or harpoons and to create thrust and therefore fuel for engines. Some Dust lamps were made using the crystal. It is the crystal that attracts the Dust and uses the Dust to create action.

Today, as technology has progressed, the lore, language, and culture of the Communicators is passed down and recorded into writing. Knowledge of the existence of a Council of Meniya, with eight Shishilms was passed on. In Communicators' esotericism, the modern Towers are considered the heirs to the Shishilms. Knowledge and fear of the Flares' blasts have been passed on, though it is acknowledged that the Flares are made of Cosmic Dust, a force as much creative as it is destructive. The Communicators came to be a body of Albrimir knowledge. This body exists in parallel with each local Land's knowledge and wisdom keepers. Both co-exist harmoniously for the most part. It must be said that among the Communicators, no knowledge has remained concerning the Exiled Woman. She and vision-communication practices were forgotten, as she herself had wished. All that remained were legends in local lore, quite different from one another, but containing some element of truth. And there were the occasional communications from the outside, which led Communicators to speculate that there were crystals outside the Eight Towers.

In the search for the World Beyond, attention was given to outer space, and in the year 948, a signal came from another planet. However, while the Eight Towers can receive alien transmission on their frequencies, every time they do, the receiving crystals move in a strange and peculiar way. The only possible explanation for this movement is that there is another crystal of equal or superior strength acting from within Albrimir upon the others.

This "crystal," which acted upon others during broadcasts from outside Albrimir, along with the local lore of the Wandering Woman, were all that remained of she who was the source of vision-communication, she who was the reason behind Meniya's fall.

It must be said that the Wandering Woman's vow to cut human ties was not categorical. After she smashed her crystal, she picked up one of its shards to keep in her back pocket and took off for a spot deep in the most distant mountains of the known world.

"I will communicate on occasion with this mini-crystal shard. If ever any human is sensitive enough to receive my communications from it and if ever any human is then able to seek me out and find me, then I will return and share my gifts and my magic."

But these conditions were not impossible conditions for the Master of the Flares. For as long as she was still out there, he vowed to call out to her until she returned. She would return when humans were ready for her. He would do all in his power to make them ready.

That is where the world stands in this year 963. The above-mentioned story of the exiled Wandering Woman, the Flares, and the Crystal, is known only in fragments, as part of the lore of different Lands.

Chapter 1
Lands' Visions

On the Tenth of Fifteenmonth, in the year 963 of the Modern Era

Mikkjal

The orders were clear. It was now Skadi's Time. Sigfather had his chosen ones in every Land, touched by his powerful Dust. Representatives from all Eight Lands must go to Ancient Meniya, but not alone. They must also seek out the magic of the great-huntress-who-still-lives. Skadi must join them in the temple, so that Sigfather's energy may combine with Skadi's magic to usher in a new era.

If they didn't succeed, a strife like no other would befall Albrimir. War and tyranny would take over.

Sigfather's words were supported by the Oracle and the spirit of the late Bjorn. Mikkjal and Kolfinna were given twin rune staves, their journeys inscribed by Sigfather, intertwined in this mission to Meniya. Sigfather and Skadi for evolution. Or else Sigfather and Sigfather for destruction…

Mikkjal took a sip from his pitcher of cold ale. How he would go about convening the Eight plus Skadi he did not know. Neither he nor Kolfinna were even Skadisfolk but Westfolkers. That must be Sigfather's point—the uninitiated must seek Skadi out. Cold ale in his throat let him, if only for a second, ignore both his thoughts and his loud mates. Kjartan, Ginnar, and Iafri were sharing jokes at the table, while Astrid silently puffed her pipe and listened to the fiddle music that filled the tavern.

Eight days had passed since the Solidarity Reaffirmation and Sigfather's revelations at the Gap. The Guides and everyone else were trying to get back to a normal life. Mikkjal had to admit that everything appeared rather normal on the outside, despite the event that so recently uprooted all his beliefs. Nothing would be normal for him, though. Mikkjal bore several reminders of his fall into the Gap, a fall from which none had been thought able to return. He still had the two red dots on his left hand. He still had his birch staff at home, now complete with engraved runes from Sigfather to enshrine his quest. And most significantly, he still had Kolfinna.

Kolfinna Helensdottir was as far from a boring woman as humanly possible. In the time since their return, she regularly gave herself passionately in bed and accompanied Mikkjal on intense snowmobile rides. Yet the girl always maintained an element of mystery and seriousness no matter what she was saying or doing. She knew things that few understood, the byproduct of being a Storyteller's daughter no doubt. Mikkjal couldn't decide how he felt about being paired with her, not merely as a part-time lover but in a cosmic alliance wherein each was bound to one another and to Sigfather. Physically, their union was off to a great start. Yet it would take more time for him to understand her mind, if he ever could.

"Mikkjal!" Kjartan shook his mate out of his thoughtful stupor. "Toast time." He turned to see the impressively-bearded ginger man. But it wasn't Kjartan's toast. Astrid was leaning in with her pitcher, her mood rather celebratory ever since they finished the hunt and made way for the tavern.

"Tonight we make it official. No tiptoeing around. Iafri, Ginnar, and Kjartan shack up with Rikey. And Mikkjal and Kolfinna weather the storm of public approval!" The Chieftain gave Mikkjal a wink after she spoke. "You'd think that would come easier to them than flying through the Gap, but then again not everyone is Aldisson and Helensdottir." All five raised their clay goblets and toasted heartily.

As if on cue, the band struck up a new, lively piece, and some tavern-goers got up from their tables to dance. With the new beat, Iafri was inspired, standing to give his version of a toast. "To a completed two-thirds of winter. A month and a half till the snow melts!" Again the five Guides raised their goblets.

"To spring rebirth and new families!" Astrid replied. "To the lucky ladies! Long live Rikey Sifsdottir and Kolfinna Helensdottir!"

Everyone cheered. Kjartan roared so loud that even the fiddlers turned their heads. The lad was a friend for the ages.

"Dance, dance, Kjartan. Tonight the ale flows plenty!" continued Astrid.

Even the head of the Guides was in a less preoccupied mood than Mikkjal, whose senses today had failed him. He didn't pick up on a bear their hunting party was chasing this afternoon. No thanks to him, the Hunters did eventually spot the beast and haul it in. Astrid insisted that the group go straight to the tavern after dropping the carcass off with Jann the Butcher. But she had certainly sensed Mikkjal's ungroundedness on the hunt, reminding him, as the snowmobiles revved up for the return to town, that he was the boss of himself, no matter what Kolfinna, Sigfather, or the Oracle said.

On the stage people, including Kjartan, held hands and formed two parallel circles to spin around the fiddlers Sigurd and Helen, while folks at tables and the bar clapped their hands. Mikkjal and Iafri looked at each other as the latter was getting up to join the dancing.

"Looks like people stopped fixating on that big secret, eh, Mikkjal? You know, the Oracle's rantings about the plot to see Skadi return?" The lad with the ever-youthful face laughed fully.

Mikkjal nodded. *But I haven't stopped,* he thought to himself. Astrid leaned over, having overheard the two. "Lads, I have something to say about big secrets. One more thing I have to say tonight before you go your merry way. Forgive my language, but fuck big secrets!"

"Boss?!" Ginnar cackled.

"What, Ginnar? Dust master Sigfather tells us he's been calling us for years, that everything happened so that we might be called to this big war that's coming. The truth's out. Either we can't handle it and we fall back into conflict between Westfolk and Mountainers, Njordsfolk against Skadisfolk, a miserable and everlasting divorce, or else we grow. I'm for growing!"

Fiddlers and singers played louder than ever, and the clapping made any conversation almost impossible. It wasn't necessary to talk, though. Astrid's surprising humour and the music contributed to the lightening of the mood for Mikkjal's mates and wasn't without impact on Mikkjal himself. A group of warriors entered the tavern and were summoned to jump and clap their hands before they even made it to the bar. The next who entered was a familiar old face, who somehow spotted Mikkjal in the crowd and walked over to the table where he and Iafri had sat back down while Astrid still stood.

"My hero!" Magar shouted, putting his arm around Mikkjal's neck. "Give me a taste of your brew!" The old man, who of course still wore his orange jumpsuit, grabbed the mug of ale out of Mikkjal's hand and took a big gulp.

Astrid turned to the new arrival. "You'll address him as 'sir,' good fool," she said with straight eyes that, for a second, appeared to throw the oldster off guard. But once she saw him hesitate she patted his shoulder with fierce joy. "If it weren't for you, Aibmu would now be dead. Cheers to the sir who helped save my son!" She held out her goblet and toasted Magar, who chugged down more of Mikkjal's brew. "The orange legend!" she exclaimed.

"A compliment from one legend to another." Magar patted Astrid's shoulder.

"Enough, old man! Before the winter's over, we may be dead legends still. I'm for drinking till the next battle!"

Nodding a gentle fist into Astrid's shoulder, Magar replied with a mischievous smile, "No battles, only adventures! That's the way you have to see it!"

At the table Iafri addressed Mikkjal's distractions. "What's on your mind, mate? I mean, other than the Gap journey and Kolfinna."

Mikkjal sighed and looked intently for another subject that would provide suitable conversation. "I miss summertime. Fishing, sailing, driving in the mud!"

"Here's to twenty-three summers of life!" Ginnar lifted his glass with his thick arms. "And damn it, no one will get in my way, not even Sigfather." He smiled with his intense blue eyes.

"Yes, let's liven it up!" the muscular Guide continued. "Tell us about what it's like in bed with Kolfinna."

"Oh, I bet he's got stories to tell there!" Iafri jumped in, bearing a giant smile from his brown beard. And as if called over from the dance floor by the conversation, Kjartan's red beard was there, rubbing against Mikkjal's shoulder. Back to the table just in time. *Embarrassing moment to come...*

"Really rapacious and ravenous I bet," cackled Kjartan as he turned around and toasted his pint against Mikkjal's head, swaying his shoulder-length hair. "You got what we all wanted as teens, little lad."

"What we wanted but couldn't have," said Ginnar with a nod, his short-cut blond head a complement to Kjartan's mane.

"Oh yeah, she was weird," chuckled Kjartan, a few years senior to the other three. "But who wants a boring life?" he asked with a wink as he took a seat beside Mikkjal. The ginger took a break from dancing to amuse the serious Gap traveller. Astrid had made her way to the bar, leaving Magar standing to tell his stories to anyone and everyone he could oblige to listen.

"Iafri, Ginnar, Mikkjal," Kjartan started, "I have something to confess."

"Watch what this fool has to say this time," laughed Ginnar.

"That time during your training when we walked along the coast from South Village to Westport… when I met you guys in the dingy on the second day of the excursion? Well, I was supposed to give you a motivational speech on the first day but I was too drunk to get out of bed. Woke up in the arms of a most delightful lover, too—a daughter of one of the former Wild Women. Anyway, you got no speech because of me, and for that I'm sorry."

Mikkjal couldn't help but burst into laughter, along with the other Guides. Iafri almost spat out his ale. "Wait, it wasn't planned for you to meet us on the second day?" Mikkjal asked.

"No way. Astrid had it all planned out, the speech and all."

"What happened?"

"Well, she was pissed, I can tell you that. She had me sleep alone in a cave the night I finally arrived. Then she let it go and went on as if nothing had happened."

"Wow, I never would've known," said Iafri, looking at the others. "You acted so professional!"

"I was professional because I was so proud of myself. You don't know female company until you've been with a Wild Woman."

"*Daughter* of Wild Women, Kjartan. Don't get ahead of yourself. You don't know the era of the actual Wild Women." Ginnar's bald head gleamed light off its dome. "Otherwise, you'd have gotten torn to shreds!"

"Yeah, yeah, you get what I mean. I'm sorry to have let you down, brothers, but I can see that you've become excellent Guides, nonetheless. It would be an honour to go on a camping and fishing trip with you this summer."

"Hear! Hear!" shouted Iafri, raising his glass and inviting all to follow suit.

Then a familiar female voice chimed in. "Not if I have any objections." Rikey's long, dark hair would have given away her presence from afar, but she'd snuck in between the dancers to approach the tables. "Don't forget I can be wild, too!"

"Our dear!" the three Guides raised their glasses to their wife-to-be, who sat down among them.

"I'm sorry you won't be joining us, Mikkjal," Rikey spoke, intentionally seducing him her eyes as she removed her coat. "I would have enjoyed wedding you, too. But I'm sure you will make Kolfinna happy." She gave a kiss in Mikkjal's direction and winked playfully. The three Guides and their betrothed all burst out laughing.

"He doesn't know what he's missing," chuckled Kjartan. "But then again, think about it. A Guide who's really serious, only focused on guiding and leading, and a girl who's *out there*, speaking to real and imagined mad folk. They're made for each other!" All laughed while Mikkjal looked away. She was strange but originally beautiful, Kolfinna. Following her meant a unique path, one whose uniqueness shined strong as Mikkjal observed the familiarly seductive Rikey. Kjartan was wrong. Mikkjal knew exactly what he was missing, and he was not sure he actually wanted to miss it. A Guide household with good mates and an earthy woman was always how he had seen his settling-down.

He lifted his glass to toast Rikey, then got up to walk over to the dimly lit bar to refill his ale mug. There, a group of five or so Guards were playfully dancing, clapping, and shoving each other. As Mikkjal came near, two of these warriors stopped to pat him on the back, a wearying side effect of suddenly becoming known by everyone. Eyeing Amber the energetic bartender, he lifted his mug to ask for a refill. The girl gladly did so with a smile.

Astrid was standing against the far wall next to a mounted lantern, where she was smoking her pipe and chatting with an obscure figure that was most likely Richard. Seeing Astrid's part-time lover made him ponder whether he wanted to see Kolfinna tonight. Perhaps he did, but only if she truly wanted to see him and only if they could avoid the topic of Sigfather's quest. If Kolfinna could be present and at ease in the energy of that evening at the tavern with his mates, it would be perfect. It would be perfect but it would never happen. He shook his head, grabbed his neck and looked back at the bar.

Amber handed Mikkjal the clay goblet filled to the brim, but emphatically shook her head when he took bear teeth from his pocket to pay for it. "All was paid for by Astrid. The only thing you need to worry about is drinking. Have fun!" Amber winked. Yet just as he grabbed the ale and was about to go back to the table, his left hand pierced his stillness, becoming gripped by the red dots and sending short bursts of agony. In the shock, he dropped his mug, spilling the ale on his feet and the floor.

That wasn't all. With folks at the bar now looking over, Mikkjal noticed a thick cloud of Dust pulsating in and out of his hand, seething the skin and hazing the room. *The Call returns.* He took a step back but was beaten by the wooden tavern door bursting open with a frantic boom. A high-pitched shriek shattered the air and brought the whole room to silence. No more music played, and the scream repeated, louder still. Mikkjal's hand scorched, with the cloud of white Dust emanating all around him—an engulfing swarm of bright, odourless smoke and fire intertwined as one. The scream repeated and everyone got to their feet. They could see very little, as the Dust was already beginning to cloud the tavern air. Three screeches were all that would ring. As the hell bell turned off, Kolfinna thrust herself into the alehouse, where she fell to her knees not far from the bar. Mikkjal made out her bright blond mane in the midst of the white cloud of Dust that surrounded and penetrated her as much as him.

"Kolfinna!" Mikkjal shouted. The girl was shivering and speaking to herself incoherently amidst the white cloud. He sifted through the airy white grime to kneel next to her and place his hand on her shoulder. He sensed Astrid approaching from the other direction.

"What's happening, Kolfinna?" Mikkjal shook her arm.

"*Joooorg! … War!*" she screamed in such an unrestrained cry that the walls shook.
Mikkjal grabbed his left hand, agonizing from her beastly shout.

Unaware, he had stood back up to retreat from such force. Kolfinna continued, "*Sigfod!… Jackrabbit rider!… Mik-Mik—*"

"I'm here," Mikkjal replied, kneeling again.

"*Mik-Mikhail Joooorgsoon!*" With this cry she shook her partner on the inside. She wasn't calling him. She was evoking someone else. But her evocation was coming from some*where* else. Mikkjal looked to Astrid, behind him, who stared at Kolfinna, her face showing her to be equally bewildered and frightened.

"Who?" Mikkjal asked.

"*Mik-Mik-Mikhail!*" she shouted again. As she bellowed her fingers clawed at her neck beneath her green jacket. This time Mikkjal resisted the urge to recoil from her despairing animalistic howls.

"Mikhail Jorgson, the leader of the Land of Jorg," came a female voice from the tavern door. It was Communicator Chieftain Marja, standing tall and grave-faced as she walked through the Dust cloud with another male Communicator. Once he saw who it was, Mikkjal stood back up at attention. The Chieftain walked stern-faced toward him and Astrid. "She's had a vision this evening in the Tower and has been like this ever since, accompanied by the Dust and everything. I've worked with her for years but have never seen her like this. It's almost like something else was speaking through her."

"What does she say about Mikhail Jorgson?" Astrid asked, alert.

Marja, standing close to Astrid to be seen in the white veil, looked down at her shaking work disciple. "She says she saw Mikhail of Jorg attack all Lands of Albrimir in the same manner as Sigfather—with Dust from the Gap. Only Jorgson destroyed all the Communications Towers and recovered the Towers' crystals for himself. She sees Jorgson waging war on Albrimir and controlling crystal communication. Yet she claims to have spoken without radio, by means of Sigfather's Dust, with a woman from the Land of Jorg. By these means, she says she knows of the Land's leader's actions."

Mikkjal let the Chieftains speak, but hearing of Kolfinna's vision immediately reminded him of the one against whom Sigfather had warned them in the Gap. *A man exactly as you expected me to be. A man of the Dust who selects his own and slaughters the rest. Without Skadi's magic, he is all that Albrimir shall receive of my power.* This man from Jorg was him. Sigfather as they had expected Sigfather to be, but far worse.

"Is there any news that leads you to believe that this is true?" Astrid asked the leader of the Communicators.

Marja sighed. "Jorg's Communicators have been acting rather strange of late. They listened intently to Kolfinna's narration of her journey to the Gap at first, and now they refuse to talk to us for reasons we don't comprehend. But we must be cautious before leaping to any conclusions. And we in the Tower possess no technology to communicate in the way Kolfinna says she now can. These are spirit matters, Astrid."

Astrid nodded. On the floor Kolfinna was shaking but no longer shouted. The Guide leader motioned for Mikkjal to kneel with her and lift Helensdottir up. As they lifted her, Mikkjal saw that the white cloud emerged from her right hand, but also from the four-pointed circle necklace Bjorn had given her in the Gap. The pulses were painful in the skin and hand's nerves, while the stagnating Dust gave the feeling of a continual painless burn. They supported her and walked her over to the nearest table. Kolfinna, calmer, looked at Mikkjal then blew on her hand in his direction. In the floating Dust, he caught a glimpse of a city, with many buildings, and then of very high mountains.

She can share visions through Sigfather's Dust?!

Mikkjal and Astrid sat down next to her. "What did you just do, Kolfinna?" he asked.

"Showed you something," the girl answered, shaking. "If I can talk to you like this, so can I talk to Lia."

"Lia?"

"Lia Jackrabbit," Kolfinna answered, looking at Mikkjal with calming eyes.

"The woman from Jorg she says she spoke to," added Marja, squinting in the cloudy air as she approached.

"Lia is Sigfather's Chosen from Jorg. Jorgson tried to kill her. She fled to Torvall."

"Kolfinna, I radioed Torvall," Marja tried to reassure her. "They'll let us know if this indeed happened."

"I know," Kolfinna sighed. Her energy was now spent and the Dust clouds were slowly beginning to fade away. She leaned her head against Mikkjal. "Sorry you saw me that way."

Was that really you I saw? Mikkjal thought. Though he grabbed her hand and stroked her long blond hair, his body still shook inwardly with the shockwave of her mighty output.

The cloud of white soot nearly gone, Astrid stood up and took her place beside Marja. "Kolfinna, I somehow believe you, though I can't explain why," spoke the Guide Chieftain. "You speak from some place that is somehow frightening yet familiar, and so I believe you. We must discuss further at some point."

Kolfinna looked at Astrid and gave a slight bow of the neck. "Thank you."

Mikkjal knew the vision was somehow true as well, for it fit so clearly with Sigfather's warning about who was coming. He could, of course, offer no advice, counsel, insight, or spiritual visions of his own. He could suggest no precise course of action to take.

"How do you communicate with this woman, Kolfinna?" asked Marja, now somewhat less tense.

"I don't know. I mean, I can control it but I also can't control it. I see visions—a brown woman riding across the plains. A rider. Her hair is dark. She has dots on her hand like me. Then I move my hand and I see more. She sees me. She and I speak *through the Dust*. It only works sometimes."

"And what you saw, you saw it clearly?" Marja asked.

She answered strongly. "Lia of Jackrabbit Clan in Jorg. She is fighting against he who will be enemy to all." Astrid took a deep breath and gave a glance both satisfied and worried at Marja and Mikkjal.

"Urgent decisions must be made at tomorrow's assembly," the Guide Chieftain spoke. "Hopefully, we'll get news from Torvall by then."

Just then, an unexpected figure appeared from nowhere and walked up next to Astrid and Marja. "Indeed, Chieftains. But Helensdottir has shown that she has intuitive knowledge of a form of communication that is both new and ancient. It is the Spell of Ansuz, a tool that can ensure victory." The voice came from a man beneath a dark cloak, who now stood over them. "Her skills surpass mine and her father's." The man pulled back the hood to reveal Eirà the Mountaineer Storyteller's thin and chiselled face, breathing out a raw and frightening aura.

Everyone's breath lay still, choking on the frightful change to the energetic space the dark man instilled. "Those are legends, Eirà. We don't know what we don't know. Communicators' knowledge all over Albrimir is only spotty on what you evoke."

"Correct, Marja," Eirà replied calmly. "You don't know and I don't know. But it is increasingly clear that Kolfinna knows…"

A shiver went up Mikkjal's spine at his words. Astrid must have been sensing the malaise as well because she spoke rather quickly, as if to satisfy the man so he would leave. "*All* things will be discussed tomorrow at the assembly, including magic if need be. Let us hope by then there is news from the Tower."

"Of course," replied Eirà, nodding politely. "But the magic we speak of is already in action. Ansuz is the key."

Marja was stiff. It wasn't the first time she had heard that word. The Mountaineer magician then smiled and turned to walk out of the room in silence. Kolfinna shivered again and Mikkjal again stroked her hair. All in the tavern were deep in thought. There would be no more music that night. Mikkjal looked across the room at his Guide mates. They and he were beginning to belong to two different worlds.

Chapter 2
Passing the Flame

On the Eleventh of Fifteenmonth, 963 of the Modern Era

Kolfinna

Marja was already in tears the moment she arrived at Kolfinna's cabin. She had to deliver news Kolfinna already knew. Last night at the Tower and tavern hadn't been some random vision but a sign of events to come, the first of which had now transpired. Mikhail Jorgson made an announcement on the all-Albrimir frequency today saying that Jorg would invade Torvall unless it returned the sorceress Lia of Jackrabbit Clan and her conspirators. These Jorgians had sought refuge in Torvall to the north. Lia was Jorgson's enemy because she spoke with Kolfinna. Kolfinna was Jorgson's enemy because of her ability to communicate with the Dust. Sigfather's Chosen threatened Mikhail Jorgson.

The world was on the cusp of war for the first time in more than a generation. Only this time the stakes were of cosmic proportions. Jorgson's rule would end everything that made each Land unique, even his own.

Eight days ago, Marja accepted Sigfather's revelations at the Gap about Skadi's Time beginning and the balance of life energy on the planet shifting. The winds, the climate, and the animals had been growing wilder and more unpredictable for years now. As a woman of Mountaineer origin, the shift did not threaten her position or her family. Yet, she adamantly opposed Eirà's notion that Ansuz had anything to do with Skadi.

Communicators' more esoteric beliefs posited that Ansuz may have existed as a technique of divination communication that the ancient Seers of Meniya used to connect with people far away. But until Sigfather's mention at the Gap, no one made mention of any link between it and Skadi. In fact, no Communicator had ever spoken of the goddess existing outside the borders of Gorrland. Of course, Communicators did not know all…

Eirà upset Marja with his belief and with his peculiar spiritual practices. So it was all the more upsetting for her to find him seated on Kolfinna's carpet when she arrived. Thin, lanky, and old, the man meditated with rune staves in front of him. He had been giving her counsel all afternoon. More than a bit protectively, Marja implored him to leave, with his dark energy, and go back to the tree stump he called a temple. Marja was in shock at the news from the radio waves and did not like seeing Kolfinna distraught like that. Such was apparent in her motherly expression. But it was the "dark sorcerer," as she referred to Eirà, who had correctly shown Kolfinna and Mikkjal not to resist Sigfather's Dust blasts. It was thanks to him that an unnecessary foe became an ally. Such words as Kolfinna uttered them to her supervisor were truth, and the fair Marja finally acknowledged it. Soon she accepted to sit with the two for tea and discuss how to proceed.

The Chieftain was clearly on Kolfinna's side, but she would never understand the realness of last night's vision. That what she saw in the Tower and in the tavern might *not* come to pass was unimaginable. It was reality. Eirà saw that. Even Mikkjal saw that once she sent him her vision by Dust. The nocturnal hermit of Utgard was the only human in Gorrland who could give useful counsel before the pair set off, and the time for them to set off to Meniya was now. So, he gave her a training routine to help her understand the spell and maximize its usage to convene with the Eight and Skadi in Meniya, before the temple was destroyed a second time by the hands of Mikhail Jorgson. Contrary to what Marja, Astrid, and other Skadisfolk had long believed, Eirà believed the Huntress still existed in physical living form somewhere on the planet. Ansuz's communication would bring her out of hiding. That is why Kolfinna chose to seek out Eirà for spiritual guidance instead of the old Oracle.

In the afternoon, before Marja confirmed the move that the despot of Jorg had made, Eirà told Kolfinna a hard truth that, as an afflicted girl, offered a certain comfort—to succeed in convening the Nine through Ansuz, she would have to die to her old self. Her life with a troubled mind would end, and her life as a Communicator for Skadi would begin, bringing glory for ages to come!

Eirà taught her to seek peace with Utgard. To let the Outer World penetrate her. To release thoughts and become only Shadow.

Marja's love didn't agree with him, but she had no choice but to accept. In Kolfinna's house, Communicator and Storyteller came to an understanding. Gorrland needed the dark hermit. Marja radioed her fellow leaders to prepare them for the type of assembly to come.

So now, Marja and Eirà sat together, next to Kolfinna, in the first row of the Scarlett Pyre amphitheatre. The village sat around the flame, silent before roaring, crackling, and smoke. Everyone's face was kissed by the orange light, reflecting what remained of the Life Fire of a Folk that had made it two-thirds of the way through winter but could not yet see spring. The three had arrived directly from the cabin and were about to make an announcement that was the first of its kind in the Modern Era.

Five flame keepers were standing watch before the pews as a full house awaited its leaders, who had somewhat of a delay. Of course, even Astrid and Ivaldi couldn't know how best to present these matters to the public. Such was understandable, for they were not prepared.

ANSUZ

Nor was Kolfinna truly prepared. But in continuing with the theme of Eirà's teachings, she wore black as she sat puffing on her pipe on the cold, wooden bench. Black dress made no attempt to hide from the Darkness that was engulfing Albrimir at the moment. It made no attempt to show a Kolfinna that tried and tried but couldn't meet the demands put on normal people. She bundled her black cloak around her and kept the hood covering her eyes. Only her mouth and nose touched the cold, midwinter air that offered no rest for the weary.

Darkness would also allow any and all light that may emerge to shine freely in contrast. She stood in front of Eirà, also dressed in black, as such was his custom. For those unable to heed the signs years in the making, they should heed the words the hermit spoke last night. The time for Skadi's magic had come. No more farming, no more sedentary growth, no more seafaring life support. Nomad Hunters were of Utgard. They were the ones most adapted to change. And as for the Huntress of Utgard, she not only knew runes but developed her knowledge enough to communicate over air through Dust. She learned Sigfather's language and magic but honed it in her own unique way. Both beings' magic would pass on to the girl born as Kolfinna Helensdottir.

With furs cloaked tight around their bodies, Astrid and Ivaldi strode slowly to the entrance of the amphitheatre, then walked over the snow in front of the flame to face the assembly. Embers shattered and high sparks flew. The bearded warrior wore brown bear fur and the land woman wore white reindeer, matching the colour of her aging hair. They had both been born into Mountaineer reindeer-herding families, Kolfinna remembered. Their culture, older than Westfolk's, would never die. Skadi's return would ensure that. Hunters, trappers, herders, any and all ancient folk of the forest and tundra were the best hope for the future. She breathed softly, feeling Marja and Eirà's presence and equally noting Mikkjal to her left. Her pineweed pipe spewed a twinge of flavour in their area, sweetening the ambient wood smoke from the Pyre.

Though the old Oracle had been a friend to her and was still unjustly decried for the manner in which he revealed the truth about Skadi's mounting strength, his powers were waning in this world. The Mountaineer Storyteller had answers for this uncertain period. He was not a man for everyone's taste. Before the Gap travels, Kolfinna herself would have been wary of his words. But however non-social his ways, his beliefs and soul were part of something. Her father had seen that and had not been afraid of the man. During this afternoon's practice, he already did the Death-Release trance with her. Kolfinna felt no fear as she dove her soul into the unknown. There was relief instead. Then excitement. Eirà's Skadi devotion was an offer of new possibilities—for Kolfinna as much as for Albrimir. Soon she would be free of being owned by her wretched Curse of the Visions. She would be free of her ailment of Bad Fate.

Astrid eyed Ivaldi, who took initiative in the warrior way. "Guards of Gorrland, *hwa*!" he shouted, crossing his arms over his head.

"*Hwa!*" thundered all Guards present.

"Thwa!"

"*Thwa!*"

"Ya!"

"*Ya!*"

"I greet you at a perilous time, but nonetheless a time when events of the past week are taking a form as clear as a winter's night and as solid as a potter's clay. We can take comfort in coming out of what was uncertain. To explain the news I call Marja Fjallsdottir, chief of Communicators, to address the assembly," bellowed Ivaldi solemnly. Marja, her silver hair hidden beneath a thick, woollen cap, stepped forward and joined Ivaldi and Astrid. She took a deep breath and warmed her eyes in the blaze.

"My dearest Folk. Eight days ago, Kolfinna Helensdottir and Mikkjal Aldisson confronted Sigfather at the Gap and heard a powerful message. Last night, Kolfinna had a powerful vision that confirmed this message and suggested the identity of the one who poses a danger to us. Today, we have received confirmation on the physical plane that Sigfather's prediction is coming to pass... I would much rather not believe in the magic unfolding, but today's news has obliged me to recognize the evidence of its truth. I shall speak first on the news we've received today at the Central Communications Tower. Torvall has informed the all-Albrimir frequency that a group of about one hundred people from Jorg has crossed their borders and been granted asylum. They were fleeing persecution at the hands of leader Mikhail Jorgson. Once asylum was granted, Jorgson demanded that Torvall hand over the refugees if they wanted diplomatic relations to continue. Torvall refused this demand."

Folks seemed startled but hushed. "So, what is this? A declaration of war?" came a loud voice from the rising smoke.

"That I cannot say. But Jorgson's tone was menacing," Marja continued.

Hushed chatter continued.

"Who are these refugees?" asked a warrior.

Marja turned to make sure people on all sides could hear. "Farmers and traders, accused of plotting to overthrow Jorg's leaders and government." She strained her voice to be heard over the roar of the flames.

"*Accused* of?" came the voice of Westfolk farmer Gudmand. "You sound like you don't believe it."

"*I don't* believe it," Marja exclaimed. "But that's not due to my being partial to Torvall." She removed her hat and continued, letting her silver hair flow. "After the all-Albrimir broadcast I mentioned, a secret signal was sent on a shorter-range frequency from Torvall's north tower. It was meant for us. It was just barely heard on the other side of the Isaveg by *Taqraup Nunaat* East Tower, but the Skrallanders relayed the message to us." The crowd held its breath while Marja took a moment to catch hers. "Torvall's leader himself, the Shishilm Anavend, spoke with the Jorgian refugees. They told him of horrors, of farmers being chased from their lands by hordes of killers, of torture."

Ivaldi shouted loudly, his anger and defiance getting the better of his composure. "*Why?!*"

"According to them, there was never a plot against Jorgson. Instead it was Jorgson who was obsessed with finding a woman who was of his own Land—a woman who has entered into communication with our Kolfinna by means that I can only classify as a magic belonging to another epoch."

Startled chatter struck up within the audience. An unidentifiable voice from the rear of the group shouted, "*Magical communication?* What is this?"

Eirà stood up, his hooded cloak still covering his forehead. He spoke calmly and precisely, loud enough without shouting. "It is the Spell of Ansuz, the technique that the ancient Shishilms of Meniya used to communicate with each other even when at a distance. The ancient seers could transmit visions, words, thoughts to each other and to other persons they chose, through use of the Cosmic Dust emanating from the Gap. And now that we understand, thanks to Kolfinna and Mikkjal's Gap travels and the Oracle's unfortunate ordeal, that Skadi's time is returning, I must share with you my conviction. Skadi, our goddess from the mountains, used the Spell of Ansuz. Kolfinna, as she is being called to learn it as well, shall commune with Skadi and with all of the persons chosen by Sigfather, including this woman from Jorg. The Spell of Ansuz, Skadi, and Sigfather's Chosen—the new Shishilms of Meniya—are key to establishing a new epoch of peace and prosperity."

Comments, gasps, and sighs resounded through the crowd. They couldn't trust Eirà yet. The same news, as startling as it may be, would've been accepted if it had come from Kolfinna's father. She put her pipe down and promptly stood up and stepped forward from her seat to stand between her Chieftain and Eirà, removing her hood to reveal herself. "What he just said is true, my Folk," she shouted over the blaze and the chatter. Once they had recognized her, the people gave a startled silence. They were probably as surprised as Mikkjal had been to see her wearing black. "I have communicated with a Jorgian woman of the Jackrabbit clan by use of Dust emanating from my hand. Some of you present in the tavern last night were witness to the effect it produced on me. As were Chieftain Marja and my Tower mates Alvi and Gala. This woman, like Mikkjal and myself, is one of Sigfather's Chosen, to become the new Shishilms of Meniya."

Pavel, a teacher, called out from high in the pews. "You know this how? These are visions! Perhaps hallucinations!"

"She has the same name, Pavel!" Marja answered forcefully. "The woman Jorgson called for has the same name and clan identity as the name Kolfinna heard through her magic. Lia Jackrabbit. She heard it before Jorgson's broadcast."

"Still, it's too outrageous," Pavel shouted, motioning his hand toward Eirà. "Plus, now this man of darkness is involved. I don't want to believe it."

"Neither did I, Pavel," spoke Marja, calmer. "But if you're worried that what we're saying is part of some plot by us Mountaineer Skadisfolk to take over Gorrland for our own benefit, I'll remind you that Kolfinna is a Westfolker like you. I'll also remind you that both Alvi and Gala are also Westfolkers from farming families, and they can confirm every bit of what Kolfinna spoke of yesterday in her turmoil. As can several tavern-goers."

Pavel calmed down and sat down. He had no argument against that fact. The teacher chose to listen rather than argue.

"Just to get things straight," rose Aibmu Astridsson from about five rows back. "The reason Jorgson was after the woman in the first place was because Kolfinna spoke to her with Dust with this Spell of Ansuz?"

"It would appear so," Marja said. "Jorgson sees this… spell, or technique, or however you want to call this magic as somehow a threat to him. We do not yet know why." She looked to Eirà as she finished speaking.

"But has Jorgson issued any threat against us? Against Gorrland?" Aibmu continued.

"As of now, no threat has been made against Gorrland, Aibmu," said Marja. She continued slowly and hesitantly. "However, after discussing with Eirà, I believe that since Kolfinna is the human at the origin of this *magic communication*"—she looked at the dark hermit while speaking—"that she will eventually be targeted by him. If Kolfinna is his enemy, he may threaten us."

"Let him try, Aibmu" Ivaldi bellowed deeply from his chest in the centre of the floor. "Jorg has never been a Folk of fighters. If he tries against Gorrland, he'll wish he never left his mother's cradle." Aibmu himself chuckled at his Chieftain's remark, as did several others in the crowd, but a chill went up Kolfinna's spine. At the same time as she felt the chill, the fire emitted a pop, sparks exploding at Ivaldi and Astrid. *No. Jorg has developed something else. This will not be battle like we are used to.*

Marja looked at Kolfinna, then at Eirà, thinking about the words she would use to describe something of which she still had no confirmation. She looked down and spoke with a tone similar to the smoke. "Fellow Chieftain, we cannot be so confident lest we miss something crucial. We have reason to believe that Jorg has made recent technological progress in crystal power extraction. They've been silent about their Communicators' technology division for more than seven years. No Gorrlander has visited them in more than seven years. Lia Jackrabbit's words have confirmed that Jorgson and Communicator Chieftain Fraick Abbott have overseen the development of new and more destructive types of weapons over the past seven years."

Ivaldi's expression changed dramatically. But he knew not to question another Chieftain's area of expertise in front of everyone, so he quickly diverted any interrogation on the matter. "I see, Marja. If he challenges us, given our reputation, it means he has confidence in his technology."

Aibmu remained standing but looked at a select few of his Guard mates around the fire, scratching his thin beard. "*Is* he challenging us, though? He's said he hates Kolfinna and her... *co-magicals*... but will he fight us because of that? I'm sure I'm not the only one to think this so I'll say it. I ask, *why should Gorrland consider going to war with Jorg just because he threatens Torvall?* If Kolfinna and Mikkjal stay in Gorrland, Jorgson has his fight with Torvall. How would that be a problem for *us?*"

Several cheers and shouts erupted, along with a round of applause from some. Kolfinna's eyes stung with smoke. She had been looking so intently at Aibmu's pew that she didn't even notice the wind changing the direction of the flame. She took a few steps forward on the snow, past Ivaldi and Astrid, eying the boy whose mother was a Chieftain. *You selfish, closed-visioned weasel! No thinking beyond your own neighbourhood! You think you can keep me here and just feed Lia and Torvall to Jorg? You know nothing of what has changed in the world! All you who applaud, you will be slaves under Jorgson!*

Mikkjal stood and took a few steps forward to join Kolfinna. "Friends, I hear your concern. But we aren't going to war just yet. Sigfather is calling his chosen— Kolfinna, myself, Lia, and others from all Lands—back to the fortress of Ancient Meniya, which is in Torvall. Lia from Jorg crossed the border, reaching her destination. Aibmu, we have a way to avoid war while not sacrificing anyone to Jorgson. If Kolfinna and I leave for Torvall and we convene the new Shishilms of Meniya, we can stop this. The planet will evolve and Jorgson's clique will be defeated. That's what Sigfather and Skadi's energy uniting means."

Mikkjal, you see! You almost understand everything. Sweet Mikkjal, you stand by me still. I need you on this journey, too. I still don't know you well, but I know you are a good person. You serve your family, your Order, and your Folk well. You feel my visions when I send them to you. And now you speak wisdom and common sense to the skeptics. Please follow me on my journey!

"Alone, Mikkjal?" Aibmu shouted. "Let me try to believe this stuff about Sigfather, Skadi, Jorgson and so on. Who will be your backup along the way? You really expect to go there alone, just the two of you?!"

"All the more so if you two are indeed some wizard's divine creations or another type of cocked up legend," shouted Magar, the absent-minded orange fool that Mikkjal somehow found time to show some affection for. *You have to have an opinion about everything, don't you, oldster? We don't need more warriors to accompany us. You must understand that! Aibmu the proud and Magar the fool, stubborn folk of the Old World! Neither one of you see! You think your objection-mongering and provincial piety will be rewarded by a privileged place in Jorgson's slave pits?! You want to shoot his guns and not get shot by them?! He's coming to take over everything...* But they wouldn't understand, and neither would half the people in attendance. So Kolfinna remained silent. A log cracked, scattering dozens of sparks in front of the speakers' faces.

In the crowd's reflected silence, Ivaldi approached them and spoke in a hushed tone, to Kolfinna and Mikkjal. "It's true I wouldn't feel right letting you go without an escort. I happen to believe you two can stop this mess before war even starts. But in case you're too late and caught in Torvall, I don't want you to be sacrificed meaninglessly to Jorg's army."

Kolfinna felt a lightening in her chest. "Thank you, Chieftain." She realized that she'd begun to sweat, and so removed her black cloak to be more at ease next to the blaze. Her green jacket was bright in the light.

"Friends, a suggestion have I," spoke Soren, who Marja called up from South Tower immediately after Jorgson's transmission. He sat in the second row. "Marja, you shared with me Torvall's secret message for us, which Akinisie of Skralland agreed to relay. There was no direct request for Gorrlander intervention in any sense. It only implied that Kolfinna would continue her work in contacting the Dust-sensitives—the *New Shishilms*. Her and Mikkjal's convoy can perhaps be inconspicuous. They only have to travel to Torvall, and both Torvall and Skralland have shown themselves sympathetic to Kolfinna and her... comrades... up until now. They can travel by land discreetly."

Marja nodded while Ivaldi opened his mouth in a voiceless protest. *Land travel via Skralland fits well with the times. And I will surely be able to contact the Skralland Shishilm and convince him or her to accompany us.* Sensing where the warrior Chieftain was preparing to object, Soren went on. "But that doesn't mean we are indifferent to the danger Kolfinna and Mikkjal face. I propose that a Guard team follow them, remaining at an accessible distance in case anything goes awry." Soren had always been an impressive Communicator with his verbal arguing skills, Kolfinna thought to herself.

"Stationed at a post in Skralland. Perhaps East Tower post at the edge of the Isaveg," Astrid spoke from the front for the first time tonight, her voice firm and solid. "I believe they would allow us to station at the limits of North Island, accessible from Torvall's North Tower by short-range radio frequency." Her eyes went off in Marja's direction, and the Communicator Chieftain nodded.

"I favour the proposal," resonated Ivaldi. "Mikkjal and Kolfinna will travel by land, by way of Skralland on snowmobile. Tomorrow morning, a crew of fighters led by Captain Fálgeir will sail between the icebergs and lay anchor beside the sea ice on the eastern tip of the island." Kolfinna felt her chest loosen somewhat. For someone who harboured a mistrust for Eirà, Marja had done a good job convincing the Chieftains to support the mission. Astrid and Ivaldi were Skadisfolk like her and must have similar combinations of support and reservations about the mission. As for Petr and Evan, who hadn't spoken tonight, they must have followed the lead of the other three.

Ivaldi eyed Astrid, as if seeking her approval as he prepared to continue. "So we understand, Mikkjal and Kolfinna will go east by snowmobile through Skralland Village, then across the Isaveg into Torvall—if Mikkjal is fit to guide such a journey. In Skralland, Kolfinna may connect directly with whoever is *called* from that Land. You'll both carry your swords, of course."

A combination of cheers and protests abounded, while Mikkjal stood still. Kolfinna knew what was going through his mind. He wouldn't believe in his ability to ride over the Isaveg. Rumours circulated about North Islanders from Gorrland and Skralland who had managed to cross, but to this date nothing had been officially recorded by the Communicators. Amidst all the noise Aibmu's voice managed to break through. "But chief, have we already decided that we're even sending Mikkjal and Kolfinna to Torvall? Are we such true believers in Sigfather's prophecies?"

Aibmu doesn't see. Ivaldi seemed to realize as much as he sighed loudly. "I speak for myself. I don't place faith in Sigfather's prophecy. I, for one, never spoke with him. But I do place faith in my Quest. *"You shall partake in a battle across the sea that the entire planet will remember"* was what I was told by my goddess Skadi herself when I came of age. I sense that my destiny will soon be fulfilled. Yes, with a heavy heart, I share that I sense that war is indeed coming, whether or not we chose it. Whether or not we choose to honour Sigfather, what Sigfather said will come to pass. And whether or not we like the hermit storyteller Eirà, his knowledge is necessary in our new world."

The smoke and flame cut clearly through the silent air. The great Ivaldi never shared his personal visions and feelings publicly.

"Jorgson brings war to all," Kolfinna added. "He acts as Sigfather, as we had thought Sigfather would be. Only he is no god, no spirit, but a human like any of us. He is the one to whom Sigfather referred as 'One far worse than me.' And in my visions last night, I saw the type of world he brings—engines, guns, and screens. Fast travel, fast weapons, and quick communication, but all under his control. Technology but with slavery attached to it."

"For him to have developed the technology Lia mentioned to Torvall, it would mean that he's discovered new and unseen ways to augment the Dust crystals and fine-tune their properties," Marja spoke. "He and his right-hand man Abbott are magicians at crystal communications technology. But between technical mastery without soul and reviving the ancient communications techniques as Kolfinna does, I'll choose the latter every time."

Cheers erupted from around two-thirds of the amphitheatre.

"Do I need to call a vote?" asked Ivaldi. "Or have interrogations about the proposal been satisfied?" The bald beast warrior made no point of hiding to whom his words were addressed, staring adamantly at Aibmu with intense blue eyes. The lad was feisty and robust but the son of Astrid must be taught to feel the call of forces greater than himself at this time.

Aibmu returned Ivaldi's stare at length but then subtly lowered his gaze. "I remove my objection."

"Good," Ivaldi reverted from menacing beast to booming, jolly leader. "Mikkjal and Kolfinna will leave the day after tomorrow at dawn. Travel to Skralland Village takes ten time-lapses. You can radio us from there at the end of the day, then let us know your travel plans from there."

"I'll contact Chieftain Akinisie of Skralland and arrange everything," said Marja. "If anything goes wrong en route they'll be able to use belt radio to us up until Yggram's Pass, almost halfway to Skralland. Then about seventy kilometres from there, they'll be within range of Skralland low-range frequency and can contact them. I will also let Akinisie know about the planned Guard ship that will anchor off the tip of the Isaveg."

"Does this plan abide with both of you?" Astrid asked.

Kolfinna and Mikkjal nodded at the same time. But she had one more point to make. "What do the gods say?" Kolfinna beseeched. "We never have an assembly without spirit guidance."

"Kolfinna, you know more than any other Seer ever has, you with your visions from Sigfather, your Dust communications, your—"

"My guidance comes from ones who have guided me." She pulled her quadrated circle necklace forward and the pendant glowed white with Dust above her green attire. Her father was present. While the assembly let in the presence of the deceased Bjorn Njordson's spirit, Kolfinna made a point of walking closer to Eirà, still cloaked and still dressed in black. "Our Land has been without an official Storyteller since my father died. It is time we fix that."

And with that cue Eirà removed his hood and spoke from his fine-featured face and flaming grey eyes. "Two Storytellers worked on the same problem, one in the Mountains, one in the Village. Bjorn experimented in runes better than any. And though I'm no master, I'm far from ignorant in such spirit speech. But the girl here, with Sigfather's blessing, has intuitive knowledge of it naturally. All along, Sigfather had been guiding us to the present moment. He has been guiding us in his lasting quest to unite the Eight Towers with the Wandering Huntress. Skadi used Ansuz. Kolfinna will use Ansuz to convene with her." Bjorn's pendant glowed ever brighter still with the words, producing the familiar white odourless smoke that was the Dust, though it stayed still within the pendent this time. It lit up beside Scarlett Pyre. "Our Kolfinna is both a woman of the crystal radio waves and a Storyteller's daughter. *Ansuzdottir* is to go, inspired by Skadi, her spell radiating, to contact all who must be contacted to fulfill the needs of the times. She has contacted one from the other Seven Lands. Six remain. And Mikkjal, young man of the land, is to be her personal Guide."

No one spoke. The glow of Bjorn's pendant reminded them that the frightening obscure mountain man's advice was shared by their beloved speaker and healer of old. Kolfinna had gone to Eirà. Bjorn supported this move. Eirà's magic was the only kind that could help them in the present turmoil. Yet there came a most unlikely voice that broke the silence to vouch for the strange man of the woodland Skadi temple. "Here's to the words of the good man of the hills," the Oracle spoke quietly, rising across the way. He eyed Eirà and Kolfinna, then Mikkjal, whose brown eyes looked unsteady. "What do the gods want before the journey is to take place, Eirà? *You* tell *me*."

"The gods want an offering from the ways of old to the ways of new," said Eirà, nodding at the Oracle in reverence. "A celebration among the farmers of Westfolk in honour of the Hunt, of Skadi, and of the way of life of the old clans. Njord himself would want this."

"Very well," spoke the Oracle, loud before all. "Skadi shall receive her due in the land of farmers and sea folk." Then, adding, much lower, "And there she shall have her sacrifice."

Kolfinna's heart fell tender upon hearing the Oracle's grace. He had not foreseen things going this way but he had given his life to a path of serving forces greater than himself. "Thank you for understanding, old friend," she spoke, the pendant still glowing. The words that came forward in that moment had been both her own and those of her father speaking through the amulet. "Astrid, Ivaldi, do we have your approval for what shall transpire? A ceremony in Westport tomorrow evening before our journey to Torvall at dawn?"

The pair of Chieftains looked at each other for several seconds, and Astrid broke the silence. "I grant approval for this ceremony. If you depart from Westport, then be sure to allow fifteen time-lapses for your travel to Skralland Village. A full half-day is appropriate."

Marja followed Astrid's lead. "I also grant approval for this ceremony. The Five Chieftains shall be present in Westport tomorrow evening."

"Thank you, Marja," said Kolfinna with a nod. "It shall be at Hrafnshemma Dune."

Stifled applause followed, though it was not cheerful. It was a resigned acceptance of what was fated to happen. The old world was falling apart. The new world was yet to be born, and Kolfinna accepted the impending death of her former self with eager anticipation. She placed her black cloak again over her bright vest during the closing remarks, looking at once at her grounded lover Mikkjal, then back to Eirà. She must again seek his counsel tonight and tomorrow before the ceremony. Their plan was to seek ways to visualize and identify the other New Shishilms in addition to Lia. If she could identify and contact Sigfather's red-dotted Chosen One in Skralland, and contact him or her before leaving, it would make the journey to Meniya that much quicker. She stepped away from the fire and went back to her cold wooden bench.

Chapter 3
Brighter Fire

Attention! Attention!

Attention please on the long-range frequency of one thousand crystal waves per second.

Attention please on the all-Albrimir Communicators' frequency.

It is midday, on the Twelfth of Fifteenmonth, 963. I again reach out to you. Communicator Chieftain Fraick Abbott and I extend greetings from Iorki to the Towers of the other seven Lands. Today I reiterate the message we broadcast yesterday. On behalf of our Folk, I, Chief Mikhail Iorki-Son, repeat my demand to Shishilm Anavend of Kalyim. You now give quarter to a band of criminals and a sorceress. Such is an act against the sovereignty and dignity of the Folk of Iorki.

Sir Anavend, you should understand that if you do not comply with my demand to turn the group over, you are committing an act of hostility, for which there will be consequences.

I shall also use this announcement to inform you all, esteemed Communicators, that we have made a great bound forward in technology. Our Communicators have worked tirelessly on crystals and have built machines that will enable rapid travel all over Albrimir and even to other planets. Our work will also allow for quick communications between any people in any Land at any moment. With this technology, Albrimir can pass from a divided mass of separate and sometimes warring Lands to a unified world of progress, prosperity, and discovery. Before spring, we will share this technology with you, for the future belongs to all of us united!

And so, I return to you, Shishilm Anavend. Your reputation precedes you as a man who enjoys comfort, both for yourself and your people, not a man who is stuck in old superstition. What do you gain from Miss Lia? She is but a common witch who seems to have received a transmission from an even more dangerous sorceress in Gorrland. I trust Chieftain Marja Fjalsdottir to do something about the woman in her Land. But you, Anavend, must choose whether you are an ally to an Albrimir of unity and progress or to superstition, spells, and backwards wizards. Make the right choice for your people, sir.

As we began our struggle against backward elements in Iorki thirty years ago, so we shall continue. I would ask of other Lands that they do the same. Marja of Gorrland, do not underestimate the treachery of your sorceress. She may seek to subvert others still, as she did with Lia. For that, I ask you all, Communicators, to be on the lookout for anyone who contacts her. The world is changing but not in the way Gap Traveller Kolfinna Helensdottir says it is. I can assure you that this shall be the last winter of darkness. Greetings from Iorki!

***

Kolfinna

Wind made her cloak flutter as she trudged toward the dune. Mother held her hand in comfort from the change that would've meant her death if it had happened just a few years earlier. They led a procession of thirty people from Grandfather's homestead over crunchy thin snow to the edge of the island. They would accept Skadi's way of life more into their world. From now on, Hunters would be allowed to roam northward from the farms, extending along the western hills up to Nordhemma on occasion. Agriculture would be part-time, its yield having been below average for ten years straight. It was time for acknowledgement. Utgard was coming closer, with its darkness, with its danger, with its somber tones. The World Beyond, where the winter goddess was most at home, must enter the hearts of all Gorrlanders and, eventually, all Albrimese. Kolfinna's heart trembled as she walked, torn within about what needed to be done. The Oracle had been a support. Though he was old, he saw the truth of the turning time, and he knew that his recognition of Skadi must take a specific form. He must be given so that the Land may not perish.

Heidi sang a somber tune from atop the tall dune, with the people waiting below. *Carry the cry for all of us, little sister.* For the souls of farmers, fishers, and free-living seamstresses she cried out in the cold, clear twilight while Bjarni Alfredson's fiddle fused into the windy sea. The procession of family and Westfolk clan heads nodded to Heidi and Bjarni before turning to take the stairs down to the beach.

The other five heads of clans hadn't needed much convincing of the need for this offering. They'd lived stagnant lives as their children and grandchildren had joined one of the Five Orders and lived actively in town or on the land. Able-bodied farmers barely got by with their weakened yields. If this spring were to be anything like the last one, it would begin well after Sixteenmonth's end, and only begin growth in mid-Twomonth. The Mountaineers were a more adaptable people. Although tonight's sacrifice would be hard, it would be preferable to life as usual. Father Siraz stood beside Mother, and Father Haral stood beside Kolfinna. And through the pendant, Father Bjorn was present. He recognized the Mountaineers' epoch and the six clan heads still recognized him.

This afternoon during Death-release training Kolfinna only felt total darkness for a few seconds before clarity came. As she lay on her hard wooden floor, with Eirà's hands massaging her skull, she let go as she was supposed to. She hit the depths of her soul and the collective's soul, and saw more. The destroyed room of then, its renewed form of now: Meniya.

There, she spoke with Lia, if "speaking" were the right word to describe this communication. It was a Dust pulsation in her hand, which she did without any thoughts, for thinking and Death-release state were incompatible. Her hand spoke to Lia's, through the magic of the Flares, whom Gorrlanders called Sigfather. *We are coming,* Kolfinna messaged without thought, across land and sea.

Come soon. His announcement was not a bluff. He can harm you.

Is it true what he says he has? Kolfinna messaged.

It is true. And he has the support of many. I'm grateful to be in a good place now, though.

And as Lia pulsated the last message Kolfinna could see the woman, around the beginning of her fifth decade of life, seated in a throne of eight in the Temple of Ancient Meniya. In the seat to her left, she could now identify one more of the grouping of New Shishilms, the council of Sigfather's Chosen. Beside the woman of brown complexion and dark eyes sat a man of similar age and skin a small bit fairer. *Who are you?* Kolfinna asked with her hand into the darkened hall.

Caskil Anavend of Kalyim, he answered with his Dust pulse. *The Flares called me, too.*

Sigfather's Chosen from Torvall was none other than the Shishilm Anavend himself. Continuity, this man expressed. He was a Shisilm in the ancient spiritual sense and in the modern political sense. So interesting that Torvall kept the ancient Meniyan word for leader! This man Anavend protected Lia not just because he believed her, but because he had the Call as well.

Other humans sat at the other thrones, but she couldn't make them out in the shadows they cast. Even Gorrland's New Shishilms—herself and Mikkjal—were shrouded in black.

She couldn't see the Skrallander's face either beneath the shadow, though he was indeed there.

But there was no sign of Skadi.

Kolfinna came back to life, sitting up beside Eirà. She would try again after the sacrifice ceremony.

On the beach, the Westfolk procession stopped, in front of the assembled public, and facing the vessel that would be given. Heidi and Bjarni, on the dune above, ceased their pure, haunting tune and let the wind accompany the sights of the crowd, bundled up for a coastal winter's evening.

Father Siraz had chosen the most beautiful wooden ship he had ever helped built. The Westfolkers universally revered it. For Kolfinna, it held a special significance, for Father had begun working on it the summer she left on her Quest and had finished it when she returned. The ship was confirmed, in its own way, at the same time she was. Its smooth dark brown wood contrasted against the white of the snow and sand. Its mast stood taller than five men. The steed was a product of the finest craftsmanship and could have sailed down to Solicia, around the southern tip of the world at Kaltland, and back up the east coast of Albrimir's mainland to Torvall's high peaks and fjords. Instead it was to be burnt as a sacrifice to Skadi and to Sigfather. Although sign after sign was there that all must be done to herald Skadi's Time and promote her and Sigfather's energetic union, Kolfinna's heart still ached at the decisions and actions she was making. *The new era would either be upon us by spring, or else winter will never end.*

Five men with torches stood alongside the vessel, while the Chieftains of the Five Orders stood in a circle in front of it. Eirà stood in the centre of this circle. A dark man but a survivor, he shared tales from Utgard, which were tales of Truth. Once people overcame their fear of Shadow, they would be free. That Gorrland accepted his appointment by the Oracle as the more powerful spirit man and recognized him as the new Storyteller for the Land gave Kolfinna faith. Jorgson offered all Lands a choice between progress and fear and backwards superstition. Gorrland chose Skadi and Kolfinna, even if it came through darkness. Skadi's magic brought resilience, for she and her Spell of Ansuz were still there.

Still, gentle summer, bright fields, you I will miss most of all!

A team of twenty Guides and twenty Guards stood in impressive rows behind Astrid and Ivaldi on opposite sides of the Chieftains' circle. Kolfinna spotted Mikkjal standing with the general public, alongside his Guide mates Iafri, Ginnar and Kjartan, all Westfolkers themselves. Mikkjal dutifully agreed to the plan to leave immediately after the ceremony and sleep at Skadi's Temple in the mountains, rather than conduct the whole journey from morning tomorrow. He agreed to Eirà the Storyteller's counsel. He would agree to what Kolfinna suggested, without understanding it, but he couldn't hide the fact that he would miss his men-of-action mates and even Astrid. He was giving up a lot in this mission. She had perhaps paid him less affectionate attention than a grounded man would like. The sexual magic ritual she'd foreseen tonight should help him in that.

Eirà walked out from the circle to greet them.

"Helen Hrafnsdottir," he nodded from his dark cloak. "People of Westfolk. Welcome. I thank you for agreeing to this ceremony, which is necessary to earn the favour of the spirits in guiding Kolfinna Helensdottir and Mikkjal Aldisson, two descendants of your Westfolk clans, across the bridge of land and time to Meniya. As has been revealed, Kolfinna possesses a special ability to communicate to those who feel Sigfather's Dust, a spell possessed by our mountain goddess, Skadi—the Spell of Ansuz!"

"Ansuz!" repeated the five Chieftains, after which came a sudden, short gust of wind. Father's necklace began to shimmer over her neck, white Dust gathering around her hand. *Please, let me know that I'm making the right choice, Father.* Throbbing came at her red dots and at her heart. Fleeing would be simplest now. She reached under her cloak and pulled out her birch staff with Sigfather's rune inscription on it. The letters didn't form a pronounceable word but, according to Eirà, would have an impact when pronounced individually when in the proper state of mind. Mikkjal had been sure to bring his own birch staff to the ceremony. *Let go, Kolfinna Helensdottir. Release. Accept death. You are part of Utgard, the darkness that is beyond the comprehension of the human mind. There you will see. You will see all—the Shishilms, Skadi, the end, the beginning. Your choice is your destiny.* Her chest pressure lessened, though her hand remained alight with inner churning of Cosmic Dust. She was more than just herself at this gathering.

"Tonight is a night of sacrifice," Eirà continued, his hood drawn from his head. "But what is burnt tonight shall be breathed into the air for ages to come. It shall be reaped by our world tenfold!" A chill went up Kolfinna's spine. The man had powers, for sure, but he could never be a familiar force to her. Such was the nature of Utgard magic, she supposed. He retreated back into the circle and Marja came out.

"Kolfinna, daughter of Helen Hrafnsdottir, daughter of Siraz Himinnson, daughter of Haral Vindursson, daughter of Bjorn Njordsson. The Five Chieftains call you to light the torch. Do you have the blessing of your family?" asked Chieftain Marja, who had not stopped for one second to consider whether Jorgson's radio depiction of her was to any degree true.

Pulling her dark cloak tight, Kolfinna looked to Siraz, Haral, and Helen in their farmers' attire, who all nodded their heads.

"I do." She looked Marja in the eye.

"Understood. I call you then, Kolfinna, Helen, Siraz, and Haral, to take the torches. In the name of Westfolk you are called to give this offering to Skadi, to Sigfather, and to the ancestors and descendants of all Gorrland." She walked slowly forward with Mother and her two living Fathers past the circle to the side of the ship's hull, where four Guards gave each of them a torch. Marja came around and took the fifth torch. Back on the dune above, Heidi began to sing the same tune as before, while playing her shoulder fiddle. Another singer, Eivor Nilsdottir, joined her, as did Bjarni and Hilgur on the drums. Although the wind still blew, it didn't stifle the song but made the music reverberate to all below, amplified by the blowing air. The music echoed against the sand and rock, while the sea remained calm.

The song took on a more determined and resolute beat with the drums. Hearing the singers' age-old lyrics of a young farmer-lad who had to sacrifice his crops due to a freak hailstorm, but who had faith that the future would provide for himself, his wife, and his young child, was surely bringing hope to the audience's ears. They had been through a lot over the years—surviving clan raids, kidnappings, the ever-continuous merger with the ways of the Mountaineers. Even though farming's prospects had been bleak for some time, even though icebergs were becoming ever more present even in Westfolk Harbour, they would find a way for their culture to survive and thrive. Hunters and farmers would continue to influence each other, side by side. Kolfinna looked up with a smile at little Hei as she sang in the twilight, then took in the glances of Siraz, Haral, and Mother.

"We owe it to ourselves, to those who came before us, and to those who will come after us," Siraz professed in an elevated tone. "No one will destroy Gorrland. Hail to the Njord the Ship Master, his children the fishers and farmers. Hail to Skadi the Huntress, her children the Mountaineers. Hail to their union, temporary though it was, for it produced their children the Gorrlanders." Kolfinna, her parents, plus Marja, brought their torches up to their faces, while Mother gave the final word.

"Our Folk knows and understands. I trust in my late husband, who has spoken to Kolfinna from the other side. For Bjorn and for the world!" Kolfinna shivered with Helen Hrafnsdottir's exclamation, then tossed her torch inside the ship's helm. She followed suit, as did her Fathers and finally Marja. All stepped back to observe the ship catch flame, gushes of crackling air accompanying planks that caught fire. As if on cue, the wind picked up to quicken the flame's spread, engulfing the vessel up to the mast. Marja rejoined the Chieftains' circle. In the quickening wind Kolfinna caught a familiar fleeting vision. The Eight New Shishilms were seated there in the room. Only Jorg and Torvall had faces; Lia Jackrabbit and Caskil Anavend. The rest awaited contact. Hear me! Kolfinna tried to call out but was brought back to the present plane by the heat from the flaming ship.

The singers changed tunes, singing to the flame as the sun drifted below the horizon. Blue twilight sat still in contrast to the mighty and expansive blaze. With the solemn tune and drummers in the background, the crowd looked on with humbled eyes, souls partly burning and partly awakening. The fire was bright and strong in the wind, sparks spitting higher than the cliff. Heidi kept singing and fiddling, her strong but pure voice never wavering. Around the ship, Helen gave a nod to the rest of her family. *I love you, too, dearest Mother. I hope to all the gods that this sacrifice is worth it.*

In front of the fire, Eirà again left the circle and walked forward to address the assembly. "Helas, we have one more sacrifice to make." And with that the signing stopped. Steady drumming was now the only music that accompanied the wind. The Oracle emerged from behind Mikkjal and his Guide mates to greet the new Storyteller. In his long purple robe, the old Seer simply raised his forehead. The wind was shuffling his beard, which now contained scattered specks of blowing sand.

"Is this indeed your own decision, Seer? Your own choice?" Eirà asked.

"It is, Storyteller. My time has come." And so, Eirà motioned for the tired old soul to follow him in the direction of the light. Kolfinna looked down, squinting. A tear was leaving her eyes. The Chieftains' circle opened to leave Ivaldi standing directly in front of the flaming ship. As Eirà brought the Oracle before him, the warrior bowed his head, then placed a hand on his wrist. His own eyes clearly quivering, the warrior drew his sword and held it skyward. Its Dust-throwing properties were activated, lighting its white outer cover.

You served us well, old Seer. I wish you could still confront this monster with us, Kolfinna thought with another tear. *But your immediate future is better than ours. You will get to experience the Release once and for all. In your memory, we will fight well.* She would have to take the old man by his right arm, while Eirà took him by the left.

Looking from one of them to the other, the Oracle smiled. "I'll give your regards to old Bjorn." Kolfinna could no longer hold back her tears, which rolled down her face. "You are serving Gorrland until the last," she gasped.

Even Eirà patted him on the shoulder. "It's okay, Man of Mystery," spoke the Oracle quietly. "We have different ways but you'll be a fine Storyteller for all—Mountaineers, Westfolkers, villagers, plain dwellers—and for the Five Chieftains. And if there's anyone I can trust to carry me into the next world its Kolfinna. I shall see you through to Meniya, girl. And to a new epoch for the planet."

Kolfinna sobbed and put her arm around the man's neck. "I'm so sorry. I'm sorry you were cast aside. I'm sorry it has to be you here tonight." She couldn't keep herself from breaking the ceremonial neutrality of sacrifice ritual. A knot edged in her throat. She couldn't find the words to describe her conflicted state. *You're more than a pawn in Skadi and Sigfather's dance, Oracle.*

A smile came across the Oracle's face. "Cast aside? Girl, I am receiving the highest honour. Seeing you on your journey to our Land's future is the best end I could wish for. It is my destiny."

"Aye," spoke Ivaldi. "And it is not the end. We shall meet on the other side in the Eternal Lands, old friend." The warrior chieftain lowered his sword to his chest level. The time was now. It had been fourteen years since a human was last sacrificed. But as one of the two chosen to hold the offered one's body, Kolfinna had to look the

Oracle directly in the eye until she and Eirà saw his soul leave his body. Ivaldi placed his blade to the Oracle's heart, pulled it back, then shoved it in quickly with all his force. White Dust entered the Oracle's open wound and the Seer quickly became listless. The holders took his heavy, drooping body over to the blaze, still staring at his eyes. Slowly, ever so slowly, his soul began to stir, moving outside his body. Kolfinna felt this movement around her heart's space.

With all their might, the two lifted him in their arms and heaved the man onto the burning ship. Once on the pyre it was clear that the Oracle's soul left the flesh, dancing about in the flames as the body caught alight. Beyond them, the music had stopped and folks bowed their heads, leaving the sound of mighty sparks in the flames as the pyre took on and consumed the once powerful man's body. Dozens, if not hundreds of sparks flew over Eirà and Kolfinna, the torchbearers, and the Five Chieftains.

Now was their time to shine—the moment Eirà would redeem himself and everyone would see. Even as sacrifice ceremonies go, this one wasn't ordinary. With the Seer's parting, the people must gain insight, at the very least. Her cheeks alight and her hair fuming, Kolfinna again took her birch baton in her hands, while Eirà removed a smaller branch from his cloak. On it were inscribed runes unreadable to Kolfinna. The Storyteller, however, read it several times, his head undulating with the incantation. The man's torso rotated in circles, and every time he tilted forward he spat at the ground. An ugly sight it was. It was Eirà's trance, though, and not Kolfinna's. Finally, after a dozen or so rotations, he stood tall and calm and recited the word that was increasingly defining this Westfolker who would die to her culture in order to find Skadi.

"Ansuz!" Eirà shouted.

"Ansuz!" Kolfinna repeated, at which point Dust floated outward from her birch, her necklace, and her hand directly into the flames. With it the Pyre crackled and roared twice as high, with hundreds of vibrant sparks rising ten metres further still. The folks closest to the ship took a few steps back from the blaze. Fear clearly struck them.

I don't mind that you fear. Just, please, see like me. Don't leave me alone to see and feel all that is awry. Living in ignorant inertia will save you negative thoughts now, but you will be enslaved, dear Gorrlanders. You are not a people to live in Jorgson's way! Neither are you, Skrallanders, for that matter. North Island, feel what I feel! The call of old will give you a better future than Mikhail...

As the large flame occupied the space newly liberated from the closest members of the crowd, the Oracle's soul was allowed to dance there. Fire mixed with Dust and the glare became a blinding whitish-yellow, while the old Seer's voice boomed.

"Thanks to Gorrland. Yours shall be glory!"
Spectators gasped. Some put their hands over their own mouths. *They heard that, too! When had that ever happened?* Indeed, there was no known knowledge of any departing soul having spoken words understandable to all present. The new magic was working. Kolfinna's spine thrilled and in her sudden ecstatic burst a gleeful burst of joy could not be contained. The Oracle must be thanked, and so must Eirà.

Now, as planned, Kolfinna blew Dust from her birch-gripped hand into the fire, making it brighter and strong enough to take over everyone's field of vision. As it did so, she heard shouts—unrecognizable shouts that weren't those of joy. Booms and clanging came from deep within the flame. The fire within her could not be contained now, as the incantation produced the consequences Eirà had anticipated. Kolfinna gave in to Ansuz. And the things that she saw and felt made her shriek, recoil, and scream, while the red dots of her hand burned and she breathed in that white smoke without smell. Kolfinna hit the ground in terror, hearing the suffering of others, at present and yet to come. But out of the corner of her eye she could still observe the reactions of some of the folks around her. They gasped and shrieked, covering their ears and eyes, horrified at the same sights and sounds. They could indeed see.

And if they should see anything, it should be this. There was the new kind of weapon Lia had mentioned. With it, humans shot other humans down from afar, feeling no threat to themselves and pursuing no bravery in combat. An army was ravaging Land after Land, shooting people unequally armed, then pillaging, killing, raping, and finally taking over every Communications Tower, whose crystals were then shattered. Then there came visions of the old stone fortress of Meniya being consumed by Dust energy itself a thousand years ago. The Dust pierced through stone and into a room where eight people sat—men and women, each one sitting on a throne with a torch by their side. One by one, the eight flames went out, leaving stone-cold darkness. The eight beings scrambled to at least salvage the crystals which were placed beneath their thrones. But neither flesh, nor soul, nor crystal was spared by the blast, which in its wake left but a scorched wasteland. On this Land of ash and ruin walked mechanical men with their distance rifles, screens, and radios. They were backed up by armoured vehicles patrolling and scouting for enemies. This was to be the new rule.

The last image that Ansuz was to give Kolfinna and which she would be able to send to others through the Dust in the flames was of lines of steel protruding out from the ruins of Albrimir's Lands into space, binding it to other planets. As the visions receded and Kolfinna was able to sit up, Sigfather's voice returned to her.

"Jorgson is me without the Huntress—destruction and servitude. You must convene the Nine! Kolfinna and Mikkjal, you are to awaken Skadi!"

Kolfinna turned to notice that Mikkjal, too, was lying on the ground, his hand extended with white Dust extending to and from it. He was hit by this as well.

Now it finally receded, and Kolfinna could feel the earth-plane elements once again. She breathed as she felt the heat on her cheeks and the wind against her cloak and her floating hair. The flame returned to its familiar colour and size. Sitting on the sandy beach, she looked at the shocked audience. Eirà, still standing, looked over her with a concerned glance. The sight had been intense, even for him. But now, realizing herself safe, Kolfinna felt a burst of relief. She had gone further away than at any point with the exception of her Gap travels. She hadn't seen as Kolfinna Helensdottir, eccentric, witty, disturbed daughter of Hrafnshemma but as a vector. As with the exercises, she had died to herself, albeit briefly. Danger and tragedy were there, but they were not the visions that were her lifelong curse of Bad Fate. They were the truth. Or rather, they were a *potential* truth. She chuckled as she rose, staggering to regain herself on the sand. The message in the visions was dire, but she was freer than before, following its course.

Though she laughed, Eirà looked at her, worried. The Storyteller was coming towards her, but Mikkjal beat him there. Her partner grabbed her elbow. "I can see, dear one. That is why we're both here," he said to her, his dark eyes intensely aglow. The Guide could see the chain of events unleashed. "We will find her. We will rebuild the old Council. We will fight along the way. I'm ready to ride to Skralland and to Torvall. I'll ride across the Isaveg. We will ride and convene the Nine, and we will be back by spring."

"Indeed, Mikkjal," spoke Eirà, nodding. "But Kolfinna, you must calm down your personal motivations. Concentrate on Skadi, and specifically on finding the New Shishilm from Skralland. You must contact him or her on your journey there."

Kolfinna was at a lack of words. *Personal motivations?* If anything, her trying to exceed herself was in the service of Skadi and the universe. Wasn't it?

ANSUZ

Eirà calmly allowed the assembly's energy to fall and let Astrid and Ivaldi give the closing remarks. The travellers would embark for Skadi's Temple by snowmobile once they had physically recovered from the experience and their machines had been fuelled up. There was about one time-lapse to go for that.

Chapter 4
Chieftains' Response

Mikkjal

She was overdoing it. Yes, the threat was considerable and the visions she shared were frightening to all, but her every breathing second was now devoted to the mission. She couldn't relax at all.

Trachtsin plants soothed Mikkjal's thoughts and muscles, as he sipped its warm, sweet tea. From the armchair he had a view of the moonlit hills and forest.

Skadi's Temple didn't even have a bed the last time he visited. Everything tonight was prearranged. Eirà and whoever else maintained the cabin had placed candles and warm furs around this new mattress, encouraging a meaningful sexual encounter. Kolfinna dutifully followed the script, this being work for her. Before, during, and after the time she spent fucking her partner, she recited prayers and poems for Skadi. Then, when she was again clothed, came time for the famous Huldra Prayer and Death-relase exercise. She spent time next to Mikkjal without being with him. Even now, as she slept, he wondered whether the slumber was for her or if it was part of another plan or ritual.

An overgenerous Guide's estimate, Mikkjal brought three days' worth of food. They would have storm provisions, even though the air promised clear weather until their arrival in Skralland after sunset tomorrow. He also supplied the machines with an extra two days' worth of fuel in stone pots he packed in the rear of both supply sleds.

ANSUZ

Would his path cross the two Guides he and Kjartan spent time with during last winter's supply visit? Jaani and Kunuut were their names. After the Providers had secured the new goods in the sleds, the four Guides spent the rest of the day racing their machines on the bay and target shooting their arrows in the hills. Although humans may go to war and although spirits above may get upset, the Land stays the same. Guides live off it. May there be a small amount of fun in Skralland, before Kolfinna ushers the poor Skrallander Shishilm onward with them across the Isaveg!

"It looks like the plan is for us to be inspired and cozy on our first night." Kolfinna spoke plainly as Eirà rode away on his machine and they kicked the snow off their boots in the Temple's entrance. The sorcerer's men left candles and fur everywhere and removed the daggers from the central table. Mikkjal was enjoying the coziness but was doing so alone.

Finishing his tea, he looked down at his hand, then back at his birch staff extending from his brown parka at the door. "Can you feel me, Mikhail Jorgson?" he chuckled. "I have the marks, so I guess I'm your enemy, too. You don't want to share your world and ways with sorcerers, Mikhail?"

Alas, not every person on the planet would see through him. Gorrlanders had so recently been tested by Sigfather's blasts. Their Gap initiation was barely a week before, where Sigfather had given a precise warning about a figure like Jorgson. Folk on Lands that weren't recently called by Sigfather from the Gap may well believe Mikhail's broadcast. That must be why he singled out Kolfinna. Only two days after she shared on the airwaves that she'd been to the Gap and returned initiated into Sigfather's mysteries, Jorgson brandished her an evil sorceress. If he didn't offer the world his vision, large numbers of people may begin to believe her story. Luckily for him, most people would more readily choose progress and prosperity than esoteric superstition, which was what he painted Kolfinna's magic out to be.

They were not most people, Mikkjal thought, standing up and looking at Kolfinna. He scratched his bare chest and went to put an extra log on the fire, preferring indoor heat to layers. Ordinary folks want what's best for themselves and their families. Extraordinary folks can defend their loved ones against external threats. Exceptional folks are able to discern when a threat is external or internal and adapt their defence accordingly.

Astrid, Marja, and Ivaldi all recognized an internal threat arising if Gorrlanders refused to change. Insistence on moving "forward" in farming and not heeding the flexibility of the more "backwards" nomads, hunters, and herders would make time ripe for someone like Jorgson. If Jorgson had come to Gorrland after the Nordhemma Tragedy and the ensuing despair, he could have easily turned the "forward-thinking" Westfolkers against the "backwards" Mountaineers. In fact, were it not for Storyteller Bjorn's astuteness and flexibility, Gorrland may have produced its own Jorgson. Many a Westfolker already thought war on the "primitives" was a preferable response to the kidnappings than Bjorn's family model flexibility.

Such were Astrid's words to Mikkjal after the ceremony, just before they rode eastward. Astuteness and flexibility was her explanation as to why she personally accepted Old Man Eirà as new Storyteller.

Bjorn, Astrid, and the other Chieftains were exceptional, but what of the ordinary in Albrimir, who may be seduced by Mikhail's promises? Kolfinna, for all her attempts to contact Shishilms and Skadi, did not think enough about those people. It would be the ordinary who would have to choose to embrace Skadi's Time, the beliefs, and the way of life involved. The other Lands would need to have good leadership, as Gorrland did, to make this matter understood by their ordinary folk.

They would start off by seeing Skralland's leaders. Though Mikkjal had been there five times in his life, the only leader he'd met was Guide Chieftain Ungilattaqi. Akinisie, the Communicator Chieftain, seemed sympathetic to their cause, else she wouldn't have transmitted Torvall's secret message. But how would she act if and when her own "sorcerer" was threatened by an army with Jorgson's weapons? *These* were the kind of matters Kolfinna and Mikkjal would have to think about as they set out to unite the Lands with a goddess whose ways many considered uncivilized.

Sigfather trusts Skadi. But, as the master of the Flares, a god of many names, all Folks dealt with him in many ways. To get to Sigfather's desire for the Huntress, they would have to dialogue with every Folk's representation of him.

Mikkjal sighed. He'd gone farther from his Westfolk farm than he'd ever dreamed as a child. He'd seen Skralland five times and Torvall once. He led the Folk at the Solidarity Reaffirmation, an event his educators had prepared him for since he was a child. Even though the truth about Sigfather's Dust attacks was nothing he'd expected, he stood on the front line to see it. "If anyone can convince Skrallanders or Torvallians of what we know, it's you," Father Heike had said before departure.

Did that mean Mikkjal should speak first when they came before the Skralland leaders? He couldn't take attention away from the girl whose name Jorgson had broadcast on the air to every Land in Albrimir. Still, he could add perspective to the discussions Kolfinna began.

Unconvinced he was ready to join his partner in the bed, Mikkjal went to put on his bearskin parka and boots and take a step outside. He wouldn't be going far enough to need either the snowshoes or skis that adorned the side wall of the cabin. Nor would he need Sigfather's presence, so he took his runic birch out of the pocket and left it on the table before stepping out into the cold.

Kolfinna woke up with neither hunger nor presence, only staring out the window and smoking her pipe. "We should go" would be her only words to him until midday. Mikkjal took his time, frying a dozen or so chunks of frozen reindeer from the box. She only ate two. She drank no tea, preferring to consume her trachtsin by smoking. He breakfasted, drank tea, and packed up the supplies to the sound of the burning hearth.

Both snow machines needed a cold start, and Mikkjal let them warm up for twenty minutes. With fuel tanks still nearly full and the crystal's autonomous power strong, Mikkjal sheathed his sword. Kolfinna remembered to radio Marja, and they were off. It was at nine-thirty—five and a half time-lapses before midday—and rays of sunshine were starting to emerge between the rolling peaks. Mikkjal led the way between pines and shrubs, quickly gaining speed in the thick powder. There were some quick turns between trees and some side slopes that required leaning but the terrain wasn't challenging. Mountaineer territory was beautiful. It soothed his breath and body. Turning behind, he saw Kolfinna had kept up with him. Whatever was on her mind that stole her hunger had no impact on her riding skills.

As they went further east, they came to a section that levelled out and they could advance on flat ground in the thin forest. Their snowmobiles' hums shuffled life around them as much as their skis sprayed snow in all directions. For another thirty kilometres or so Mikkjal spotted tracks in his peripheral vision—some from riders and others from skiers. None were suitable to follow, though, so he blazed the eastbound trail himself. The snow held life well. Fresh fox and caribou tracks emerged here and there, and ptarmigan tracks were almost everywhere. As he approached any small group of leafless shrubs, flocks of these white birds swarmed from hiding like snow squalls, flying on to the next group of shrubs. Hunting them was fun. He thought about stopping to get his bow from the back sled to carry over his shoulder in case he got a good shot along the way but looked at Kolfinna and thought better of it. She clearly had the mission on her mind as she rode. From the grey fur of her hat and hood edge, her bright hair blew in the wind. Under the black-bodied duck down coat, she surely wasn't cold. This attire was obviously more fit for the forest than the green leather jacket she often wore.

With the morning sky perfectly clear, they steered over a rolling hill that took them beyond the tree line. From there, even in descent, they remained in a moderately wide treeless valley, with rocky peaks on either side. Mikkjal tuned his senses. Winding between peaks, the tundra advanced and receded, with groups of short pines or bare, ptarmigan-sheltering shrubs coming and going. Once they braked for lunch, he'd get his arrows and shoot some in the afternoon, for sure.

Last winter's trip was in Tenmonth, when the snows were thin and lakes barely frozen. He couldn't ride nearly as fast and had to rely a lot more on his land senses. Gorrland vegetables from several farms, including the one his parents owned, exported vegetables in exchange for seal meat. It was the fourth North Island supply exchange of the year, and the first by snowmobile since snow's return in late Ninemonth. Provider Chieftain Petr accompanied his host of eight farmers. The Skralland Hunter he spoke to joked about the excessive formalism of Westfolk Gorrlanders. The trip was precisely organized, leaving little room for down time. According to him, such was the mark of sedentary folk. Mountaineer Hunters visited Skralland more often, more informally, and often exchanged meat and berries.

In the Taqraup Village the ground was free from snow for a mere three months out of sixteen. In the eastern hills, near North Island's tip, it was only two months. As such, they were happy to get those vegetables. While lengthening winters made farming more and more difficult in Gorrland, it had never even been considered on Skralland's part of the island. That made life harder.

But, on the other hand, they did not have a thick, uninhabited zone to their north like Gorrlanders did, which was ripe for hostile clans. Instead, they made use of the wide tundra to the northeast. There were regular ice outposts for fishing and hunting, and a few nomadic groups still camped at varying locations there. According to Jaani and Kunuut, the Guides that operated there conducted peculiar stealth training under the supervision of "The Girl from the East." From what Mikkjal had heard, this Guide didn't particularly care for village life.

Mikkjal's motor buzzed its bug-pitched noise and barrelled through powder as thin as the air itself. They seared through the valley until the snow cover began to harden as they cut around some rocky cliffs and climbed once more. The land was solid and without risk. Nothing had yet been communicated on their radios from Gorrland Tower, which was good news. He intensified his hold on the throttle, making good speed up a hill, with Kolfinna riding smoothly behind, her hair still fluttering. He slowed to cut around several large boulders and came to a long, treeless straightaway. Just before he squeezed the throttle for all it was worth in a hard acceleration, he noticed Kolfinna had slowed down. He eased back and let her catch up with him.

"What is it?" he shouted above the motor, now rumbling rather than humming.

Kolfinna stopped and cut her motor altogether. "The time. Midday."

Mikkjal pulled out his belt radio and verified. "It is indeed," he shouted, then cut his own engine. "Does that mean anything in particular?"

"It's time for Mikhail Jorgson's message. He goes on the air at midday."

"I see." Mikkjal breathed heavily into the air. He stepped off his snowmobile and walked on the snow to Kolfinna's machine. "He did that yesterday. You think he'll do it again today?"

"He will," said Kolfinna, her green eyes showing worry. She hadn't been pondering rituals in her head all morning.

"Right. Well, we're still in Gorrland. Would you like to check in with Marja before we continue?" asked Mikkjal.

"I don't want to hear him or hear about him," she implored. "Can't we just not listen?"

Mikkjal looked around. "I mean, it's a clear day with no obstruction. We won't have trouble reaching Skralland Village. I guess we could turn off our radios."

"Splendid!" Kolfinna shouted, then grabbed her radio from her belt and turned the knob off. She kissed Mikkjal on the cheek. "This makes me happy."

"We should try to be happy," said Mikkjal. "Are you ready to eat lunch?"

"I'm starving."

Mikkjal was puzzled by her response. She chose to hardly eat breakfast. "Right. Let's make it then," he said with a nod and walked towards the sled. "So, this morning, you didn't... *see* or *hear* anything?"

Kolfinna sighed and smiled. "I tried. But the airwaves were calm. Since then, I started to enjoy the calm."

"I won't say no to enjoying the calm, Kolfinna." Mikkjal ran his hand through her long blond hair and took off his fur hat. They would make a fire next to one of the boulders. Moosemeat stew with potatoes would be the meal.

Over lunch the couple discussed what would have been, if it weren't for Lia's revelation about his weapons, the most awe-striking part of Jorgson's technological announcement—space travel. It had been the dream of every Communicator ever since they had received signals from Ragnik and Boldein fifteen years ago. People will want to travel in space and visit other planets and their beings. No matter what hidden knowledge the Ancient Meniyans possessed, no matter who they may have been able to communicate with through Ansuz, physical travel to another world was something that should be attempted if the means exist. Such was common thought and was even the thought of Kolfinna and Mikkjal. Even if they were victorious in uniting the New Shishilms in Meniya with Skadi, it would be a shame if Sigfather and Skadi's energy destroyed Jorgson's space technology altogether. If it must be destroyed with Jorgson, at least allow good people to learn how it works first.

Mikkjal wondered if maybe they were not meant to use the Dust and its crystals in that way, and that maybe it was the price to pay for being independent. Kolfinna acknowledged that she couldn't see Skadi championing space machines but knew that there were Communicators like Marja and Akinisie who would put such equipment to good use.

It wasn't Marja or Akinisie that invented it, though. It was Mikhail Iorki-Son, Kolfinna and Mikkjal both knew.

With the tyrant defeated, could they take his equipment without reviving what he stood for? Could they avoid trying to control animals, plants, spirits, other humans? Perhaps they could keep the space vessels and destroy the weapons. The space vessels could be put to a positive use. Gorrlanders would all agree on that. Then again, the weapons could also be put to a positive use. If Kieran had had one of those so-called rifles when he went out on his jubilant solo ride in the Outlands, he could have defended himself. If those tools had existed, Mikkjal would still have a little brother. They could save so many people.

And it wouldn't only be the so-called rifles that could help. If Läckjell were to decide to raid again, after more than three decades, Jorgson's armoured vehicles with so-called cannons could protect Gorrland from them. Canons on Gorrland ships would save them from attacks…

But Gorrlanders attack, too…

If, once space contact is made with Ragnik, Boldein, or extra-solar planets and one of these planet's beings are hostile, an arsenal of Jorgson's equipment will be of positive, protective use…

But Albrimir can attack, too. We can attack, and we can take power from the gods. We should never have that power. Even space technology alone. It would be better for Skadi and Sigfather to destroy everything Jorgson made. Don't tempt Albrimir with that power!

Upon reaching such a conclusion over lunch they breathed deeper. They both knew the stand they would take with the Skrallanders, the Torvallians, and any other people.

"Did you contact the Skralland Shishilm yet?" Mikkjal asked Kolfinna as they sat on the snow, finishing their bowls of moose stew.

"No. I tried. It's as though he or she doesn't want to make contact," she replied.

"Hmm. You think Skralland's leaders, like Akinisie, are pro-Jorgson and maybe the Shishilm just doesn't want to risk being found out?"

Kolfinna looked around with a long pause. "It's something that would be so improbable to me it almost sounds mad. Taqramiut are more like Skadi than any single Folk. Then again, Akinisie is a masterful Communicator who has made much progress on radios. Maybe she could be tempted…"

Mikkjal looked down at his boots. North Island's two peoples had been allied for nearly two hundred years. Being on opposing sides was simply not natural. But nor was it natural for one person to have the things Jorgson had. Nor was it natural for one person to try to take over the planet thanks to these things.

Mikkjal would bring up fonder matters for discussion over tea.

***

CHIEFTAINS' RESPONSE

Attention! Attention!

Attention please on the long-range frequency of one thousand crystal waves per second. Attention please on the all-Albrimir Communicators' frequency.

It is midday, on the Thirteenth of Fifteenmonth, 963. We reach out to you, good Communicators of Albrimir. It is with pleasure that I announce that we've received a messages from Communicator Chieftain Arban of Khairtai on the medium-range 1800 wave per second frequency. Chieftain Arban has announced that both Khairtai and Shá have issued statements condemning sorcery. Both Lands will do their best to prevent any backwards elements in their people from plotting against Iorki's progressive aims. The leaders of both Lands urge all other peoples to do the same, most notably Anavend of Kalyim. Communicator Chieftain Arban of Khairtai urges Communicator Chieftain Ilmari of Kalyim to use his rhetorical powers to persuade Shishilm Anavend of the right choices.

Those were the diplomatic words of Chieftain Arban. Now Chieftain Abbott of Iorki and I say this to you, Anavend: if Khairtai and Shá can develop resolve, then so can you. Give the word to Ilmari and he can radio us on medium-range, like Arban did. Let us know you'll hand the thieves and sorceress over.

Abbott and myself urge the other Communicators to convince their Lands to make resolutions like Khairtai and Shá did. The southern mainland Folks have chosen peace. Will the folks of the South Islands, Wanautipun and Solicia, so chose? Will the folks of North Island so choose, Gorrland and Taqraup Nunaat? I ask the Communicator Chieftains of the four undecided Lands by name: Tia, Ehukai, Marja, Akinisie, convince your leaders! Make the right choice against barbarism and the sorceress. A glorious Spring awaits.

Greetings from Iorki!

***

ANSUZ

Kolfinna

The red of Mikkjal's taillight soothed the white snow that made the dim twilight sing. A rising waxing moon shone on land more rugged, even alien, to what Kolfinna had seen before. Here it was distinctly colder than at the cabin temple in the morning. The snow cover was shallower and harder, which made Mikkjal have to swerve to avoid rocks while blazing downhill on more than one occasion. He was a Guide who never faltered, always the most dependable of them. Marja had referred to him as the sturdiest young Guide, from what she'd heard about him from expeditions, hunting parties, and scouting trips.

Only the normal variety of visions came that morning —scenes from past misery signalling some or another kind of failure. She saw the Oracle speaking of Siljol the family fleer, who confessed in the amphitheatre eighteen years ago and was never allowed to sleep with another woman. She saw Ivaldi speaking of numerous cowards, who were tied to ship masts or dragged behind snowmobiles as punishment. She saw Father Bjorn speaking of the late Haral Oggsson, a trickster who lied about receiving a prophecy. Haral was given a cave on the hills north of Egilman's Plateau to live the rest of his life in solitude. She saw Westfolk clan head Arnold condemning Susanne for not waiting until her Quest to pursue sexual companions. She was to wear the Necklace of Bad Fate until she turned thirty years old. "You who are without patience before fifteen years of life shall wait another fifteen years for joy."

Susanne got caught. But one need not get caught to be cursed with Bad Fate…

She saw the Oracle sitting with Bjorn, giving the Storyteller his daughter's diagnosis. *Curse of the Visions.* Healing session one. *Failure.* Healing session two. *Failure.* Healing session three. *She will just live with it.* Kolfinna would live but wouldn't care for years. She would have lovers before her Quest, too. What did rules matter when she had already been told she'd have to live her whole life with a Curse? Because of the words of her Quest, she'd been initiated into Marja's Order, though she believed nothing. One year onward she just lay on the bed in her family home. If Mother hadn't shaken her back to something resembling life, she may still be on her bed.

Why can't all of this be gone? Skadi, hear my rituals and prayers!

She'd heard nothing after the Huldra Prayer and sex ritual. Thank the gods Kolfinna had thought to turn off her radio at midday so as to not have news from Jorgson, if none was forthcoming from her allies. Soon, though, she'd hear about whatever Mikhail had said from Akinisie.

Mikkjal zoomed around a rugged cliff and began waving his hand, nodding and pointing at the frozen valley below. The snow and ice lit up the night sky so much that very few stars could be seen. Icy Ragnik must look just like this! She squinted and strained. Was it there? Yes ! Oh-so-small and oh-so-far were a few yellow lights shining from Skralland's only full-time settlement. Beyond that village was the bay that would eventually open to the sea. Mikkjal was smiling at her. Of course he saw and sensed better than she could. Perhaps he saw all the way to the cape past the village—the point where the sea began. While she allowed the sensory pleasure of the present valley, her mind couldn't stray far from the duty Sigfather bestowed upon her. *Please receive me, neighbour Folk.*

With the hum of the two snowmobiles, she would've missed an important sign had she not looked down at her belt. The radio receiving light was on. It flickered stronger and stronger. Now it was real. She was within one-to-one radio distance, so she decided to switch the device back on. It was ten minutes until time-lapse twenty-one. They were almost there and things were beginning to settle in Kolfinna's mind with a calm excitement. But Mikkjal looked back at her a couple of times, an expression of thoughtfulness and worry visible from beneath his fur hood.

Say something if you feel something!

It was then that Kolfinna saw something. It only lasted a second—an intense and jolting flicker before her mind's eye. A village of snow houses sat beneath a mountain. Down from the mountain came a giant, who crushed the village beneath its feet.

Then the flicker was gone. As if it had never happened, the gentle sloping deep valley returned beneath the bright moonlit sky.

Did you feel it too, Mikkjal?

He no longer looked back at her but didn't slow down or stop either. Kolfinna's heart beat fast. There could be danger for Skralland, although the giant she saw didn't seem associated with Mikhail Jorgson. Whatever else it was, though, its energy wasn't a good sign. It wasn't altogether unfamiliar, though.

With a seeking mind, Kolfinna rode for several minutes as they descended into the widening valley. Nothing foreign, nothing menacing was there now; only the rocks they weaved around, the thinning snow cover, and the outline of the great frozen bay. From here, she could no longer make out the settlement's lights because of the way the land plateaued before the upcoming sharp downward slope. On either side of the bay extending out were mountains that were quite high themselves, though lower than the highlands from which they had just descended.

Mikkjal cried indiscernibly above the engines as he pulled back next to her. She nodded and didn't ask him to repeat it. Where are the houses? She wanted to speed up and arrive sooner, even considered taking the lead from Mikkjal. But that wouldn't be wise. Close though they may be, the ground still had time to present treachery, so following the Guide was the best option. Mikkjal's throttle rose in tone, or so it seemed at first before

Kolfinna saw lights zeroing in on them from both sides. Their hums echoed off the rocks and vibrated up through the snow's surface.

"Here are my mates!" Mikkjal shouted.

A new pressure in her chest formed before her heart could relax. Soon, she would have to explain herself to a new Folk, all the while Mikhail Jorgson was calling for her head! She prayed Akinisie would take her side, though there was little reason to believe she wouldn't. After all, she had agreed with Marja to allow their passage through their Land. From a hidden nook on the left, two snowmobiles emerged, and another appeared almost directly behind them, quickly taking a spot on their right. One of the riders took the lead, a hand waving and a face becoming visible inside a thick, furry hood. He was a robust and muscular man and cried in Albrimese in a heavy voice, "Gorrlanders, you made it! You're early!" The strong man smiled.

Mikkjal smiled back at him. It was clear that they already knew each other. It was also clear that he was the leader of the group. He motioned with his left hand for Gorrlanders and Skrallanders alike to follow him.

To the left was a young man and to the right was a woman with radiant brown streaks of hair emerging from within her parka. She nodded at each of the Western riders, then looked at her leader. Five snowmobilers zigged and zagged, avoiding rocks and crevasses with ease.

A few lights came into the picture before the bay, becoming more and more until two dozen dwellings or so could be made out. It quickly became easy to distinguish the colours of the permanent dwellings under the bright moonlight over the bay straight ahead. Some houses were red, some yellow, some blue; all resembled the houses of Gorrland's South Port. Only by looking at the dwellings that surrounded these wooden houses could one know that she was *not* in South Village.

ANSUZ

Kolfinna had learned that in Skralland in wintertime, many nomadic clans settled around the central village, building houses of turf and others of snow. At this time of year, around two-thirds of the Land's population would be housed in or near the village. A family's commitment to living in the village zone—as well as the degree of hunting luck they'd enjoyed in previous years—could be determined by the permanence or transience of their town dwelling structures. They passed scattered snow house domes here and there, and saw more up on a slope to the left. Every so often someone would stick their head out the door from one of the permanent wooden houses to take a look at the riders. Sometimes children accompanied the adults, waving away at the passersby.

Scattered small snow houses gave way to larger snow houses and eventually turf houses. For those people who tended to have two dwelling places—one for summer, one for winter—the turf houses were large, held up by bone and built into the ground. They were warmer than the snow houses, so they required more investment. And they were warmer ever more so that they were inhabited by at least five families at one time. These houses were among the warmest places in all North Island. Kolfinna remembered the cultural training session the retired Skrallander Communicator Elisapie had given during her Gorrland visit four years ago.

From these turf houses more people emerged, waving to the new guests from the west. The trail gave way to clear village streets, as the leader slowed down even more and the others followed suit on the now thickly packed snow till they reached a large red permanent house standing on a hill. On one side of this house were turf houses and to the other side were wooden houses. In front of it stood a host of around ten people, half of whom were holding torches. Everyone turned off their machines. The large man came over to Mikkjal, shaking his hand warmly and uttering a welcoming word in his language with a large smile. Mikkjal replied with a few words in the Skrallander tongue. The large man presented his colleagues, a young man and woman, to Mikkjal. Then he walked over to Kolfinna.

At this point he pushed back his hood and spoke clearly in Communications Albrimese. "Greetings. You are the Communicator Kolfinna, are you not?"
She nodded.

"We have heard about your journeys," said the man. "I am Ungilattaqi, Guide Chieftain of Taqraup Nunaat. There is Olaf and Alaraq." He motioned to his two riders. "Come, Kolfinna, I will present to you someone you already know." He gestured to a tall and beautiful woman in a fox fur hat. "This is Akinisie Narralik, Taqraup Nunaat's Communicator Chieftain."

This is her?! She was radiant and warm with a glowing face and gentle dark hair.

"Akinisie?" Kolfinna smiled and bowed.

"Greetings, colleague. A pleasure to finally meet you, Kolfinna," she said, grabbing her forearm beneath the elbow. "Your name is known to all."

Kolfinna removed her hood and hat, and adjusted her hair, while Akinisie elegantly walked over and shook hands with Mikkjal.

"I should introduce you to all these people," Akinisie said. She proceeded to a stout man with a thin beard in a dark brown parka. "This is Singataaq, Hunter. This man to his left is Ittoq, also a Hunter member of our Land Council." Ittoq was taller and younger than Singataaq, a bit large but not round, and bore an enthusiastic face. "To Ittoq's right are Mikisoq and Taamusi, our two Elder members." Though the two were more or less elderly, they both had youthful eyes and nodded with a smile in the bright torchlight.

"Another person you'll have to know," continued the Chieftain, "is this woman here. She's the one whose house you'll be staying in. A stoutish young woman came over and shook the Gorrlanders' hands. Her hood was down, revealing long black hair and a welcoming face.

"My name is Naujaq. I hope you like my place. I'll take you there now."

After feeling the warmth of the welcoming party, Kolfinna remembered the urgency of the mission. They had to be forewarned and prepared. She took a step away from Naujaq and spoke to the Chieftain, still loud enough for those around to hear. "Akinisie, did Iorki-Son make an announcement today, like yesterday?"

Akinisie repositioned her loose hair within her hood. "He did. It turns out Khairtai and Shá have said they side with Jorg and will reign in their... hmm... *those who hear your call.*"

Kolfinna's heart sunk. Jorgson didn't appear dangerous to everyone.

"He explicitly asked the South Islands and North Island to state our positions," Akinisie continued. "He personally asked it of Tia, Ehukai, Marja, and myself. He wants us to disavow you before we even understand you."

"And will you?"

Akinisie stared directly into Kolfinna's eyes. With her own brown eyes, the leader emanated a strange mix of confidence and uncertainty, or so Kolfinna intuited. "Well, with that warrior ship Ivaldi sent to the glacier edge, you Gorrlanders made sure I wouldn't really have a choice now, didn't you? Could we ever oppose Albrimir's greatest warriors?"

A silence came upon them, each Communicator observing the steam coming from their breath amidst the burning torches. Kolfinna felt a knot in her gut. "Relax, girl." Akinisie broke the tension with a smile. "We won't do anything that would make problems between the Folks of North Island. And we won't put the life of any of our own people at risk to please Iorki-Son, even if this person does have a sorcerer's magic and red marks."

"That's reassuring for us. Which begs me to ask, *do* you know of someone that has sorcerer's magic and red marks? They would look like this." Kolfinna removed her bearskin mitt and pulled back her right sleeve to show the red dots. "Any person with these marks has been called by the Flares, whom we name Sigfather, to travel to Meniya across the Glacier. I've become able to communicate by Dust to all who receive the mark and the call."

Akinisie looked without emotion at Kolfinna's hand and back to her eyes. "No. We have no one like that."

"Oh. Well, as Marja must have told you, we must unite the heirs to ancient Meniya—the *New Shishilms*—as a way to stop Mikhail Iorki-Son. The Flares and Skadi's combined energies will stop him. They're the balance that the world always needed… *combined*. Skadi—or perhaps you know her by another name—was the one who used the ancient Ansuz spell. You know, from the esoteric teachings we received. I am sensitive to it and can use it now." Only when she stopped talking did Kolfinna realize how fast she'd been speaking.

"You've taken Eirà's counsel. You're not the only one who has spoken with him."

"*What?!*"

"You think a hermit like him stays on his side of the mountains? He travels to Taqraup Nunaat often. In fact, he was just here this morning, speaking what you just said with some of the more nomadic of our Folk."

Kolfinna gasped and shifted her weight to maintain her bearings. "How could he? We saw him just last night and he—"

"He didn't tell you he was already in touch with us? Of course not. He does things on his own time. But he left at midday, so don't go looking for him tonight. One thing's for certain—he's no friend of Mikhail Iorki-Son. His ideas about you and Ansuz and your Skadi-goddess-who-still-lives-in-the-flesh are something I'd love to believe, but I'm a bit more empirical than Eirà. I'll believe it when I see it. And now we've got plenty of our own problems here in Taqraup Nunaat."

Akinisie took the torch from the Elder Mikisoq's hand and motioned with it back to Naujaq. "Now I ask you to go to your guest house, Kolfinna and Mikkjal. I believe we are on the same side. We've heard about your Gap journey. Personally, if I were your Chieftain, I would not have allowed you to broadcast it on the air upon return. Now Iorki-Son knows who to target. That being said, we have no direct experience with your red dots or your spirit communication. We'll speak of all this in due time. Perhaps Eirà is right. But for now, enjoy the next few days in our Land. You will have several activities to take part in. You two must forgive us, though. Things are not as they usually are. Don't be surprised if you come across sadness and sickness here that has nothing to do with you. We are faced with some… issues." Akinisie finished with a sorrow in her eye that she'd suppressed in her initial presentation.

"The Tower. Marja—

"I will inform her of your arrival, Kolfinna. Please, follow Naujaq now," Akinisie spoke from under her breath and looked down.

Kolfinna looked at Mikkjal. There was nothing else to do. They walked over to the stout young woman, who walked with her torch away from the crowd. The other Council members, their faces unresponsive, turned and followed Akinisie in the other direction, inside the red house.

Naujaq motioned for the visitors to start their machines and follow her to where her own snowmobile was parked beside a snow house. As they reignited Kolfinna was able to see, just over a small hill, the immense structure that was Skralland's main Tower.

They rode behind Naujaq between alleys and streets, which let them see it even more. It was a structure by the bay's shore, a bit away from the village but still looming over everything else. It must be at least twice as tall as Gorrland's Tower, with a bright metal structure glowing beneath the mighty antenna.

Kolfinna's face was glued to the structure as they rode between village houses. Akinisie clearly had more means than Marja did, in terms of technology and likely also in terms of range. But what was that light that glowed from inside and outside the Tower? Unfortunately, they turned away from it as Naujaq showed them through an area with several houses, lit by fuel lamps, torches, or hearths. Finally, she pulled up to a small green house with a cozy smoking chimney.

"Tunngasutsiaritsi!" she called out as she turned her engine off in the driveway. "I live here alone, but it should be big enough for the two of you." Naujaq spoke very good Communications Albrimese.

"Anything is fine," Mikkjal replied, stepping off his machine. "In fact, I thought we'd have to share a big turf house." He spoke a mixture of Albrimese and a few Skrallander words.

Naujaq laughed. "Yes, I'm aware of what Gorrlanders like to say about our turf houses. It's not all it's cracked up to be with fifty people spending a whole winter under one roof. You'll be glad you're alone, the two of you."

"Thank you, welcoming woman," replied Kolfinna, following Naujaq to the doorway.

"Thank you for your visit," Naujaq replied with a smile. I have one question. What was the word you said ? Sig-fodr ? Father… victory father?"

Kolfinna nodded.

"That's the word you use in Gorrlander to designate *the Flares?*"

It must be true. "Are you a Communicator? You speak Albrimese and know Communicators' terms."

"No, I'm not. But my husband is. He speaks of his work to me. In our Land, the Flares is referred to as the Evolver."

"The Flares are here now, I know. Sigfather, the Evolver is calling all Lands," Kolfinna uttered quietly in Albrimese. Naujaq pushed the door open and motioned for the guests to walk into the small house.

The wide-set Skrallander woman simply raised her eyebrows and removed her fur cap, revealing long black hair that fluttered around her deerskin parka.

Naujaq spoke again. "Something is here in Taqraup Nunaat. Something that isn't good. But we haven't had any experience like yours. No dots, no call."

"What have you experienced?" asked Mikkjal.

"Sickness. Sickness bringing isolation," she answered. Mikkjal grunted and looked to and fro. "They will let you know soon. You can trust Akinisie and the other Chieftains and Council members. I must go home for dinner. On the back porch, there is a sealed cooler with plenty of food in it. Meat and even vegetables, traded from your Land last summer."

"Thank you," Kolfinna replied in Taqraup Nunaat's language while trying to smile.

Naujaq smiled without surprise. "You're welcome, Kolfinna Helensdottir," she replied in her native tongue. She turned around and walked over the wooden floor and out the front door.

The house was simple and cozy. There was one floor with a high mezzanine containing the bed. Beside the wood stove was a couch and a chair. Kolfinna went straight to the couch, leaving Mikkjal to take care of the dwindling fire. He put two large logs on it.

Before going back out to the snowmobiles to unload their supplies, he made a revelation to her. "I'm glad she doesn't believe Eirà's words so blindly. He's the Storyteller Gorrland needs, but the world has different perspectives that we can also listen to." He slowed down his word pace, hesitating so as not to stumble. "Please forgive me for not fully understanding you. I hope I do one day..." And with that he looked down and walked back out the door to fetch their belongings.

Kolfinna looked at him as he exited but then simply lay down on her stomach on the couch. Was he criticizing her or was he seriously apologizing for not fully understanding her? If it was the latter, it would be the first time anyone had ever done so.

Chapter 5
A Long First Day

Conniving hermit! Since there's obviously stuff you aren't telling me, I'll follow my own path to Skadi. I'll find out where she is and find the Shishilms, too. Just keep wandering so that you'll have some good poems to recite. I'll save the world for us!

Kolfinna descended the ladder from the mezzanine bed and went straight to put wood in the stove. With it fired up she could be comfortable enough to lie on the wood floor in her underwear. It was time for Death-release once again. She quickly looked at her belt radio on the kitchen table and breathed a sigh of relief. Time-lapse four past midnight. Mikkjal wouldn't wake up for at least another three. She had plenty of time to disappear and seek before then.

She lay her bare legs out on the hard floor, placed her birch stave beside her, closed her eyes, and breathed in. Once, twice, three times. Darkness came. The room disappeared in black and Kolfinna floated.

The room was the Gap, she realized.

The Shishilms would show up.

Breathing, floating, she feels Lia in her pulsating hand. Her Dust is activated.

There she appears, on her throne, the white odourless smoke swirling around and through her. She is safe. And the Torvallian appears next to her. He is robust and well-dressed, a ceremonial brown tunic going from knees to neck.

Anavend and I are together, Lia pulsates.

I won't betray you, Lia, or the others, Anavend communicates. *But we don't have the weapons or warriors to repel him. We're not fighters.*

Kolfinna breathed, darkness separating her from Naujaq's cabin room by more than an age. We will send our people. No one from Gorrland supports his aims.

That is good, pulsated Anavend's energy to Kolfinna's hand. *That's more than I can say for my people.*

Of course. *The closed-minded fools they were.*

They are afraid, came Lia.

They were. Kolfinna, though, had learned to let go of her fears. She'd learned that thanks to the wise Eirà, who was pursuing his own mission independent of her. Focus, focus, she told herself, coming back to the comfortable release of death. Breathe into the abyss. You are the Gap. Who else is there?

The room was there, with beings seated at eight thrones. They sat; they emanated; they breathed. Faces were shrouded but one head flickered. Blue-white light overcame the figure's shadow. One, then two, then three, then four… they were activated.

Who are you? Kolfinna spoke through the energy. They couldn't hear yet, so she cut away all thought, hope, expectation, and desire as best she could. *Die to yourself, truly, Kolfinna Helensdottir.*

Then, as she finished talking only to herself she received an unexpected response.

You're not Kolfinna Helensdottir. You're an old soul. At that moment a male face took form from one of the four flickering throne beings. He was young, similar to Kolfinna's age. A young man with dark hair and brown skin. *You're our only chance now.*

And who are you? Kolfinna pulsated with her hand.

Ashkii from Khairtai. We must come to you now. All of us.

And there the other three shadows were clarified. In addition to Ashkii, there was one other male and two females, all with southern features.

ANSUZ

Come. I am in Taqraup Nunaat, soon to go to Kalyim. Ashkii, and you? She looked at the woman from the tip of the southern mainland, Kaltland. *From Shá…*

Lowanna.

Ashkii and Lowanna. Your leaders sided with Mikhail…

They did. We are not safe here.

Come join me and Mikkjal in Taqraup Nunaat if you can. By ship. She tried to reach out to the two thrones who didn't identify themselves yet. One for Skralland, one for Gorrland. But how? She and Mikkjal were *both* called by Sigfather from Gorrland. How come no one showed up in the room of eight? One of the figures breathed but didn't respond. The Skrallander who is still hiding. But the other, the Gorrlander, was shifting back and forth. A shrill scream came from there but no face revealed itself.

It was time for Kolfinna to return to life. She slammed her feet on the wood and watched the throne room disappear, the darkness recede, and saw her hand glowing white with Dust. She sat up and breathed quickly.

She'd woken up Mikkjal, who was sitting up on the mezzanine bed. It looked like he was just now waking up, so she wouldn't have to do that much explaining.

"What are you doing up?" he asked. "It's still really early."

"Meditating." She looked up at him. "Practicing Death-release. Looking for signals and visions. Don't worry. Go back to sleep."

Instead of accepting her callous excuses, her partner peered over the edge, shirtless, his muscular body still half asleep. "Is it important that you look for that *now*? You don't want to get back in bed for a little bit?"

That wasn't fair. She was doing all the contact work with Ansuz, repeatedly training to die to her old self, while he was acting like they were there on a marriage getaway. How could he be so calm in the midst of it all?

"Sex isn't going to solve our problems, Mikkjal. Serious matters are happening. South Islands, Kaltland, and Steigson's Shishilms just spoke to me. And something's off here in Skralland." She turned away from him and attuned herself to her breathing, her birch in her hand once more.

But Mikkjal wouldn't allow that. He threw himself back on the bed and pulled the bearskin blankets over himself. *Now she wouldn't be able to meditate even if she wanted to. What the fuck are you thinking about all this time, Mikkjal? I'm here, overtaking my whole self to become someone capable of dialoguing with Skadi. And you're in your harmonious calm mode.* She fumed inside.

Mikkjal himself sighed loudly, threw the skin off and descended the mezzanine ladder. He picked up the lantern on the dining table and took it to the door, where he pulled on his parka and slipped his boots over his thin deerskin underpants; He must be going out for a piss.

Kolfinna stood up and put another log in the tiny stove. She watched the sparks before putting the lid back on, sighing and scratching her neck. *If he wanted a normal relationship, he chose the wrong woman. That was true even before this world-shattering Calling was thrust upon me.* She wished she could say it was all the fault of Sigfather and the Spell of Ansuz, but that would be a dishonest assessment. The truth was she could never maintain a relationship with a man even before then. Heidi had told her a few years back that perhaps she just wasn't meant to unite with anyone, that hers was a different path and that she should just accept it. Yet solitude had never given her assurances either. Partners were good for the body always, good for the heart sometimes, and good for the mind never.

Accepting her sister's advice was too hard, but she hadn't received any better advice. She grabbed the tea kettle that hung from the kitchen wall and opened the door quickly to fetch the ice from the wooden box on the front porch. She filled it with nice large ice chunks and came back in from the cold. It would be long before the sun would rise. She estimated from the fresh tracks he left leading away from the house that Mikkjal must have gone for a walk. Kolfinna place the kettle on the stove, taking brief pleasure in the sizzling sound of melting ice on burning steel.

She'd spoken to Shishilms from the South but wasn't able to learn anything from Skralland yet. Akinisie hadn't told them everything. Plus, there was her vision of the giant suffocating the village as they approached. And Naujaq spoke of sickness.

Once the water was boiling, and the dark trachtsin-filled pouch well infused, Mikkjal re-entered. "Tea's almost ready." Kolfinna had filled two of her backpack's pockets with the plant since it would be more difficult to find in Skralland and would be completely inexistent beyond North Island's shores.

"Fine, all right."

"We could both use a stress reliever." She relaxed her gaze and smiled. *Thank the gods I didn't tell him the stupid things I was thinking about him.*

"Yes," Mikkjal agreed. She was once again kneeling by the stove in her reindeer skin undergarments. Her partner brought two of Naujaq's clay mugs over and poured the tea. Mikkjal first took his mug and walked to look out the window at the dimly protruding edges of light from the distant dawn over the sharp white mountains to the Northeast. He sipped calmly, slowly and purposefully. And after a long while sipping and contemplating whatever it is that Mikkjal contemplates—his thoughts, the landscape, or perhaps the neighbouring houses—he turned back and sat cross-legged in front of her. He had something to talk about.

"Kolfinna, we've both been confirmed in our orders for five years now. Tell me, what's one thing you miss about the Testing Period?

A peculiar question, as he had never shown any interest in this part of her life before. What was there to say? "I guess I miss the fun," Kolfinna answered, as truthfully as she could about a time period that was by no means her favourite.

"The fun?"

"The carefree fun, you know. The fun parties." She let herself think a little more about the year or so of her life after Quest and before Confirmation. "And sex. Having sex was fun that year. There was the occasional month with nearly a new lover every night. You must've had that, too, in Testing Period?"

Mikkjal stared blankly, frozen. His eyes gave hardly a blink but scurried about as though he were looking for a starting point. Finally, he jolted his head back. "A few but not a new one every night. I had family responsibilities. Plus, Astrid's training is always grueling, even for apprentices."

"I see," Kolfinna said calmly as she sipped her tea. "Yes, I always saw you as a shy and serious kid. I wouldn't have thought you to have been a big partier." She'd seen through Mikkjal's thin veil of exaggeration.

But his eyes were flaming. "Well, forgive me for having people to look after and not being able to ask just anyone to screw!" He stood up and walked away before shooting his shoulders back around. "And by the way, I'll point out how insensitive it is to chide me for *suggesting* something that could *possibly* lead to you and me having sex this morning, only for you to throw in my face how much you miss sleeping with randoms. I'm that pathetic for you?!" He turned around definitively and made for the doorway.

"Mikkjal, it was the past, the Testing Period. I've cha —"

"You've changed?" Mikkjal glared. "No, you haven't. You're just as cold as before! You want new human contact only when *you* want it or when it suits you for your rituals. Well, I won't bore you today. Enjoy the thrills! They might get in the way of your current, fleeting death obsession, though." And with that the Guide slammed the door to the small wooden house. A few seconds later Kolfinna heard him ignite his engine. He hardly warmed up his snowmobile before taking off.

ANSUZ

As she sat frozen before the stove, her first tear was slow to form, even slower to fall. But the ones thereafter lacked neither speed nor vigour. She was shaken. No one had ever directly put her down for her past. Then again, the only actual partner she'd had before Mikkjal was Gjarbid, and he went more insane than she was. Kolfinna slammed her hand on the floor.

"Damn it all!" She didn't truly want to return to the thrills. Mikkjal should know that. But… he just asked that random question out of nowhere and she answered with the truth of what the Testing Period had been like for her. Some of its memories were fond ones. Even the thrills. With the Curse of the Visions, a person with Bad Fate, she had to deal with the good thrills and the bad thrills and make the most out of it.

People change. No one is determined by their past. Though people are determined by their fates. Maybe I won't ever die to myself. Maybe Skadi will just ignore me after all. *Maybe the thrills were my fate*, Kolfinna thought.

As she placed another log through the door of the stove, she thought of coldness. She had been accused of coldness by from others before. Others who didn't know her had said she was cold. She preferred solitary places like Karlstad Treehouse, Sjalkland Lake, or even Hrafnshemmas Dune when no one was around. The village stressed her, even her solo cabin. There she was too close to others—others who didn't know her, wouldn't know her, and wouldn't understand her even if they tried. So she had to keep it to herself. The Steigsonland Shishilm told her that she wasn't Kolfinna, but an old soul. At least he felt something coming from her. Mikkjal felt nothing.

She hadn't thought. To him her remark about him wanting her in bed must have sounded cold. And in that context speaking of missing the thrills of many lovers, it was cruel. She had communicated terribly wrong. A heavy lump formed in her throat.

Mikkjal was her grounding source even more now that she didn't have her family or Marja and her colleagues with her. She did feel for him… and not only when it suited her. It was love she felt for him, as much as she was capable of feeling love. She lay down on the couch, extending and retracting her legs in alternating rhythms. Still, vigorous movement couldn't warm herself in air that was well-heated by the fire. So, she let herself become still and she let her tears flow.

Kolfinna had been called to become a Communicator. *From the darkness below, you shall communicate with worlds above in ways unknown to any soul of the age* were the words she'd heard pronounced at her Quest. And so, she joined Marja's Order. She fell into the Gap, down below. She was learning Ansuz communication, the first in the modern era to do so. She touched six people scattered across the planet. Yet when it came to communicating love or affection for the man to whom she was fated, she was at a loss for words. Kolfinna Helensdottir was cursed. She couldn't even successfully die to herself.

Kolfinna Helensdottir, not the old soul Shishilm Ashkii mentioned, cried herself back to sleep as the sun was rising.

A good while later, she was awakened by the sound of the door closing. Startled, she sat up and saw Naujaq in the doorway. Kolfinna quickly walked to the entry hall to greet the welcoming woman who had entered.

"Hi Kolfinna," she said with a smile. "Are you all right?"

"Hello," Kolfinna said, startled and coughing, her eyes avoiding Naujaq's direct gaze. Her throat lump was now a full-fledged burning. She rubbed her eyes but felt she had no more tears left. Then she was struck by the degree of light pouring in the window, spotting the sun's position in the sky. "It's late!" Such was an understatement, for it was clearly less than a time-lapse before midday.

"Morning's in its later stages, yes. You went back to sleep?"

"Yes, I-I was tired. Come in, Naujaq. Have tea and eat if you want. Sorry I wasn't ready." She coughed some more.

"That's quite all right, Kolfinna," chimed the stout Naujaq. "Are you sure you're okay?"

"Yeah, well I guess you could say I didn't get the best night's sleep. But it's not because of your bed or your house. I've got a lot on my mind."

"I see. Mikkjal's not here?"

Kolfinna bit her lip and looked down. "No. He wanted to explore a bit on his own," she said, coughing and fighting back the tears.

"Asuu… I see. In that case I wanted to ask if you would like to come with me and see my aunt at the sewing house. She's a master seamstress and she already told me that you'll be needing a new parka during your stay in Taqraup Nunaat."

"She said that? I'm not cold. I just need answers from Akinisie."

Naujaq reacted with extended silence. "Chieftain Akinisie is busy at the moment. But she advised my aunt to help you make a parka. And if you go out riding around here, you will be cold."

Kolfinna sighed. She didn't plan on spending enough time in Skralland to go riding around enough to notice the cold. Akinisie was stalling them. Still, she might as well follow Naujaq to this sewing house. In the absence of leaders giving her the kind of attention she needed, it wasn't as though she had a whole lot else to do. Going alone from house to house and asking people randomly about red dots would be seen as disrespectful to their host Land."

"Okay. I'll come with you. You're leaving now?"

"Yeah. We'll have lunch over there."

"But Mikkjal? He might worry if I'm gone when he comes back!" Kolfinna tried to convince herself as much as inform Naujaq of this stress.

"He won't have time. I think he's going to spend the full day outside."

Kolfinna was shocked as she started walking towards the entryway to get her parka. "What do you mean? You saw him leave? Darn, I didn't mean for us to fight!" She broke again into a cough and a few tears again flowed down her golden cheeks.

Naujaq immediately placed a hand on her shoulder. "It's okay. That's not what I meant. I meant that someone told me that Mikkjal was helping Ittoq, my uncle, over at the fishery. He'll be busy there till evening. My uncle works a lot."

"Oh." Kolfinna cleared her throat, embarrassed. Luckily Naujaq responded with tact.

"Whatever happened will fade away. You two are on a journey bigger than yourselves. I can see that. Now come on, follow me!"

Kolfinna nodded and put on her black parka and followed the dark-haired woman out the door.

"How's your fuel?" Naujaq asked, eyeing Kolfinna's snow machine.

"About a quarter of a tank. It should be enough for today."

"Eeeeh, no, hop on with me. We'll probably do some riding today."

No choice, Kolfinna hopped on the back of Naujaq's machine and the two whizzed off. She had no idea what a Skralland sewing house would be like. The Gorrland equivalent was a crafts shop in Central Village just down from the blacksmith's, in which a large room was dedicated to sewing and weaving. This, of course, was the only community-wide centre for sewing. The duties of every household woman included much of this type of activity.

The snow machine hummed through the streets, and they crossed few people until they came to the first turf houses, for apparently the sewing house was on the outskirts of town and not in the centre. Outside snow-covered turf houses, several men and women were getting their supplies out and filling up the trailers to be pulled by their snowmobiles. Everyone seemed to be busy, going on with their day-to-day activities. Yet despite the business, or perhaps because of it, Kolfinna again felt strange about the energy in the village. It was, at the moment, not at all like the energy they felt when they crossed the Land's threshold. There was a dissonance between what she felt Skralland was and what was being given off at the moment in town. Those were the words her feelings could lend themselves to as of now. Words were especially lacking in a Land in which she didn't know the tongue.

They rode a distance that was surprisingly long for Kolfinna, driving by turf houses and snow houses in areas off the path that they'd ridden yesterday. People nodded to Naujaq, then to Kolfinna, who had to pull her hood back up due to the wind. They kept going outwards until the houses became more and more sparse. Taqraup turf houses, on the outside, looked nearly identical to those from Westfolk. Noticing this, Kolfinna wondered just how long ago Gorrlanders and Skrallanders split apart and became separate peoples. All Folks came from Meniya in the beginning, it was true, but the North Islanders must have split far more recently than the 815 years Kolfinna and her generation had learned in school. Still, she wondered how the Skrallanders were able to make these dwellings useful in their winters which were much harsher than Westfolk had to offer.

The thoughts were a distraction from her troubles with Mikkjal, but they were also a distraction from the mission. She shouldn't allow herself to get distracted. Jorgson ever tightened his grip. She would have to convince the Skrallanders to find their Dust-sensitive individual and send him or her to Meniya, then convince Akinisie to broadcast to the whole planet Taqraup Nunaat's support for the New Shishilms' journeying to ancient Meniya. If another Land openly supported

Gorrland, then Kolfinna's words, visions and truths from Sigfather would be seen as credible. Even more so if Skralland and Torvall joined Gorrland, in a united effort of all Northern Folks.

On top of a hill stood one large turf house across from which were three snow houses. "Tikisimaratta, we've arrived," exclaimed Naujaq, coming to a stop and turning off her motor. "This way." Naujaq started off towards the turf house outside of which were parked two snowmobiles.

"It's a good ways out of town," Kolfinna said. The Gorrland Communicator couldn't help but notice the large quantity of dogs tied up around the snow houses opposite the great turf house. They lay still, however, most certainly having recently eaten. The turf house was long and bland with a roof covered with snow on the outside. Yet once they set foot inside it was another story. The floor was covered with a dark blanket and lanterns could be seen hanging from the ceiling. Around the edges were a dozen or so women engaged in sewing activities.

Kolfinna took her hat off on the inside and nodded a general nod to all who were around her. Most of the women nodded back or gave a smile to the newcomer, who followed Naujaq, going forward without saying a word to the wall on the far edge. She now noticed one very big difference between these turf houses and the less cold-proof ones of her native Westport The entire inner structure was beset with massive whale bones so that one could almost appear to be looking at a whale's ribcage from within. On the far end where Naujaq was headed was one of the two wood stoves and chimneys the turf house contained. On this wall were wooden shelves upon which lay various furs, and next to the shelves were cubbies holding threads and needles. "This is my aunt's area. These are her furs. One of these will be for you."

"They're so beautiful. I don't want to take them away from anyone who needs them more than me. I'm just a guest here."

"No one needs them more than you, and no one needs them more than your partner. You both shall have them." Naujaq walked along the edge of the house, stepping behind a few elderly ladies and going to a stove beside one of the whalebone arches. She came back with two bowls of stew and presented one to Kolfinna. "Here you go. Seal stew."

"Thank you." The two ate the delicious stew, which contained potatoes and vegetables in addition to seal meat, in silence, while the other women sewed or drank some tea. No one seemed to pay undue attention to the newcomer.

The meal soothed Kolfinna on the inside, removing several distressing thoughts of adolescence and the onset of the Curse of the Visions. But removing these individual distressing thoughts brought out more of the collective distressing thoughts. Finally, while eating, Kolfinna decided she wouldn't stay silent about them with her host and companion.

"Naujaq, I'm afraid I'm the bearer of bad news. Like I said yesterday when we arrived and we told the Communicators, we've been to the Gap and we've received dismaying news from the Flares. Iorki-son—"

"You're here now. You began your journey. You are following your path. We're all aware of what happened. Don't worry. You mustn't be too full of thought at this time. Much has happened and much will continue to happen. And much has happened in our Land, too." Naujaq sat up, eyeing Kolfinna calmly, which made the Gorrland Communicator look down at her hand.

But I feel it, here, inside, she said to herself looking at her red dots. *I have to tell them. Things have to get done.* Burning up inside, she took a deep breath and on her exhale said, "Okay," and proceeded to finish her bowl of stew.

At the very moment she finished eating appeared a woman who had been part of the greeting party the night before. Kolfinna had forgotten her name. She was a woman of Naujaq's stature but with greying hair—aging but not quite old. She approached from one of the groups against the wall and said something in her native language to her niece, before addressing the foreign woman with a smile. To Kolfinna's surprise, this lady spoke adequate Communications Albrimese.

"Hello. Kolfinna, yes?"

"Yes, yes."

"My name is Mikisoq. I'm Naujaq's aunt. Welcome to Taqraup Nunaat."

"Thank you." She remembered the name Mikisoq from the night before.

"Now come here. It is my job to make sure you don't freeze while you're here." And at that point aunt and niece broke into laughter, which made Kolfinna, standing up to follow Mikisoq, give a reserved smile herself.

"Let's see…" The lady went to her shelves and took out a white fur. "You'll have a great coat made out of the finest reindeer. With sealskin lining on the inside. What do you have for mitts?"

Kolfinna showed her her mitts. "That will do. Those will do." She held one mitt in her hand and felt the sealskin from the West. "If you were staying here longer I'd make you newer ones, warmer ones. But they'll keep your hands from freezing. You're not from a Southern Land I must say."

"No, I'm not," Kolfinna said, this time with a more earnest smile.

"Atii, let's get to work. Sit beside me. What Naujaq may not have said was that I'm not going to show you. I'm going to give you the fur and the thread and show you, but you're going to sew your own parka."

"Am I?"

"Of course." And at that all of a sudden lighthearted cackles could be made from many of the women in the house. All had been listening, although they seemed far away. Mikisoq and Kolfinna found a comfortable spot on the floor to sit.

ANSUZ

"And when we're done, you'll have to remember your partner's build so that the good Guide Mikkjal will have a fur coat and stand as an aid to Ungilattaqi."

Kolfinna sighed. "I hope he finds his way here, but I made him angry today," said Kolfinna.

"It's okay. You'll make him un-angry. Besides, even an angry man needs to stay warm." More cackling could be heard. Kolfinna relaxed and laughed herself. The Communicator was surprised at just how many Skrallanders appeared to speak or understand Communications Albrimese. Knowledge appeared far more widespread among the general population than in Gorrland.

"Don't worry about him. He's with my husband now at the fish factory by the bay. We'll all meet for dinner, if you don't mind fish!" The woman chuckled again.

"I have nothing against that," said Kolfinna. The three women sat down before Naujaq's aunt's shelves and began to work on the clothing for the guests. Aside from Mikisoq's brief but poignant instructions, work would be done in near silence. The dozen or so women sewed and weaved to the sound of the crackling fireplaces and the faint smell of leftover seal stew.

***

Attention! Attention!

Midday, on the Fourteenth of Fifteenmonth, 963

Attention please on the long-range frequency of one thousand crystal waves per second.

Attention on the all-Albrimir Communicators' frequency.

This is Tia of Wanautipun Tower. I have met with the fellow leaders of our island Land, who have asked for clarifications from Iorki Tower. I therefore broadcast for Chieftain Abbott and Mikhail Iorki-Son.

We respond that we do have knowledge of a person who has received a mark of red dots. We are also not afraid of this person, especially as there is no way this person can convene with the girl Kolfinna Helensdottir. As you know, Wanautipun and Gorrland have long-standing hostilities. We would not be welcome in their Land, and Kolfinna would not be welcome in ours. We shall monitor that this magic does not cause tension with your Land, however we shall not arrest this person simply because Iorki-Son asks for it.

Communicators, we accept the positions taken in Khairtai and in Shá, as expressed by Chieftain Arban yesterday. Before we make such a declaration of our own, on all-Albrimir radio no less, we must take a stand and ask you three questions, Mikhail.

What kind of world do you propose to build for Albrimir?

Will all Lands be equal in this world?

What shall be your attitude to Lands that declare themselves neutral in your combat with the group of sorcerers?

Greetings from Wanautipun!

Attention! Attention!

Midday, on the Fourteenth of Fifteenmonth, 963

In response to Chieftain Tia, my answer shall be simple.

There can be no neutrality between my world and the world of Kolfinna and her sorcerers.

From this affirmation flows the answers to your other two questions. I advise you to consider it carefully, Tia, as I advise Ehukai, Marja, and Akinisie. And of course Shishilm Anavend, though I believe he has already taken his position.

Greetings from Iorki!

ANSUZ

***

Mikkjal

Fury couldn't describe his feelings as he sped down the empty alleys. She understood nothing, the fairy chosen one. All his hardship and feelings were but fodder for her growing sense of specialness. Talking about Death-release, she was doing the opposite—growing, growing in her head, proud of exploits of all sorts. Mikkjal's sled unhitched, he navigated the town quickly and nimbly. Once he reached the bay he could let loose. There, he'd ride into the hills southeast. The higher he'd get, the better. He'd go to his spot. From it, he'd be able to scream out all that was driving him mad about this cold and distant Kolfinna.

He was Mikkjal Aldisson. He was Astrid's Pride and leader of the Solidarity Reaffirmation. He guided the whole Folk to the Gap to confront Sigfather. And he was as much called by Sigfather as she was. He was not her little plaything. The mistress of thrills had to shove in his face how special she was. *And she looks, thinks, and acts nothing like Skadi! Why does she think the Huntress will contact her just because she talks about dying and makes faint references to Utgard!* He almost hoped that Eirà was secretly plotting another course, so that Kolfinna would finally step back and think of her own accord. That would be more useful than constantly wanting to die.

Some people were walking outside their houses, packing hunting equipment in their sleds, getting ready for the day. Mikkjal put on a fake smile for them and waved. Let them spend their days in peace. He would head for his place of release. He arrived at the bay, carefully navigating the ice mounds near shore and then speeding on the sea ice parallel to the coastline. This ice had been frozen thick for at least four months now, so he sped into the wind with no caution. In Skralland his chosen spot for meditation, breathing, and occasional venting was a rocky deposit on a hill about twenty kilometres out of town. He eyed the coastline until he got to the great rock that marked the place to climb.

Despite his anger, he scolded himself. Expressing jealousy was proscribed. Solidarity was to one's order, one's clan and one's Folk, not to one's desire to please one's partner and be the only one to do it. All this was well and good, but Mikkjal couldn't see Kolfinna's solidarity to anyone. *Cold-finna indeed.*

The Guide turned his machine back to shore upon seeing the rock, and climbed the hill till he reached his destination. The rocky deposit looked exactly the same as two years ago. His intense riding and rage had caused him to sweat under his thick parka, so he unhooked his belt and took the coat off when he cut the motor. The sun was perhaps a third of the way up its winter loop over the bay, and Mikkjal jumped furiously off the snowmobile, running over to the rocks. Shouting, he grabbed a small rock and hurled it against larger ones.

"Shy and serious!" Mikkjal shouted as the rock smashed. *Nobody knew me!*

"Focused on the job!" he bellowed while heaving another rock. *Nobody knew me! No one listened to the pain.*

"Not lighthearted!" *Nobody allowed me to be lighthearted. Not... one... single... day.*

Screaming, he hurled a rock for every comment unknowing people had made about him. He made it up to ten before he lost count.

"Can't take advantage of the Testing Period!" *What life was there to test? I was a Guide even before my Quest. Astrid only solidified it. I guided my own family when my fathers were out on the land!*

"Does his duty. Does his DUTY!"

A rock wasn't enough for that comment. He definitely needed more. He stepped back to his parka on the snow, where his belt held his sword. He unsheathed the weapon and pressed his finger on the crystal activation button on the handle. This suddenly blazed the blade in a silently flaming white. He flung his sword in all directions, howling his lungs out as Dust pummelled rocks all around.

"I had to look after Kieran!" He let the words fall from his mouth, unable to hold them in. "My brother was under my wing, but the dutiful Mikkjal couldn't keep him from dying! Oh, how I wish you'd have seen me right after Kieran died! I was reckless and full of thrills. I would've thrilled you to the bone! Dutiful Mikkjal can thrill, too!" He slashed rocks and snow with Dust while screaming. Then, his body unable to take the pressure of rage anymore, he hammered the steel blade into a large stone. Shards seared past his eyes and hit his skin. And with that swing his red dots were reactivated.

The pulsating hand was startling, as it was unexpected, but Mikkjal regained his composure, his footing, and his anger. He slashed out one more time on the rock, this time taking aim at one thing that wouldn't serve him anymore—the image of Kolfinna as a special, sensitive, and strange girl, beyond the brutal reality of the world. She was as flawed as anyone, even more so. Cold and distant, self-serving. As his blade ripped through the air, sending Dust and crashing into another rock, Mikkjal didn't feel the flying shards on his skin but a puncturing pain clear across his chest. It was as if that very blade had sliced through him on its way to the rock, from his right shoulder down to his lower left back. Such pain threw him on his knees and buried his face in the snow, screaming. It was worse than anything he'd felt before.

With his chest reeling in the snow, beyond his control, he thought his actual heart was twisting and turning. A few seconds passed with the Guide immobilized before he could lift his head from the snow. Raising his head only made him feel his hand dots burning. His left hand pulsated with short bursts of agony, as it had in the tavern. And with this burning came a familiar voice.

"What is wounded must heal."

Sigfather. The Gap Master spoke but he also sent a vision. A woman, brown of hair and clad in clothing of another time, a spear strapped to her back. No doubt this was Skadi. She fled to a cave, hiding. Then Mikkjal came to the entrance of the cave and crossed over after a long hesitation.

"There she lives. And you will awaken her, Mikkjal Aldisson."

Once again Mikkjal screamed. The Guide pulled away from the snow and sat up. His biting pain had gone but his chest wasn't the same. In the space of the sword-slice wound he felt a gaping hole from right shoulder to lower left back. It was with this new space empty and open that Mikkjal got up and looked around. The land was nearly the same. The sun was halfway up its rise to midday and the snow glistened pure. The only exception in the sameness was that there was a person on the ice, just out from the large rock by the shore, with a snowmobile and sled. Since this person was looking precisely at Mikkjal and likely saw his strange behaviour, he figured it would be a good idea to go back down to the ice and greet him. It would be at the very least be necessary so as not to arouse suspicion.

Mikkjal rode a hundred metres onto the lake ice and stopped before an aging man, who it turns out had been one of the hosts' welcoming party.

"Good day," spoke Mikkjal, attempting to speak Skrallander. "Ittoq is your name, yes?"

"Ai. Yes, Ittoq. And you are Mikkjal?"

"Yes."

"What are you doing out here?" asked the man who wore thin-slit bone sunglasses for snow.

"I came to meditate," Mikkjal answered.

"Asuu."

"Yes. Sigfather—the Evolver—he revealed to me a secret." Mikkjal figured he'd just start talking to this Ittoq about matters of the journey. "The whole planet is under attack from the leader of Iorki."

"Iorki. I see," Ittoq interrupted before Mikkjal could find the words he wanted to say to continue. "You came way out here for that? You don't just ask Communicators?"

"Yes. I needed my own thoughts, I suppose. Albrimir is troubled."

But the man, with greying moustache and eyebrows above his glasses, looked at Mikkjal's sword, and smiled. "Albrimir? Or yourself?"

Mikkjal froze. He looked wide-eyed at the Skrallander, who was slightly shorter than him. "Me too, a bit. But Albrimir's trouble is more important than mine, of course."

"That is where you are mistaken." The man, well into the second half of his life, spoke calm words that broke through the bright sun over the snow. "Mik-jal, are you busy?"

"Busy?" The Guide tried to understand the Skrallander word.

"Busy. Stuff to do?"

"Oh!" Mikkjal hesitated, eying the spectacular mountains on the far shore of the bay. "Well… I thought I had stuff to do but now I think I don't."

"In that case I need your help. Cutting up and distributing fish to houses. Big ice edge catch was made yesterday. You're okay to join? Your girlfriend won't miss you?"

"No. She won't," answered the Guide. The Hunter's laugh disappeared when he heard Mikkjal's prompt negative reply.

"Good. Get in your machine and follow me to the fishery in town. Oh, fuel up before we begin. Fuel is next to the fishery." Aldisson nodded and walked back to his machine, noticing on the way that Ittoq's trailer was empty.

"Where's the fish if your trailer's empty?" Mikkjal asked.

"It's already at the fishery." Ittoq smiled with friendly eyes.

"Oh, okay." Mikkjal got onto his snowmobile and turned on the engine. He was curious as to what the old man was doing there on the bay if he hadn't been fishing. It wasn't the time or place to ask, though, as Ittoq took off. If he felt especially at ease later on, he would ask. If not, he wouldn't. As he throttled to follow the newly acquainted fisherman, he stared out at the tall hills converging in the narrow valley which bore Taqraup Village, a large town compared with any of the small villages in Gorrland. While he was open to the stunning land, riding on smooth powder over the solid frozen bay, he still felt the cut line of emptiness in his chest from the swing of the blade.

Sigfather gave him some final words as Mikkjal departed the scene of his outburst.

"Every time you move the Dust you invoke me. You must be mindful."

Chapter 6
Council

The routine was always the same. Bring out the bag, enter the snow or sod home through the low dome, and greet the family or families inside, present the individual frozen fish, then leave. Naturally, everyone was curious about the foreigner following Ittoq around. The children especially came up to Mikkjal and grabbed at his parka. They spoke many fast words that he did not understand. Often the women would get up from the fireplace and go take the offering, while the men stood up and greeted the guests with a nod and a smile. The parkas of thick grey or whitish sealskin were always exquisite whether they be adorning the people's bodies or hung at the entrance to the houses. Mikkjal was reminded of the warmth and beauty of Taqraup Nunaat.

Although there was definitely warmth when he and Ittoq visited houses for delivery, something was different on this trip. At first he'd felt it merely as a change in the quality of the air, but now he put it in more down-to-earth words. In nearly every household, there was at least one person who sat apart, secluded and saying nothing to anyone at all, be they guests or other household members. Of course the Taqramiut were a people who didn't always exchange through words, but one could always tell that they were there, present with each other. The absent ones in the houses today were completely cut off in words, gestures, and energy from those around them. In addition, some people outside would just stare straight ahead with stone-cold expressions as they rode down the alleys and around dwelling places and community buildings. Whatever this energy was, it was relatively new. Mikkjal's stomach tightened at the sight of such hardened individuals, his gaping chest feeling even emptier and more exposed than when Ittoq found him.

"That's it. That's the last house," Ittoq calmly exclaimed, putting the empty skin bag back in the trailer. "Good work, eh?"

"I'll say!" The two leaned together over the hauling sled beside a snow house and sipped tea from Ittoq's thermos.

"Tomorrow we'll go net fishing farther out. An old man needs a Guide." Ittoq burst out laughing.

"Tomorrow?"

"Yes. If you're not busy with your Father of Victory, of course." He burst out laughing again.

"Well, maybe. But I think we should talk to your Storyteller."

"Maybe you will, Mikkjal. But you should also think about what story you're telling yourself." The Hunter smiled with a squint of his thin eyes, aging but mischievous, then he walked towards his snowmobile.
Was that remark flavoured with annoyance or just with jovial and playful wisdom? Mikkjal asked himself. For whatever reason, it wouldn't be easy to bring up the subject of the Storyteller during this visit. Even bringing up the Gorrland Storyteller Eirà seemed to evoke strange reflections and discussions. The Skrallanders knew a lot more than they were letting on.

As his mind once again sobered up to this fact, he again noticed the gaping empty slash across his chest. The hole remained just as open as they rode between snow houses and sod houses on their way to Ittoq's house, where he'd announced that his wife was preparing a delicious stew.

He'd never been to the part of the village they were now visiting. No one had told him before that there were dwellings hidden behind rocks and nooks or that there were opposite far-side hills where families lived. These families likely still wanted to live in a more traditional way, with snow houses that could be constructed and deconstructed at will.

Again it was twilight. The work of gathering, axing, and distributing frozen fish left him little time to think of Kolfinna or the mission. It was a physical day, a good day, but the uncertainty over the pair's journey was returning. Had he been overly angry at her? He couldn't let his feelings or his past distract him from what needed to be done. Then, as his snowmobile hummed sharply, his mind went to the Guard ship Ivaldi sent, stationed at the floe edge. Fortunately, before such thoughts could wander too far, Ittoq's high beams illuminated a sod house with several snowmobiles parked outside. The good-humoured Hunter pulled to a stop next to the machines.

"This is where we'll stop," said Ittoq, getting off the driver's seat and promptly going to his sled to gather the bag of fish.

"This is where you live?" asked Mikkjal.

"Sometimes," the Hunter replied with a wink.

This wasn't a small dinner with Ittoq and his wife. Instead of just her as host, there were some two-dozen people seated within the sod and whalebone walls. Within the light of a few sparsely placed torches, he recognized Ungilattaqi, the Hunter Singataaq, and Communicator Akinisie. The Chieftains were here and a serious tone of concentration lent itself to the atmosphere. This was no party, though food was placed on the sod floor in the middle. At the far end, a man was speaking. He took a break from his speech to nod at Mikkjal and Ittoq, and others followed suit.

"Come on, let's get some food. Where's my wife?" Ittoq asked once the speaker started again. The Hunter found her after walking between a few people. The Hunter sat beside Mikisoq. Just as he made the realization that Ittoq and Mikisoq were paired Mikkjal saw his own partner sitting between Mikisoq and Naujaq. Kolfinna's hair and face were so bright as they reflected the light from the flaming torches.

"Hi," Mikkjal said, his shoulders tightening.

"Hi, Mikkjal." She looked at him, expressionless but there.

"What's going on?"

"A Council meeting. We were sewing here and then they came."

Mikisoq took the pot on the floor and two bowls and poured stew for Mikkjal as well as her husband. In her energy Mikisoq bore a resemblance to Astrid, warm yet commanding as she sat with a thin scarf around her greying hair.

Kolfinna had changed since the morning. She was entirely present to whatever was being discussed, which seemed urgent. They would deal with each other later, for the matters here impacted them. That Kolfinna was taken by Mikisoq to sew, and Mikkjal was taken by Ittoq to distribute was not an accident.

He tried to listen as best he could while hungrily gulping down seal stew. There being no translator, it wasn't easy. Basic conversation in the Taqraup language was one thing but listening to long speeches was a different matter. Speakers changed. Occasionally, Mikisoq would translate a few words of one or another of the speakers into Albrimese, but she was only half invested in it. One person spoke about food distribution, a discussion in which Ittoq intervened. Another, according to Mikisoq, was speaking about news from the latest hunting expeditions out to the floe edge or in the mountains. Finally, someone spoke about the nomads. A third of Taqraup Nunaat's population continued to live on the land in seasonal dwellings, coming to the village only to resupply.

"They're all out there still?" Kolfinna curiously asked the half-active translator.

"They're not doing well this year," Mikisoq answered, distress present in her tone.

Kolfinna made a clear and earnest effort to listen intently to all the speakers. And there was good reason to listen intently, as nearly every person who took the floor repeated one word more often than others. The word was "qanima" or something of the sort. It was something Mikkjal had heard before. He was almost positive it referred to sickness. And with the tone of those uttering it tonight, it was definitely not a positive word. It was the sickness Naujaq had mentioned. All speakers were grim when addressing the crowd, and the room was heavy.

By the time the third speaker's remarks were open for discussion, most everyone had finished eating. Ittoq had shared some frozen fish. Seal stew pots were emptying. As the discussion with the third speaker, Ungilattaqi, was coming to a close, Akinisie stood up from her blanket on the far wall and came to sit next to Kolfinna. She gave a quick and courteous smile and spoke in Communications Albrimese to both foreigners.

"Kolfinna, you and Mikkjal are going to talk now. Ungilattaqi is almost done. You can explain your message and your requests for Taqraup Nunaat people." Akinisie was a tall and slim woman, quite elegant as a woman in her early forties. She was well-voiced, pretty, and charming, well-fitted to her job as Communicator Chieftain.

Her translation was much more extensive than Mikisoq's. "Ungilattaqi has been saying that bears have been sighted all along the ice floe edge but some closer to town. Reindeer are in the hills to the northeast only as of now. No animals sighted to the west. Any Hunters that want to send equipment to Lake-Like Settlement must bring them to his place tomorrow morning at the latest because he's going there before middle day."

Akinisie spoke Albrimese as if it was her native language, her Taqraup accent coming through only on rare occasions. That's part of their training, of course,

Mikkjal reminded himself. She gave him somewhat mixed feelings. As her position required diplomatic reservedness, she couldn't reveal herself. Yet she wasn't as good at hiding the fact that she had some underlying unexpressed layers. "There's another bit of information about secondary fuel fill-up stations far out on the land," Akinisie continued. "Ungilattaqi's Guide mate Jaani will be taking crystal enhancers out to secondary pumps tomorrow. Communicators should radio on extended local-range frequency when the job is done. Fuel will be available on the land for at least three weeks now." Good, old Jaani—a fun guy and sharp archer. Mikkjal looked around the room but couldn't see him there, though. Of course, he wouldn't think a Guide his age would've been invited to the Council meeting.

Big Ungilattaqi finished speaking. Akinisie then rose and said a few words to the assembly before turning to the guests and, in Albrimese, inviting them to speak.

The pair looked at each other as they stood up. There was some hesitancy as to who would speak first. Despite his frustration in the morning, Mikkjal motioned to Kolfinna. She was the Communicator, the one who had had dealings with Akinisie before, even if it had only been on the radio. He'd let her try to explain Ansuz communicating and why Mikhail Jorgson wanted her head.

"My name is Kolfinna Helensdottir. I am a Communicator from Gorrland. I am here with my partner, Mikkjal Aldisson. We're here as the result of a life-altering journey into the Gap, on which we were sent at the behest of the Flares."

Akinisie translated her words into the Taqraup language.

"In the Gap, the Flares spoke to us," Kolfinna continued. "The Flares took the form of the spirit for whom they are named in Gorrland, Sigfather. Sigfather's message—the Flares' Calling to us—leads us back to the

Temple of Ancient Meniya, in the Land of Kalyim, which we call Torvall, and I believe you call Sivulliup Nunaat. By the Dust in the Gap, the same Dust which gives us energy for radio, engines, and other things, the Flares call one person from each Land to go to Meniya. There they will collectively receive the energy called out from the Gap, taking his energy and bringing it into the world for improvement, to create a new world. Times are shifting. In my visions I've seen—"

"Give me time to translate, girl!" Akinisie interrupted, grabbing her forearm. Kolfinna was red in the face and let the senior Communicator speak.

"My visions have coincided with some of the historical beliefs we Communicators study." She spoke slower. "I've seen, in vision, the Dust reach Meniya in the ancient era, which it is said made the fortress vibrate with light, and allowed the Shishilms—the ancient Council of Meniya—to enable humans to communicate with each other through thought and vision and at a great distance. This technique, which some of the more esoteric teachings of Communicators name Ansuz, was used harmoniously until tragedy happened. As you know, Meniya fell, destroyed by the very energy that brought such Light to that civilization. The first modern Communicators recovered the crystals and constructed radio communication. This technology helped us Moderns escape darkness, and for it we are immensely grateful. But it pales in comparison to what the Ancients could achieve."

Akinisie stopped translating and spoke quietly in Albrimese to Kolfinna. "Are you going to tell us that by some miraculous turn of events, Sigfather not only chose you for his new Council but also made you responsible for teaching Ansuz to the new world?"

Kolfinna was taken aback. She hesitated but chose her words carefully. "Mikhail Iorki-Son has said that I am a sorceress intent on bringing Albrimir back to barbarism and superstition. This I am not."

Akinisie continued the translation, softening her gaze at Kolfinna but still appearing on guard. She motioned her on, perhaps unable to predict what she would have to translate.

"Sigfather—the Flares—is a being whom you in Taqraup Nunaat know as the Evolver. Although we call it by a different name, Sigfather or Father of Victory, we see him in the same light—as someone who ushers in new eras."

"This you say you now believe, but up until barely more than a week ago, you advocated war against the master of the Dust. You wanted to confront 'Sigfather,' as you yourself announced on the radio." Akinisie objected. "How are you going to tell them now that you're following his guidance? Think before you ask me to translate for a different Folk. You did *not* see him as we do, as an Evolver, until very recently."

Kolfinna looked down.

An elderly male voice spoke out in Taqraup language invoking the Chieftain to allow Kolfinna to continue. She nodded to him and held out her arm to gesture to Kolfinna to keep speaking.

"We were wrong about Sigfather—the Evolver. Ever since our Gap initiation our beliefs make much more sense. The dissonance is over. Not only that, but Sigfather gave me and Mikkjal a warning: one would come to impersonate the Evolver. This person would know how to use the Dust to destroy, rather than create. He would overtake all Towers and enslave Albrimir to a new order of great progress but little communications. Since our journey to the Gap, this warning is coming to pass, as Mikhail of Iorki threatens both war and a new world of wonderful progress."

Kolfinna's words were translated. Save Akinisie's voice, the silence in the room was absolute. Their interest shifted once she mentioned that Gorrlanders were wrong about Sigfather.

ANSUZ

Mikkjal, listening to Kolfinna through his knowledge of Communications Albirmise that was far less fluent than hers, couldn't help admiring how eloquently and clearly she spoke. Her eyes and her entire body were present to the words she spoke. If there could be a state that was the complete opposite of her vacant, emotionless absences, it would be this state. Not a single fibre of her being was elsewhere than in her present thoughts and energy, and Mikkjal sensed that the Skrallanders in the audience could feel this, too. *What changed in you from this morning?*

"According to the force which we call Sigfather and you call the Evolver, a person from every Land is to receive his call to go to Meniya. But these are not the only ones who must go. The Evolver's words were that this force whom we see to be Mikhail is able to use the Dust as Sigfather can. But this use of the Dust, without the attenuating energy of our goddess Skadi, can only bring destruction, rather than the creative potential of the Evolver. For the new era of prosperity, peace and light to come, we must also make contact with Skadi and convince her to join the Eight from each land in the ancient Temple of Meniya."

This time, once Akinisie finished translating there came an interruption from a familiar voice. "I'm sorry Kolfinna," spoke Mikisoq, "but how is Skadi related to the calling you say the Evolver gives to a person from every Land in Albrimir?"

All was silent. Kolfinna looked at Mikkjal. *Skadi's Time.* Kolfinna, a bit more nervous, looked at Mikisoq on her left side. "Sigfather said something I'd never heard before, neither from my Folk, nor in Communicators' history class. He said that there are not eight but nine Towers in Albrimir, the ninth being of the nomads, who use a different kind of communication. He claimed that the ancient form of communication used in Meniya didn't completely die. It has still been used… periodically… by Skadi, who lives in the wilderness and inspires nomadic people who don't forget the wildness of Utgard, the Realm Beyond."

Akinisie squinted. As crazy as that must sound to the Skrallanders, the Gorrlanders, and even to Mikkjal, she seemed to understand, even if slightly. Did Skadi and Ansuz make sense to her?

Mikkjal jumped in to fill the ensuing silence. To Akinisie he spoke in a not-too-perfect Albrimese. "Sigfather told us that all nomads in Albrimir communicate using special magic. He told us to bring this magic to the other Dust Communicators—the other red-dotted ones called to Meniya—the New Shishilms, as we call them. But Sig—the Evolver—said this was the magic of a goddess that only exists in our Land, Skadi. I admit this makes little sense, but the Flares said that the goddess Gorrlanders call Skadi is out there among the nomads and must be brought to Meniya, too."

Akinisie squinted carefully and started to say something before deciding not to. On the far end, someone put a couple of logs in the stove during the protracted silence. But then a voice spoke out from the left of Ittoq. An elderly man who had been present at the welcoming party yesterday spoke rather slowly but clearly in his language.

Akinisie spoke for the guests' benefit. "Taamusi says the name you mention is only known in Gorrland. But it is like the name Sigfather. The being of whom you speak is known outside Gorrland, including here. He says that you, girl, must know this." Akinisie gestured to Kolfinna.

"Oh? No, I never knew that." A surprised Kolfinna looked to Akinisie. "We were never taught that by Marja." But seeing her eyes, even Mikkjal could observe that the Communicator Chieftain had some knowledge that Kolfinna didn't possess.

Slowly, the elder Taamusi spoke again. "He's asking you something, Kolfinna," Akinisie translated. "He's asking what energy is shaping your personal aura?"

That's right, Mikkjal remembered. Astrid had taught the Guides about this belief of the Skrallanders in personal auras. It was something of the image that a person gave off and was shaped by the person's ancestors, their life choices, and the beings in the natural environment they acted with. Seers, Storytellers, and even ordinary Elders were able to see and sense these auras.

"My personal aura?" Kolfinna replied. "Well, I-I suppose it could be that of the spell I'm learning— Ansuz. It's allowed me to contact six other Dust-sensitive people that way so far."

It wasn't the type of answer the Elder was looking for. The aura is more complex than just some magic a person learns, no matter how powerful the magic may be. Upon hearing the translation, Taamusi nodded and immediately replied. Yet after his words and before Akinisie could translate several gasps could be heard in the room. One person spoke a word out loud that Mikkjal couldn't understand.

Akinisie sighed and waited to translate. "What he says is surprising. He thanks you for revealing that you're still learning this magic, and that you don't master it yet. He says he's not surprised that you're called to this magic. He says that he also sees a different energy besides Dust communication. He sees with you something like an image in a mountain cave, old, faraway… you waiting to be discovered after many, many years. Shrouded by danger."

Akinisie spoke without her normal eloquence. Kolfinna widened her eyes at Mikkjal upon hearing her words. For his part, Mikkjal was wonderstruck, but was quickly brought back to the vision Sigfather gave him in the morning on the hill. He felt the empty slash in his chest that remained after the pain and after the vision itself had left. The vision of himself pursuing Skadi into a dangerous cave. Now there was hushed chatter instead of silence, as something was definitely stirred up in the thoughts of the people present. Faces seemed anxious.

"Thank you for sharing, Kolfinna and Mikkjal," said Akinisie. "We'll take your revelations into account and get back to you soon about what we intend on doing. The revelation about those chosen for Meniya, with the red dots is clouded. For no one in our Land has those dots, while *two* people from your Land have them. Nonetheless, what you have said has very important meanings for our people, too."

"But there are urgent matters," Mikkjal jumped in. "War is coming with Iorki and we haven't talked about Jorgson's threats against Torvall!"

"Yes, urgent matters. We have many very urgent matters, too, of which you're probably becoming aware. So just accept that we'll get back to you in due time." Akinisie spoke decisively but without stress or anger and then proceeded to walk back across the assembly to where she'd been seated before.

But Kolfinna wasn't without stress. Contrasting with her demeanour throughout the presentation, she shouted while the Chieftain showed her back. "It's Iorki-Son's threats against you, too! How can you not take it seriously?! Sigfather, Skadi, Meniya, it's all related to Iorki-Son and what he's planning to do. Akinisie, you told me that he threatened you, Marja, Tia, and Ehukai! You have to make a decision! Taqraup Nunaat has to!"

"We do have to," Akinisie replied calmly in her perfect Albrimese. "But that is a matter for a Chieftain to discuss with her Council, not for a traveller to make. Perhaps Marja supports you, but the Order of Communicators— of *today*, I mean, not the Order of a thousand years ago —has not decided that you are the heir to Ansuz."

While Kolfinna steamed, Mikkjal spoke quickly to avoid further tension. "We understand, Chieftain, the war is not our decision to make. But maybe, since it's all related we can talk to someone. Perhaps we could speak to a Seer? Speak to your Storyteller."

Akinisie chuckled, and so did a few others. She didn't translate the message but the Hunter Council member Singataaq decided to reply, standing up and speaking loudly in Skrallander, which made a few more people laugh. Mikkjal understood the familiar reply.

"He says maybe you can… But maybe you can't. Maybe he'll speak to you," said Akinisie, chuckling.

"You can't keep us in the dark! You didn't even let us radio to our Tower in Gorrland!" Kolfinna screamed in Albrimese, not caring about maintaining any semblance of decorum. "Do you support *him*, Akinisie?! You can't! Tell us what's going on! I know you talked with Eirà. Tell me what you talked about!!" Mikkjal went to restrain her, and she now had tears rolling down her face. "*I won't let Iorki-Son win! Where is Eirà? Where is Skaaaaadiiii?*"

Kolfinna's words shattered the turf house's thick air. Mikkjal put his arm around her. To his surprise, his partner's outburst hadn't produced emotional r e actions among anyone else. Akinisie just walked over, calmly, and stared into Kolfinna's eyes. "Communicator Helensdottir, I spoke with Chieftain Marja last night. She is aware of your arrival and is not preoccupied. As for you, you have heard our words. You have heard me, you have heard Mikisoq's question, you have heard Taamusi. I know what I have to do. I also know where Storytellers are, yours and ours. But you have a good deal of listening to do first. I suggest you start. Naujaq, take them home!"

Naujaq stood up and put her hand on Kolfinna's shoulder, while Mikkjal held the other.

"Go home, rest," Akinisie concluded. "I'm not against you, girl. You just have to *think*." And with that, the Chieftain went back to the far wall and announced another speaker. A man began a new presentation, calmly, as if completely undisturbed by the preceding events.

While Naujaq accompanied the pair outside the stone door into the clear, dark cold, Mikkjal looked at the widespread green aurora in the sky. He breathed the fresh air in deeply. "You spoke well tonight," he said to Kolfinna. "You were present. You were convincing."

"I hope we find out soon if they're going to help us," Kolfinna vented, her voice back to the obsessive and detached person she'd incarnated in the morning.

"No choice but to live in the present moment, I guess." He remained hurt inside and perhaps sensed that she was, too. But as he uttered those words, the hole in his chest began to fill with warm, comforting energy. His actions, discoveries, and vision today were not at all in vain.

Chapter 7
The Great Qivittoq

Suspended in darkness, the throne room reappeared. Lia, Anavend, Ashkii, and the three southern Shishilms: a young woman named Lowanna from Kaltland; a well-built woman in her thirties from Solicia named Filemu; and a man of Marja and Akinisie's age from Läckjell named Hunapo. The thrones vibrated with Dust, as did Kolfinna's hand in Death-release in the real world. But the shroud still wasn't lifted over the two North Islanders in that ancient and timeless room.

Our leaders are searching for us, pulsated Ashkii. *We must leave.*

We are stuck in Taqraup Nunaat for now, Kolfinna answered back. *We can't come get you it looks like.*

There are rumours of a ship coming for us, Lowanna spoke through the Dust.

A ship? From whom? It's not from us, for we're stuck here!

But there was no answer.

He's dangerous because he divides, came Lia.

You mean Mikhail? Kolfinna asked, directing her Dust energy flow strong.

Thirty years ago it started. We had clan fights for centuries. Mikhail stopped them, uniting Iorki—new culture, new ways. He built, he built, he built. But he divided. A zone for Workers, a zone for Farmers, a zone for Hunters. He takes people to work splitting, processing, creating crystals. We have beautiful streets but farmers' crops all feed the Centre. Farmers sought to do their own thing. A Hunter crossed the border and joined with them.

That was you? Kolfinna asked.

No. I was a Distributor. I saw the contrast, the Centre and the edge… Iorki-Son brings only control and tyranny.

Skadi abhors him. He is enemy to Utgard, Kolfinna pulsated back.

There was silence, darkness and waiting.

One thing, Kolfinna added with much hesitation…
I'm not sure we can trust the Order of Communicators…

The silence ensued and the darkness in the dark room became even darker. The outlines of the thrones and the light in the room faded. No one answered anymore, and Kolfinna realized it was time to end the session. She sent her bodily energy into her arms and legs and pressed against the wooden floor, as she'd learned to do. It didn't work this time, though. She tried again, but her efforts only made the blackness blacker and weakened the remaining support the floor offered. She heaved her legs to hammer them home but only found herself heaving in the void. This was weightless like in the Gap once again.

All other souls in that Ansuz space disappeared. *Was it what I said?* she asked, in thought and Dust energy, to herself and anyone who still might hear. Her hands went numb and she saw herself, her own body, standing on the ground, attempting to see without her eyes. This was her resting space. Then the walls suddenly tore open and there stood before her a tall cloaked man with a thinning grey beard and dagger-like protruding eyes. It was him, there was no question about it, standing before the tear in the black on the other side of which was a winter night in the mountains.

"Hi, Kolfinna, you've come to die," hissed the voice, sinister and echoing in the void space, his Jorgian accent making the words even more strident to the ears. Then he cackled, loud like a blizzard wind, shaking up the woman Kolfinna saw as herself.

Closing her eyes, Kolfinna centred on herself. She screamed and extended her hand in Jorgson's direction. But when she opened them, she saw, instead of Mikhail,

Mikkjal was standing before her. He took her fury but stood, tall and strong, sword sheathed around bearskin parka and bow and arrow slung over his shoulder.

"*You're home,*" spoke Mikkjal, and she felt the floor and reemerged into physical consciousness.

It was another clear day but a windy day, the air pounding strong against the wooden walls of Naujaq's cabin. Kolfinna slowly caught her breath and stood up, walking to the window. Mikkjal wasn't there, she remembered. Ittoq had stopped by early to pick him up to go fishing and reindeer hunting. Once he left she'd started today's Death-release training, the most frightening yet. Mikhail led to Mikkjal. The Southern Shishilms were in danger. Akinisie wouldn't help them.

And the Skrallander on the throne made no contact with her. Neither did the Gorrlander, who was a single figure, not the diad she and Mikkjal were supposed to be. Akinisie had been quick to point out that contradiction, too...

Could Mikhail Jorgson really know her plan? Was that him who spoke or a dream image?

Kolfinna cut some bread and made herself a sandwich with thawed out reindeer meat. She breathed and tried to ground herself once more. The wind wasn't helping her. Disturbed by its mighty howling and the chilling messages and visions, she decided to turn on the radio to distract herself. Taqraup personal radio devices like this one could receive on 1800, 2000, and 2500 crystal waves per second. It could receive and transmit on 3000 cw/s for local communication within one hundred and fifty kilometres or so from the main Village Tower or secondary Skralland Towers. On the back of the steel unit was an annex wooden speaker that was identical to Gorrlanders' belt radios. Unlike Gorrland, on 2500 cw/s there was an ongoing vibrant radio presentation. Akinisie's voice was there, making announcements every few minutes, and between these announcements there was music.

Yes, this was the recording technology Akinisie had invented early last spring. She had planned to visit Gorrland before the snow melted to teach them how to build a recorder, how to connect its small mechanical crystal to the Tower's large radio crystal, how to counter crystal erosion. She would be visiting them if this mess hadn't happened, if Sigfather hadn't called and Jorgson hadn't planned his attack. Still, Kolfinna remembered that Akinisie never announced her discovery on 1000 cw/s for all Lands. She preferred to send it on 1800 mid-range, talking personally with Marja. She said she had the same mid-range conversation from Taqraup East Tower with Torvall Chieftain Ilmari and Shishilm Anavend. Knowledge of the existence of Akinisie's methods remained in the Greater North of Albrimir. She obviously knew there was risk in sharing. Jorgson, of course, probably already knew it and more. *What is going through your mind, Chieftain?* she asked herself.

Hearing the radio used in a public manner for announcements or music was enjoyable. At times Akinisie appeared to allow persons to speak from a distance, presumably by calling in on the transceiver on 3000 cw/s, and she would place the transceiver speaker next to the microphone for retransmission on the community broadcast frequency. She is an active and public Chieftain, Kolfinna thought, immediately chiding herself for admiring the woman's charisma and knowledge. *Damn it, she could be my enemy! She hasn't let me speak to anyone back home, and she lets Eirà ride through with no message. Reveal yourself, woman!*

Unfortunately, several callers spoke who were very distraught, crying in despair. The word *qanima* came over and over again, which Kolfinna recognized from last night as referring to sickness. Other words repeated themselves, and she was beginning to decipher certain patterns in the speech. Not everyone was upset, but those who weren't appeared to be consoling those who were.

The general mood was heavy. What could be the cause of this? *They don't show anything when they talk to us!*

Nothing special appeared to have happened today. Ittoq was as humorous as before with her and Mikkjal when he picked him up early this morning. Outside, people were filling their sleds and starting up their snowmobiles, preparing for hunting outings. Others were walking down alleys, carrying their children to communal schoolhouses or wherever else kids would go in Skralland. About five people called in, interspersed with music recordings, and other announcements by Akinisie. Naujaq and Mikisoq spoke in passing yesterday about something called the "Heaviness." Neither wanted to dwell on it. Akinisie also mentioned "many very urgent matters, too, of which you're probably becoming aware." Perhaps the situation was much more serious than what they were letting on…

Amid the crying, Kolfinna was drawn to a word that didn't appear with the greatest frequency but stood out compared to other words. The first time a distraught female voice of middle age said it. Something beginning and ending with a "k" sound. The next time it was said by a man's voice, whose speaker was straightforward and clear. *Kavittok* was the word. Something like that. Kolfinna thought she remembered hearing that word from the Council Meeting, from someone in the little turf house, though she didn't remember who.

A strong gust of wind heaved against the wood and made the glass windows brace themselves. Mikisoq was supposed to be coming, she remembered. Maybe she'd stay in because of the wind. The prospect made Kolfinna unsure. While an alone day would allow her to make progress in her Ansuz communications, she had to admit she enjoyed the afternoon she'd spent sewing. Not only did Mikisoq show her new techniques and allow her to start making a new parka offering much greater warmth than the one she carried, in the back of her mind she must admit that she enjoyed the distraction of the day.

Had the Council Meeting never come to that house yesterday, with Akinisie's blasted nonsense and Taamusi's aura question, she could've had good fun working and joking with the elderly lady Mikisoq. Perhaps working was part of her recognition, she thought. After making a Taqraup Nunaat-style parka she would be noticed, and with being noticed they'd take seriously her request to go before a Seer or even the Storyteller and learn the identity of the red-dotted one in Skralland? Perhaps that was the best of both worlds.

It was likely a moot point, though. Kolfinna noticed the strength of the wind as she stepped outside to bring a few logs in from the porch. Even from under the shelter of the porch, her face was stung by blowing snow from the ground. No one would choose to go out in this.

Back inside she noticed that one song had been repeating on the radio three times. There were no more announcements or call-ins. Akinisie must not be manning the broadcast booth anymore. No one was intervening. Kolfinna took this as an opportunity to turn the radio off, but as her hand hovered over the transceiver she felt a pulsation in her hand. Oh-so-subtle and brief it was, but the twin dots were indeed tremoring and her hand was vibrating. She had no other signs of visions, Ansuz communication, or Sigfather's voice. But instead of turning off the radio, she turned it to the high tranceiving frequency. Occasional conversations happened there, much shorter and more factual than the community information frequency. So the antennas were working, just no one in the Tower was manning them at the moment.

The thought crossed her mind to send out a message for Akinisie from the machine. She thought about it for several seconds but decided against it. Many more Skrallanders than just the Communicators understood Albrimese, and what they would understand as antagonism for the Communicator Chieftain may then be perceived as hostility to their entire people.

Just then the front door jolted open. Mikisoq stood in the doorway and quickly entered, pushing the large door closed against the howling of the clear wind.

"Kolfinna-ngai!" she greeted with a smile, as she took off her boots and came into the kitchen. She pulled back her grey wolfskin hood to reveal her short hair of similar colour.

"Hi, Mikisoq. You went out in that wind?"

The older woman laughed as she made her way into the kitchen, where she opened her jacket, revealing the wooden bear necklace she wore as an amulet "This is nothing. A light breeze. You're too used to trees." She laughed again then went to take a piece of bread on the counter. "You do keep the place warm, don't you?" She motioned to the fireplace, then removed her parka completely.

"I suppose I do," Kolfinna smiled.

"And I see you discovered our radio." Mikisoq took the kettle on the counter and shook it to see if any tea remained inside.

"Oh, I can make more tea if you—"

"Not just on account of me," Mikisoq interrupted. "Besides, we should go. Did you understand any of the radio?"

Kolfinna put a hand on the device, still surprised that Mikisoq hadn't modified the day's plans. "Maybe a few words. But the talking stopped on the main channel."

"Oh?" Mikisoq chuckled. "That's the way you can know that the Communicators are getting a message. You'll hear the same song over and over again. I don't know why they don't have different microphones for their different frequency transmissions. Our Tower leader has made sure we have the best technology possible but they still always forget to better cover up when they're busy receiving messages." The small woman chuckled and started towards the door. It wasn't a matter of different microphones, which every Tower definitely had, but of available Communicators to man different broadcasts at once, Kolfinna thought to herself. Right now all Tower personnel was occupied.

She picked up her parka. "So that means she's talking to other Lands?"

"To other Lands or to other planets!" And at that Mikisoq cracked up at her own joke, though Kolfinna's smile was uneasy. "Come on, girl, your parka won't finish itself."

"Mikisoq—"

"What is it, girl?" Mikisoq, asked, adjusting her parka well while Kolfinna went to put hers on.

"Do… do you trust her? Akinisie, I mean."

Mikisoq smiled with gentle eyes. "With my life, ten times over. She isn't a Hunter or a Guide, but she is one brave soul to persevere like she does."

Kolfinna buttoned her parka closed and smiled a somewhat uneasy smile at Mikisoq. This old lady had such a kind disposition she was inclined to believe her. And so she went forward, the kind seamstress opening the door for Kolfinna into the wind, even directing her to her own snowmobile in the blowing snow.

***

Attention! Attention!
Midday, on the Fifteenth of Fifteenmonth, 963
On the long-range frequency of one thousand crystal waves per second, I call all-Albrimir Communicators to attention.
This is Communicator Chieftain Fraick Abbott, of the great Land of Iorki. At present moment, our great leader Mikhail Iorki-Son is currently involved in a heroic diplomatic mission at the Kalyim frontier at Uygalaan Pass. His excellency, having a superior sense of compromise, has allowed the group of Farmers and Hunters to remain in Kalyim as a gesture of good faith,

provided he hand over our unfortunate rebellious Lia, in league with the sorceress Kolfinna. Let us all, citizens of Albrimir, hope and pray, to the deities who inspire us, that the mission succeeds and that war may be averted. We hope and pray that Shishilm Anavend proves himself as diplomatic and forward-thinking as his excellency, Mikhail.

I take this opportunity to extend, to Chieftains Tia of Wanautipun, Ehukai of Solicia, Akinisie of Taqraup Nunaat, and Marja of Gorrland, our great leader's request for clarification of your position regarding us and the sorceress. There can be no compromise with barbarism.

I remind Marja that you need not feel the need to protect this girl, for she knows not the meaning of civilized being. She likely scares you. It is ok to admit it.

I remind Akinisie that you need not side with Gorrland on this, or any issue, just because they're known as fierce warriors. We have weapons of the sort the world has never seen, capable of defending against any aggression from Gorrlander warriors on ship or snow machine.

I remind Tia of your long lasting hostile history with Gorrland.

I remind Ehukai of the fact that your South Island neighbours consider you less culturally developed.

No one need keep faith with ancient alliances that are obsolete in the New World. No one need maintain hostility because their ancestors were enemies. The world is changing. Progress is for all.

Greetings from Iorki!
Fraick Abbott out!

THE GREAT QIVITTOQ

***

Mikkjal

All six humans worked together to prepare the three javelin-launchers without disturbing the herd of forty-something reindeer down the hill. Behind two large rocks the group sat, Ittoq pressing on the snowpack to solidify the machine's base and Etua bringing three lances from a sled. The snowmobiles were left behind a ridge some sixty metres back. Working today was all the more difficult with the wind and blowing snow, but the men in the group were very strong. In such wind, the beasts also kept moving. Unable to stick their nose under for lichen long, they kept walking down the hill and away. On the other hand, not one of them noticed the Hunters. Without a word spoken, Aiviq, Ernannaq, and Tiguak activated the tiny crystals in each long lance, brightening its blade. They then placed one in each launcher, aiming one for one of the larger beasts in the herd's centre. Ittoq, Etua, and now Mikkjal would charge in after the Dust javelin launch, their non-crystal metal spears ready to hurl at staggering reindeer for final killing blows. The three launchers, wearing yellow-white reindeer coats themselves, pulled back the tight cords under cover of howling wind and let each release to strike at the animals.

Each spear succeeded in its impact. Three reindeer were downed, and the fan flair of Dust ripples sent six more staggering and disoriented. For that the three spear throwers were there. Two out of three of these ordinary spears hit their mark. Mikkjal missed. All six men ran as fast as they could in the hardened snow, Ittoq holding another spear, in case a wounded beast decided to run.

And run one reindeer did, its lance still stuck in its back. Ittoq heaved his backup spear, but the animal somehow managed to evade it, turning to run up the hill, rather than down and away from the Hunters. In fact, it was charging in Mikkjal's direction. Having no second spear, Mikkjal took out his sword. The frightened beast, not sensing which danger to run toward and which to flee, barrelled with its nose down, dripping spots of blood on the blowing snow in its wake. He pressed the small crystal activator on his sword's hilt, and swung in the air toward the reindeer, searing the windy air with flaming Dust. The animal reeled in shock and landed on its back. But it wouldn't submit. Condemned already to die, it turned to flee, muscles pulsating in agony but not wanting to meet the sword. Mikkjal swung again with all his might, and the white energy fused with blowing snow to transform sky, ground and air into a treacherous expanding white haze.

Now the animal was stunned beyond the point of getting back up. Mikkjal hustled over to it, feeling himself sweat beneath his heavy brown bearskin. His finger still on the hilt activator, Dust still outlined his long blade. In frustration and fatigue, he pulled the weapon back to give as strong a killing blow as possible, with making good use of the mighty white cosmic energy.

But then he heard Sigfather's voice radiate to the sound of the wind, repeating the message of yesterday: *"Every time you move the Dust you invoke me. You must be mindful."*

Mikkjal took a serious notice of how hard he was breathing. He also realized that the animal was lying ever stiller in the blood-stained snow, accepting its fate. While sensing Ittoq and the others slowly coming over, he changed his mind. He removed his finger from the hilt button and pointed the blade, now of bare metal, at the animal's skull. Slowly, the reindeer turned and looked at him, staring at Mikkjal in a strangely serene calm. He turned his back to the wind and quickly plunged the blade into the easiest spot back of the head, killing it instantly.

Its eyes rolled back and resistance was released. And with the reindeer's last heartbeat, as Mikkjal had just pulled the sword out, he caught another glimpse of *her* entering the cave. Ageless yet ancient, Skadi turned around, waiting before entering the darkness.

"Be fearless but be calm. Be wild or be dead," quietly echoed a deep and foreboding female voice. And from the cave's entrance, in vision, Skadi of wolf fur and shoulder spear pulled out her bow in a fraction of a second and fired an arrow through Mikkjal's eye.

He fell down, feeling the wind stinging his cheek and snow enter his eye. Ittoq was there. "What did you do?" asked Ittoq as he approached. "You almost went crazy."

Mikkjal stood back up, rubbing the blood from his blade in the snow and placing his other hand to his eye. Skadi's wound was, of course, not physical. "Yes, I almost did. But I think I remembered wisdom."

Ittoq raised his eyebrows and nodded calmly, seeming to express approval. "Hunters are not crazy, and Hunters do not control."

As he smiled at Ittoq, Mikkjal felt a strange release of a tension he didn't even know he had in his stomach and thighs. He looked at his blade, then at his hand, then up at the hills of the surrounding wilderness. He thought he understood Sigfather's lesson—the one Sigfather and Skadi taught together. Unmindful moving of the Dust was the unmindful force of Sigfather. Skadi had no use for that... but Jorgson did.

The men got to work butchering the animals. It took a time-lapse and a half and required removing mitts, so by the time they finished everyone's fingers were numb. They loaded two sleds with meat and deposed the animals' guts to feed the ravens and foxes. White furs were tied to the back of one of the Hunter's sleds. Then, with the sun halfway between the height of its loop and the mountainous horizon, engines were started.

ANSUZ

Mikkjal took his place behind Etua and Ittoq, third in line in a group of five snowmobiles, with Aiviq and Tiguak sharing a machine. Ittoq, the elder Hunter of the group, led his youthful companions further east over gently rolling hills down to the shore of sea ice. From there, they would go on to a place where Etua had built temporary snow houses with his wife and her parents. In fact, Ernannaq was Etua's brother, while Aiviq and Tiguak were his wife's brothers. They had left Taqraup Nunaat Village two weeks ago, so Etua told Mikkjal. The young, thin Hunter with the thin goatee said that life was more peaceful and less heavy out on the land. His family's intention for an extended stay was made all the clearer by the fact that they'd gone out on the land with their team of dogs, in addition to snowmobiles. In case they would want to stay out after fuel ran out, they could always travel and hunt in the ancient way.

Riding steadily on his machine, Mikkjal's thoughts returned. Skadi had not only shown herself but actually spoken to him. She spoke when he remembered the connectivity of himself and the beasts, and the fact that Dust was what connects us in living form more than it is a weapon. Connectivity in action in Utgard. Kolfinna was going about it the wrong way. Skadi didn't speak to him through Ansuz, as Kolfinna had; Mikkjal had felt no pulsation on his hand. Yet it was Eirà who got it into her head that this ancient Meniyan technique of the Old Shishilms was Skadi's realm. Eirà was the chief Skadisman of the Mountaineers. Surely he knew what he was talking about? Or perhaps he was misleading Kolfinna entirely? In any case, his partner need worry less about the loyalties of people like Eirà and Akinisie and more about what she genuinely feels, sees, and knows. Convening with Skadi was of much greater value than identifying the Taqraup Shishilm, and if Akinisie didn't cooperate, they could always ride onward to safety, and conduct their mission in more hospitable areas.

She was holding back, that Communicator Chieftain, Mikkjal thought, but she had a plan somehow. It would be completely illogical for her to ally herself with Jorgson. If she had, she would've already arrested Kolfinna and himself. The Taqramiut wouldn't risk upsetting their neighbours to ally with a mid-mainland Folk. As unfortunately pragmatic as it was, Akinisie was telling the honest truth when she told them that Skralland didn't really have a choice but to stand with their island neighbours, Albrimir's greatest warriors. Perhaps their alliance was unbalanced in that way? Then again, for any and all land exchange, it was the Gorrlanders who relied on the Skrallanders. They would be much weaker if they only had the sea to rely on, especially with North Island's climate; even more so with this climate's growing uncertainty.

Jorgson would love to break old alliances apart in the name of his new order. Smart people would know to resist his attempts. *Let's hope the wild ones Skadi loves are smarter than the civilized ones Jorgson tries to court...*

Unfortunately, thoughts had served Mikkjal little since he arrived in Skralland, so he put them out of mind. Land was his element, and he was at home. His senses were working as well here as they had anywhere in Gorrland. He had felt the reindeer moving before the Hunters had seen them. It was thanks to his senses and instinct that the team could remain so well hidden from the herd. Like Astrid had long taught, he crouched as low and as small as he could become in order to hear the land in its awesome size and might.

Ittoq came down a hill scattered with low pine shrubs, then onto the seashore, where a hard snow cover blurred the boundary between beach and sea ice. With more space the snowmobiles flared out, riding on the ice parallel to shore. They were going with the wind so the ride was not a challenge at all. Coming up from the depths of the sea, through the frozen surface, and into

Mikkjal's feet was the sense of human dwellings ahead. And after five minutes Etua pointed his finger, about the same time Mikkjal had visual confirmation of four snow houses on the sea ice ahead of them.

As the riders pulled to a stop, two women and several young children came out to greet them. Many dogs were also there, leashed to rocks beside the snow houses, barking and howling. A tall young woman walked up to Etua and warmly embraced him before greeting the newcomers to the camp.

"Hi Mikkjal. Welcome!" She had welcoming eyes and very long black hair extending outside her parka. *This woman is truly happy. Perhaps she's the first person to appear entirely happy on this whole trip,* Mikkjal thought. By her side were two small children in thick fur coats, one boy and one girl.

"These are your children?" he asked her, feeling his smile dominate his face.

"Yes. Jaaji and Pamela. And I'm Erika."

"Nice to meet you. Your name is like a name from our Land."

"Well, it's not as if today is the first time our two peoples met each other." Erika laughed. "Come in. The hard work is done."

He did as he was told, and Ittoq followed, crawling on hands and knees through the tunnelled entrance. Behind them, the camp's regulars stayed to divide the meat into what should be brought inside, what should be cached under the ice, and what should be given to the dogs. Inside this the snow house, the group didn't have the customary oil lamp or small open fire, but an actual steel wood stove with a black chimney extending up into the snow roof. It was the same kind as those found in any wooden or turf house. Blankets were on the ground in front to serve as a floor, while in the back was a raised level where furs signalled the sleeping area. A young woman with short hair was tending a pot on the stove.

"Tea's ready," she said, looking up. "Hi Mikkjal," she added, her eyes showing emotion while her voice did not.

"This is my sister Nûsa," said Erika, removing her parka and brushing her long hair back. "And you've already met my brothers Tiguak and Aiviq."

The girl went back to the stove, then to the bed platform, where she picked up a very young child of about one year old.

"That's my little nephew Boye," said Erika. "Tiguak's son."

"My little man," said the youthful Tiguak, crawling in the snow house entrance with a reindeer thigh in his hand. "Soup time?" he asked all.

"Of course, Brother," said Erika, taking the meat. "But go help my husband feed the dogs first." Tiguak obeyed his older sister but not before kissing his son then gently roughing up his younger sister's short hair with his hand.

"I can help, too," said Mikkjal, gesturing to the outside. He noticed his understanding of the Taqraup language was getting better and better.

"Yes, you and Ittoq can help by talking to me as I make lunch." Erika placed the meat on a large flat stone and began slicing it with a round-bladed knife. Nûsa, holding Boye, brought the tea pot to the floor, where Ittoq and Mikkjal sat, placing clay cups beside it. Mikkjal poured tea for all.

"So? Tell me the terrible adventure that saw you come east and get adopted by this old man!" Then, she added in a well-pronounced Gorrlander speech, "You're from Westfolk, are you not?"

"Yes. You can tell?"

"Yes, the accent never truly goes away. But you're learning our language well. Now tell me your story, in Gorrlander, Taqraup, or in Albrimese. I sense we're about to learn something."

By the time Mikkjal had finished telling his story, all his hunting companions, as well as Aiviq's wife and kids, had come into the snow house and were sitting, listening intently. Stew was cooking on the stove and the snow house's interior had gotten warm enough for all to shed their parkas. He spoke a simple but understandable Taqraup, and he could get across the words he didn't know by using a mixture of Gorrlander and Albrimese.

When the story that he was beginning to grow tired of repeating was finished there was a long pause, broken when Erika picked up Mikkjal's left hand and looked at his two red dots. "The Evolver definitely spoke to you. But if anyone here had these red dots, we would know about it."

A cold gust managed to blow through the entryway, its long howl masking the shouts from the children.

"Maybe he spoke to you in riddle. He spoke a trick," said Tiguak, sitting with Boye on his knee.

"Kolfinna doesn't think so," sighed Mikkjal. "But I admit, we're still searching."

"Does Kolfinna know everything, Mikkjal?" came the sharp voice of Nûsa staring at him from the side with bright piercing eyes from beneath her short dark hair. "All hail the magical Kolfinna!"

Mikkjal looked down and bit his lip. All were silent, watching him and feeling him. The trigger for him went off, but he hoped no one else noticed it. "What do *you* think, Mikkjal?" asked Etua finally, playfully striking his new hunting buddy with his mitt.

He paused and made sure to plant both feet on the ground. "I am very worried. But I must admit that I do not know what to think." He looked at Ittoq, then Erika, and then upwards at the majestic spiral of snow blocks that composed the ceiling. "Actually, I'm interested in what you think. Kolfinna and I have reached the extent of our understanding. This is how I see it. That is what I *think*, but I *know* that something is going on."

All looked at each other. *Do they approve of what I said? Maybe I'll never know.* Erika, seated on one knee, clasped her hands and smiled. "I'll get lunch." Standing, she added, almost gleefully, "Ask Ittoq to tell you a story."

"You know a lot of stories, Ittoq?" he asked as Erika went to the stove to get a pot of stew. *But again they don't really want to talk about what I have to say if they're asking me to listen to the old man.*

"Not a lot. I'm not a trained Storyteller or Seer or whatnot. But I know one I think you're ready to hear." The man went to pick up one of the furs from the hunt, which he folded more than once so as to have a place to sit slightly higher than the others. Only once the clay bowls had been filled with reindeer stew for all who desired to eat it did he begin.

Ittoq moved to light his pipe. "Mikkjal, you've seen our Land," the Hunter spoke to everyone present. "You know how we live. One large village, a city perhaps even. A few small settlements. And temporary camps. What's all around us?"

"If there's anything you don't understand I can translate," Erika reminded.

Mikkjal nodded to Erika. "Snow? Mountains?"

"Yes, mountains," answered Ittoq. "And ice. Even in summertime, a bay that is full of icebergs. Do you think our Land is suitable to someone who wants to live alone?"

"Well, no, not at all."

"Precisely. We need the group. We need each other. But there are some who have chosen to live alone in the mountains. There are also some who have had that choice made for them by others. These people have been forced them to live on the outside, alone, as punishment for their offences. The naive among us used to think that these people went to die on the Outside, but they did not die."

"They lived? Alone?" Mikkjal almost choked on his spoonful of stew.

"They still do," Ittoq replied, puffing thin smoke out of his long wooden pipe. "One who leaves becomes wild and mad, possessed by the mountains themselves, which gives the person killer instincts, superhuman strength and near immortality. This person becomes a *Qivittoq.*"

"What does a Qivittoq do?"

"He or she lives a life of absolute freedom, at one with the spirit of the mountains. For some people, this represents the greatest allure, for others the greatest danger. No one thinks neutrally about those from the Outside, though. These free wild ones become one, in body and soul, with the Great-One-Who-Left, an ancient woman some simply call the *Great Qivittoq.* She is their master, but they also compose and strengthen her. She left the human world centuries ago, yet through the mountain magic she is still alive, luring more and more free minds away. And her magic creates social strife so that other humans become banished from villages, sentenced to join her ranks. She is said to get ever stronger until humans relinquish their fear of what is Beyond and reckon with her."

"This is Skadi! It's Utgard's magic!" Mikkjal spoke with wide eyes and an uncontrollable chill running up his spine.

"As Taamusi said, you call by one name someone who exists in every culture's lore. The Great-One-Who-Left was a strong and energetic young woman, feisty and talented at hunting, sewing and communing with the spirits. She intimidated her husband many years back, who tried to forbid her from hunting. Wanting to be the sole provider, he confined her to the snow house while he went to hunt. After a long day, when he tried to kill animals of all sorts to show his prowess to his wife and to the camp, he returned to find his wife had left him. He was alone to tend to the family snow house and the dogs until from the mountains she

134

called forth a wind that untied the dogs, leaving the man all alone. He died that winter, unable to provide even for himself—the man who strived to be more powerful than his wife and dominate the camp.

"His wife, rejected by the social order of the time, went on to become master over that social order. In absolute freedom she became the most feared force on the planet. Due to her and her many *Qivittut* we are taught not to venture away from our settlements alone."

"But if she is to create problems by taking more and more people away from civilization, won't it continue until she is confronted?"

"Now you're asking the questions you need to be asking!" Ittoq beamed proudly. "You're thinking like someone who knows the mountains. And you are correct. She must be confronted and sought out. But she must be loved; she, the source of the greatest fear, must be loved. That is what the Elders have taught me. And this is what we've neglected to do. For this reason we are getting sick. The ones who should know—the Elders and Seers—are taken away, now lacking communication. This is what we have named the heaviness."

Mikkjal was so physically present in the story that he hadn't noticed the sound of snowmobiles approaching or that of men disembarking outside the snow house. He was genuinely surprised when, through the entryway as Ittoq was ending his story, his old Guide friend Jaani appeared. And who was it who followed him? Yes, it was Kunuut, some four or five years older than Mikkjal and built like a bear. Everyone looked at the Guides, who nodded. Jaani said to Etua and Ernanaaq that they were passing through on their delivery run of fuel pump crystal enhancers, still travelling east. Then the two came and embraced Mikkjal.

"I knew we'd see you again this year," Kunuut laughed. "Where's the red man Kjartan?"

"Couldn't come. It's not a supply exchange this time," Mikkjal answered.

Jaani and Kunuut smiled, but something prevented his mates from chatting. There was business to attend to.

"Ittoq, turn on your radio. You're being called," Jaani called to the older man. Ittoq went to the entry and picked up his head-sized device while Jaani and Kunuut shook hands with the others present. Over the radio there was dead air until a person gave a message. Luckily for them the first voice to be heard was that of Akinisie calling to Ittoq. With the thick radio fuzz Mikkjal didn't understand her message.

"It's our Tower Master," spoke Ittoq. "She wants me to contact her by private message. I think she misses me." He winked and removed the small speaking capsule from the back of the radio device. He pressed the buttons on the sender to send a message, standing up and walking over to the snow-block wall. While Ittoq messaged the Communicator Chieftain, the two Guides chatted pleasantly with the men and women present, while the children began to run around freely. Folks were relaxing after a meal and a story.

As soon as Mikkjal started to think about the legend and just how much the *Great Qivittoq* ressembled Skadi, Nûsa came and sat next to him. "Hi Mikkjal."

"Hello," he answered shyly, trying to keep an eye on Ittoq's actions at his portable radio.

"You know what?"

"What is it?" Mikkjal looked at the strange girl with short hair and brightening brown eyes, then back to his teacher. Ittoq's expression had most definitely changed, becoming most grave as he typed hurriedly.

"Pay attention to me, Mikkjal," the girl said slyly, touching his hand. "I am as interesting as Kolfinna or even more so." Then, leaning in closely to speak near his ear, she added, "I am a Qivittoq."

"What?!" The Guide felt shivers in his spine but still managed to divide his attention between this girl and the actions of Ittoq, who came over to the group. He quietly called Jaani over, serious precision in his eyes and stress in his body. The two men crouched through the entryway tunnel and went outside.

"Mikkjal, listen!" Nûsa slapped his shoulder. "I am a Mountain Dweller, a Qivittoq who returned. We do exist."

His body tensed up and his stomach churned, and he forgot the mens' sudden departure from the house.

"I live among humans, but I'm as wild as the mountains." She brought her hand up Mikkjal's arm to his bare neck. "Find me when you want to know the wild." She stroked his neck and blew soft air on it, then winked and stood up to move towards the porch of the snowhouse.

Only his recent vision of Skadi allowed him to take this girl seriously in what she was saying. Physically, however, he seemed to have taken her seriously enough. To his utter embarrassment, he saw that everybody had been watching and listening. And equally to his embarrassment, he found that he had become aroused.

"Don't worry. She gets like that sometimes," said Aiviq, nodding toward his sister.

"My sister is... interesting," Erika added with an embarrassed smile on her face. "No need to worry, though." Mikkjal watched Nûsa, perhaps a year or two younger than himself, playing with her nieces and nephews. She was clearly now focused on other matters than the foreign Guide and the legends of mountain wanderers. Attempting to further distance himself from the awkwardness she caused him, Mikkjal turned to Kunuut.

"So, you have many more delivery spots?" Mikkjal asked.

"Only one," Kunuut answered in Albrimese. "Lake-Like has the easternmost fuel supply. We go there now."

Ittoq and Jaani came back inside, each with

most serious looks on their face. The older man's speech was abrupt and loud. "There's been a change of plans. I'm called to return to town for an extra Council meeting. The Guides are going to continue east to Lake-Like. However, they're going to need to spend the night there because Sivkersok is coming from East Tower to deliver an important package for Akinisie. There's one more change. Mikkjal, I want you to go with your fellow Guides Jaani, Kunuut, and Sivkersok and spend the night in *Tasiusaq*. You'll come back tomorrow."

"What? Why? What's happened?!"

"Eqorsuaq is sending a gift for his wife, too. He can't leave the Glacier Tower so you will bring it back to her for him since you're staying in her house."

Mikkjal felt another knot in his stomach. Ittoq hadn't come up with a good excuse, and it was clear that something made him not want to bring him back to town that evening.

"Don't worry about Kolfinna. My wife will inform her, and she will stay with her all evening."

"If it's important, I'll go, Ittoq," said Mikkjal, reaching for his parka. "But why is there a sudden call for an emergency Council meeting?"

Ittoq stared vacantly at the snow wall. "Meteorite metal. We're facing a metal shortage so we're calling a special expedition to Meteorite Mountain and need to start mobilizing now." The Hunter couldn't bring himself to look Mikkjal in the eye as he said it, staring instead at the snow wall.

"Don't worry about those old folks, Mikkjal," spoke the tall Jaani. "Come on, we'll have fun. It's always a great time when we stay at the Tasiusaq cabin." The Taqraup Guide put a hand on his Gorrlander colleague's shoulder. "There's a straightaway where you can go a hundred and fifty kilometres an hour on the ice." Mikkjal nodded with a reserved curt smile as all got dressed to go back to their vehicles.

"So very nice to meet you Mikkjal," spoke Erikin Gorrlander, coming to shake his hand. Her husband Etua did the same, while Ernanaaq, Aiviq, his wife, and Tiguak waved and said the young man's name. Nûsa sat by the wall with mischievous eyes but nodded respectfully nonetheless.

Outside was a twilight sky. The Hunter turned to Mikkjal as he was warming up his snowmobile. "You're learning our life quicker than expected," he shouted through the wind. I sense your passing through our Land is part of what is wanted. Thank you for listening about the Qivittoq. I know we'll talk about it again."

"Thank you Ittoq," he replied, genuinely glad that he'd taken him under his wing. But the speed at which the man took off over the sea ice suggested a matter of much greater urgency than the supposed metal collecting expedition. Ittoq knew that Mikkjal, a Guide, could sense the speed at which objects moved across land. He couldn't hide from him that his snowmobile was going at full throttle in the direction of the village. And one only went maximum speed against the wind when one was in a definite hurry.

The truth would be known very soon. Ittoq's sudden ride would only be an addition to the list of potential causes of panic or worry—sensations that he would decide to forego in exchange for a ride and a camping trip with friends.

"I'm ready to go," Mikkjal said to Jaani and Kunuut, climbing atop his own snow machine. "Who is the Guide we're meeting there?"

"Sivkersok," Jaani answered, coming over so he wouldn't have to shout over wind and engine. "I mentioned her last time."

And for a reason inexplicable to him, Mikkjal's heart beat faster. "You mean the Girl from the East? The one doing stealth hunting, training, and sleeping on the tundra?"

"Hers truly," Jaani shouted back, then going back to his machine, warming strong with its headlight piercing the sea ice.

Then, in the second Kunuut revved his engine for the final time before turning to head out, Mikkjal again saw Skadi shoot her arrow, from the cave directly into his eye.

"*Be wild or be dead,*" she echoed.

Mikkjal followed his mates as they advanced in the dimming twilight, away from the sun and along the ice, en route to a remote settlement he'd never seen, the realm of a Guide he'd never met.

Chapter 8
The Raven Visit

Kolfinna

Mikisoq was trying. She invited her for supper, along with her daughter and husband, along with Naujaq. She served her fish chowder, potatoes, and Westfolk vegetables, as well as reindeer steaks. She filled the kitchen and the dining room with wonderfully pleasant smells to make her, forget the reality of the cruel, cold night. The wind had bothered no one, but by the time Kolfinna finished dining in Mikisoq and Kaataq's wood cabin, it had died down to virtually zero. Yet despite the warmth of the food, Kolfinna felt chilled as she sat there. Ittoq was called to an emergency Council meeting barely a time-lapse after Mikisoq had explained that Council wouldn't meet again for five days. While she had given her the unsettling news about the meeting when they were still at the sewing house, she waited until they'd reached her home before announcing the second bit of news—Mikkjal would be spending the night with his Taqraup Guide comrades at an outpost in the East.

During the day, she had finally seen him. Without engaging in Death-release or other preparations, she saw a quick vision of the New Shishilms, and on the throne for Gorrland was Mikkjal Aldisson. His face unshrouded, he sat there as clear as day with his familiar darkish hair and comforting smile. Without Dust agitation, without throbbing hand dots, Mikkjal showed himself. Somehow she communicated to him, without trying. And the others were there, too—Lia, Anavend, Ashkii, Lowanna, Filemu, and Hunapo. Seven Shishilms showed, minus whoever from Skralland would eventually show. Kolfinna wasn't to be found, only Mikkjal appeared from Gorrland, showing himself calmly and without tumultuous message. As for the others, it would appear that there was some sort of plan for them to leave Steigsonland and Kaltland, and maybe for the others to leave Solicia and Lackjell.

Mikisoq tried to make conversation. Her family were Providers. Her daughter Êla was a Seamstress like herself, and her husband Kataaq was a Hunter. It was the most typical couple pairing. The weather had been clear and cold recently, they said, but the winds were changing, meaning that the blizzards of the latter third of winter would be on their way soon. While wall-mounted torches lit the room, somewhat unnecessarily due to the bright full moon over the snow outdoors, the Skrallanders engaged her in informal discussion. Kolfinna didn't feel talkative, but she obliged them, putting aside her angst as best she could. While they had all heard about the Gorrland family structure, and the Tragedy that had made it possible, they were somewhat surprised to learn about the more formal structure of education the Gorrlanders used. Teachers were not an order in Taqraup Nunaat as they were to the west. Children were taught by their extended family at home and on the land, and periodically they were given Land instruction by Guides and technology instruction by Communicators. The Communicator leaders take an interest in how young people learn and participate in community life.

Of course you would, Akinisie. You take interest in everyone but reveal nothing.

Over the rather delicious reindeer steak, Mikisoq had exclaimed that Kolfinna would be finished with her parka tomorrow, and it would be beautiful. She really seemed to think Kolfinna knew what she was doing, despite her initial misgivings when Naujaq first brought her to her house. There was cheer in that house, some of it genuine, but it was not enough to mask the coldness eating away at Kolfinna's heart. Her mind was filled with questions, which she had to find answers to, even if they were not coming. When three time-lapses had gone by, she shook hands with her hosts as she left, agreeing to meet at the turf house sewing centre in the morning. The night would be harsh without Mikkjal, but with her unanswered thoughts. He didn't understand her, but she understood him.

After goodbyes and upon opening the door, though, she saw a snowmobile parked beside those that belonged there. On it the rider still stood, waiting for her.

"Kolfinna, I've been waiting for you. I just returned from the Council meeting," spoke the female voice, powerful but neutral. She had come to her.

"Akinisie."

"It is time we talked. I want you to follow me to the Tower and show you a few things. If you have time, of course."

"Yes." Kolfinna's heart beat faster and faster as she walked in the snow. Akinisie wore a fur hat over her thick white parka. Even in her reserve she was elegant. But with the expression she gave off, Kolfinna knew that it would be useless to ask her about what she would show her.

She stood before Akinisie, who dismounted her snowmobile and walked up to her. "I will speak to you, however, as a member of the Order of Communicators of Albrimir. Do you still consider yourself a member of this Order?"

"Of course," said Kolfinna, attempting a smile.

"In that case, turn on your machine and follow me."

She did as she was told, not without taking a look at the great Tower, which was easily visible from Mikisoq's house in the village's central area. It was a structure unlike any she had ever seen before; taller, that was certain, but also built from steel in a way she hadn't known humans able to do. In her mind, frankly, it looked extraterrestrial in comparison to Gorrland's Tower, which was essentially a lighthouse with an antenna on top. The ride toward the mighty structure was quick, and it soon became clear that there were several smaller buildings surrounding it. These were also built out of strange metal, and lit up on the inside by neither fuel lantern nor torch, but by lamps of crystal engines like those that illuminated their snowmobiles. These were likely the edifices of the mechanical division. Some of the buildings appeared occupied. Beyond them was the looming Tower that was illuminated from the ground by these strange engine-like lights. The Tower was lit so that it would be seen.

Akinisie parked beside one other snowmobile that sat by the door to the shiny steel building. Kolfinna pulled in beside her and the Chieftain wasted no time dismounting and going inside. She walked without words or expression through the doorway, where there was a compartment in a shaft. Though both compartment and shaft were dark, to Kolfinna's surprise, a mechanical device was activated and she felt a pulley bringing the compartment up. The lift up took about two minutes, and when they finally opened the door again they were in the control department.

Despite the intricacies of the Tower, the lift, and the outdoor lighting, the control room at the top was quite identical to the room beneath the antenna in Gorrland. There was a meeting space, with a large table and chairs, and above was the observation deck, a mezzanine in front of the windows where there was a barrage of machinery with lights, microphones, and monitors. Next to the machines was a large boxed-off room that housed the main crystal directly beneath the antenna. What differed were two things: a staircase leading up to further rooms above the operators' mezzanine, and an exit leading to an all-around balcony. As the two women entered the meeting space, Akinisie called out to the Communicator on duty, and a man came down the metal ladder from the mezzanine carrying a fuel lantern. Only two torches lit the space otherwise.

"This is Itassi," Akinisie introduced the man, of medium height and clean-shaven, in the Albrimese language. She removed her parka and hat and placed them on the central table.

"Pleased to meet you, Kolfinna," the man spoke. "Welcome to Taqraup Nunaat."

Kolfinna nodded, not quite easy enough to speak in a relaxed manner. Akinisie smiled back at her subordinate and engaged a short exchange with him in their own language. Once finished, the Chieftain turned back to Kolfinna. "We're ready to give you a demonstration. Go ahead, Itassi," she spoke with a proud smile.

Itassi then went to the smooth wooden wall, where there was a lever, connected by wires to the boxed room above that housed the crystal. He pushed back on the lever, which made a spark, and then the entire room lit up. From the ceiling, from the table, from the walls, lamps illuminated, bathing the entire room in a white light that made the Tower inside as clear as a bright sunny day. A high-pitched hum accompanied the switch on but then faded once the light stabilized. Warm air even came from vents at the bottom of the walls, rendering the wood stove at the other end of the room unnecessary.

Chills went up Kolfinna's spine, into her neck, and down through her legs. She had seen nothing like this anywhere before. The lights were the same as fuel lanterns, mobilizing energy from the Dust but appearing to be connected directly to the crystal. She looked in all directions, even noticing, from the window, that there was a light shining bright on the outside. "What is this?" she asked, half in awe, half in fright.

"This is part of what I had planned on sharing with Marja and you Gorrland Communicators this winter. This is what I would've done, if this whole matter with the Flares, and with Iorki-Son hadn't come up. I call it Sparklightness. Come, see how it works." Akinisie directed her to a closet door close to the lever. Itassi followed.

The door opened to a long room containing several machines and indicators. A ceiling lamp illuminated this space as well with the white light from the lever.

"I've spoken with Marja about you. In fact, since your arrival we've spoken every single day. We are very aware of what is going on on the planet. She told me that your specialty was as a radio operator, on-planet and off, and that you had limited experience working with crystal division, energy measurement, or enhancement."

"That's right," Kolfinna admitted, with some degree of embarrassment. "I mean I know how the process works and have seen others do it, just not—"

"I wasn't criticizing. Speaking is a valuable tool. I prefer it to technical work, actually. But here, you'll see all the tools that measure and monitor the properties of the main crystal directly above. As long as the Dust it emits isn't in a lull, the crystal's power can be harnessed in much the same way that a small radio captures power from a crystal fragment we've chipped off. We could provide power like this for all sorts of things."

"It's awesome," gasped Kolfinna. "It is Sparkness?"

"Spark*light*ness," Akinisie corrected. "We could *sparklight* the whole of the village if we found a way to extend wires out from the Tower. The crystal has more than enough power."

"There's no drain on energy?" she asked.

"None at all. There will be the occasional lull as there is on radios operating by fragments. With the devices you see in this room, we're able to not only monitor the energy output, but correct for imbalances. We can have the stability of the output that crystal fuel offers—so much fewer lulls than regular radios—without the complex enhancement process. This, I thought, was the future of Communication, of energy, of life for our Land, for North Island, and perhaps for Albrimir. *Sparklit* radios would mean less accidents and more rescues;

sparklit homes would provide light and heat, meaning less effort needed to maintain the fire or fuel lanterns all the time and slower use of wood for heat. Forests would last longer. We are not as blessed with trees as you are on the west end of the island. Maybe engines may someday even function this way, if one day we no longer need wires to capture the direct Dust energy. But we do not risk extinguishing the crystal's power, which is ever abundant."

"I see," said Kolfinna, amazed at the discovery.

"We're done here. We can go out," Akinisie announced, directing the group out the door. "Itassi, can you get the projectile pipe please?" she asked him in Albrimese.

The young man raised his eyebrows and did as instructed, while the Chieftain closed the door and walked over to sit at the table. "What would you have me do, Kolfinna?" she asked once both were seated, expressing a strange interrogative quality in her eyes, though elegantly holding her shoulders and head.

"I'm sorry?"

"Your presence has been announced on the air by my colleague Marja and by your hermit Storyteller, in person no less, before you came. From what he said and what you claim to say, you are an ancient-oriented one, a *Qivittoq-seeker*, who goes after the truths of the old ways and warns against the use of technology. Yet you are a Communicator, trained by the colleague whom I respect the most. What you say you learn of through the mysterious magic I thought was a bygone myth we teach our disciples then ignore turns out to be true when confirmed over the air from Shishilm Anavend or Chieftain Ilmari. I don't want to believe this Ansuz stuff, but both are true— your knowledge from Eirà, and your knowledge from Marja and me. Iorki-Son does things that are unexpected, half-mad, yet also visionary and far-reaching. He claims to know how to take us to space, human though he is. So, tell me, as a two-world straddler, what should I do?"

Kolfinna breathed heavily. "I don't know. I mean—"

But the question may well have been rhetorical, for Itassi returned with a long metal tube and a small machine he held next to it. "Thank you, Itassi. Come along, Kolfinna," the Chieftain said, standing up and taking both pieces from the young man. She opened a latch in the wooden floor just beside the lift, which faced downward into the long shaft. She turned around to explain: "Here we have a metal tube, a mini-crystal fragment, and a measure-controlled enhancer." She placed the small white rock, shining with Dust, inside the machine which held it by its edges, and it began humming. "You're aware of what an enhancer does to produce fuel, right?"

Kolfinna nodded.

"Well, this does the same thing, just in a much quicker and more localized manner. It doesn't distill the Dust in water, but it can send a projectile faster than anything known to our species, and with the power of the Dust of the Gap. Watch." And with that explanation, Itassi gave his Chieftain a small stone, which Akinisie placed in the entrance of the tube. She came down to her knees, then lay stretched out on her stomach, inviting both junior Communicators to do the same to watch. She then placed the small crystal and enhancer at the entrance of the tube and pressed hard on the power activation knob. The tube immediately made a loud boom that sent the stone down the shaft as fast as light, crashing into the wooden floor down below in a brilliant burst of white. Kolfinna, standing paralyzed in fright, looked at Itassi, who, though he must have seen the device in action before, clearly was not used to it.

"It's as if the Dust force of a hundred throwing swords were placed in one tube. This is the type of weapon that Mikahil Iorki-Son must have developed." Akinisie explained as she stood back up and returned to the room, leaving the Dust to thin and dissipate in the shaft. The hole in the floor below would be there to stay.

"Wait, you have confirmation that they exist? From Anavend?" Kolfinna asked. She had been so kept in the dark as to the real physical-plane communications that had taken place between Skralland—and even Gorrland for that matter—and the Lands who may be going to war.

"Never mind that, girl." Akinisie brushed her off with a strong but steady voice. "What I need you to know is something else. Here in Taqraup Nunaat, we could perhaps make ten weapons like that, or maybe a couple dozen, if we used all our enhancers for this purpose. So if we stopped making radios and fuel and used all the mini-crystals we chipped away from the main one, we could maybe make thirty. But for Iorki to have as many as they have—in the hundreds, it would seem—they would need more Dust than that contained in the original Dust crystals. To supply an army with these devices, Old Mikhail must have been able to harness the Dust from the Gap directly. We know that the Old Shishilms of Meniya left only one crystal in eight places, which gave us the Towers and the Lands. Each crystal functions in the same way, and we were told that no human has been able to master the Dust directly from the Gap in nearly a thousand years… that is, until *you* came along."

"What are you saying exactly?" Kolfinna asked, feeling uneasy.

"I'm saying that you are perhaps not the first to have learned the ability to manipulate this matter on your own. Iorki-Son must have had some form of similar initiation with the Flares—with the one we call the Evolver and you call Sigfather. He claims to represent progress and denounce the backwardness of your magic, yet it all comes from the same place."

"I suppose. We learn that the crystals channelled the Flares until Meniya's destruction. But the energy in them, that we use today, also comes from the Dust, which the

Flares uses." Kolfinna remembered her early lessons in training when she was still a teenager. The thoughts came back less than completely clearly, though.

"Yes. Our ancestor Sivullijjuaq was the first in Albrimir to figure out how the crystals functioned. He used its magic to communicate with the seven others. This use led to progress and survival for the scattered Folks of our planet. But a human who is initiated into the Evolver's knowledge, as you and Mikkjal are, cannot claim to choose to use it for progress *or* for sorcery. Both go together. There was always inexplicable use of the Dust from zones on the edge of the map. This we cannot explain with scientific study of the Dust, the crystals, the Towers, or world history. The initiated are out there, and they don't offer a choice between progress and sorcery, but between different manipulations of the cosmic matter, the Dust of the Gap. As long as Dust exists, we won't be able to have magical Ansuz communications without having modern technology. The two are made of the same stuff. So, I ask you, as someone with knowledge in both domains, called to follow the path of a goddess beyond human limits, and also trained to improve living standards on this physical plane, what should I do?"

Kolfinna stood up and took a step back. What Akinisie said had to be true. She had given the empirical explanation of how Jorgson had created his destructive machinery. And he was made with the same stuff as she was, initiated by the same Gap Master Sigfather, capable of manipulating this cosmic matter as she was, though in different manners. That is precisely what the spirit of the Flares had said to them, that Jorgson was who Sigfather was without Skadi's magic.

"I-I don't know. Stop asking me," she answered, shaking. She looked around at the sparklit lights, the machinery on the mezzanine, Itassi who had gone back to tend to the machines. And there was no Skadi and no Skralland Shishilm. "I've done everything I could for Skadi. I-I can't see her. I-I'll get him myself, Jorgson. The man is evil! He… he's not me!" Her voice was raised as she struggled with what was going through her. Akinisie was walking over, eyes large but expression neutral. *What is she getting at?* Kolfinna thought. *What does she want from me?*

Then her vision was pierced, and she saw him again; the jeering thin eyes of Jorgson behind his hood cackled and gawked, and the man mocked her. And again, as before, the man with the thin beard and evil eyes faded in the snowy mountains and darkness came. With the darkness in her vision, she fell to the floor, in the physical world. There Mikhail was replaced with Mikkjal, who found her in her dark spot.

"What's going on, Kolfinna?" Akinisie's voice brought her back into her body, and she came to see the tall woman standing over her, with Itassi walking over, too.

"You brought this subject up!" In a fraction of a second, she found that she had rage in her belly, and she lashed out in anger at the Chieftain. *"Why did you do that? You want him to find me?"*

Instead of lashing back, Akinisie kneeled. "What did you see?" she asked.

Could she trust her? Kolfinna's body had no answer to the question, but her mind was anxiously screaming out in the negative. She looked away from the too-knowledgeable Chieftain but decided to speak, staring in the direction of the power lever and wires nailed on the wall. "I saw him. I saw Jorgson—Iorki-Son. He was finding me. Then I also saw Mikkjal finding me."

Akinisie breathed deeply. "Alas, this has been foreseen."

"Foreseen? By whom?" Kolfinna got herself into another agitated fury on the floor, thinking about what in the world the duplicitous woman was talking about. She really wasn't saying anything to make things better. *Where are you, Shishilms of the south? Are you on your way?* she thought, grabbing at her own neck and giving herself a couple scratches. It wasn't fair to keep things like that from her. Father Haral always kept bad news from his seafaring expeditions from her. No good ever came out of his select speech and secretiveness. But this cunning leader had to tell her the madness about Jorgson being a Dust-sensitive Dust mover.

"*Come on you all from the south, come here! There's no more hope otherwise! I'm trying but I'm not being helped!*" She then got on her knees and cried out to the spirit that was responsible for the mess in the first place. "*Sigfather, what in all hell does it mean?! No Skrallander Shishilm. No Skadi! Only me with the weight of it all, and Jorgson, who you initiated, too! Tell me something, damn you!*"

Akinisie and Itassi had taken several steps back during the outburst. But to Kolfinna's surprise, Sigfather actually replied to her pleas.

"*You communicate well, Ansuzdottir, but you still do not see,*" echoed the familiar voice, deep and airy at the same time.

"I don't see what?!" she asked out loud, standing in the communications room.

"*Let your partner seek. You just need to remember.*"

"Remember what?"

But instead of Sigfather, the reply came from a mysterious female voice with an eerie call. "Shadow for light."

The words hit her beneath her ears and under the skin of her neck.

"*There is one from each Land, and there is Skadi. Unite the Nine Towers, but let your partner seek now,*" Sigfather spoke again. As his voice faded she could hear the distinct sound of a raven cawing.

Seeing that Kolfinna had become still and silent, Akinisie approached again. "What you speak of has been foreseen by your own Storyteller, Eirà. He has gone but may come back soon. As far as I am concerned I know nothing of your Ansuz method, nor do I even particularly care to know. I asked what you would have me do, considering that you straddle two worlds that are not as different as you seem to believe. You have not given an answer, so I say you must reflect on that. I don't want to keep you here against your will, save for one selfish motivation, which I must confess to you. My brother Ava is an *Angakkoq*. A Seer, Traveller and Story Finder. Two months ago he stopped sharing his gifts. He was beset with the illness that now affects so many. The heaviness. He, a man with the broadest of minds, a man who saw, fell in upon himself. The fact that our most powerful Seer and Storyteller, along with the others, could suddenly fall ill like this lets me know there is evil operating upon us. And any other Seer that may be able to treat him is also ill. His daughter and I will soon attempt to do what we can to heal him, but neither of us are spiritual people. You talk abundantly about your magic. I would like to see if it can help my niece and I try to heal him. Afterwards, regardless of the outcome, I will let you leave our Land. And I will hope and pray to our spirits that you learn to stop asking questions and notice what is said and put in motion. Give others time to seek."

Let your partner seek now…

Akinisie turned her back to Kolfinna and went to the lever to turn off the sparklight power, leaving only a dimly lit torch. She and Itassi went up the metal staircase to the mezzanine, while Kolfinna went to collect her parka in silence. As she put it on, she saw, from the window behind the control panel where Akinisie operated, the rare sight of a night-flying raven. Its caw pierced the silence, while the bird turned to fly away into the night. After it had passed, Akinisie turned around to look upon Kolfinna as she got ready to descend the staircase.

"I hope it works," she said, with an energetic tranquility in her face.

Kolfinna said nothing, turning around to walk to the lift. There, her hand pulsated twice and she immediately, albeit briefly, felt the Dust remnants of the projectile fired in this chasm. She decided to turn back around to the lady who was still technically her superior. "Thank you for showing me what you showed. And for your reflections." Then, she quickly turned to the lift compartment and started it downwards.

Chapter 9
The Girl from the East

Mikkjal

Mountains grew higher to the left, protruding into the moonlit night. In fact, mountains were growing on all sides. A long hilly island was protruding into the sea on their right, forming an impressive coast some ten kilometres out on the ice. This must be their destination, for if any place was "lake-like" it was this one. Jaani veered left to lead the climb up a steady rising slope, over hills and around turns until he reached the five cabins used as a temporary settlement by Hunters, travellers, and Guides.

No one was at the fuel station, but delivery of the crystal enhancer was quick. Kunuut used the ropes to pull the shining ball of a crystal up from the well in front of the attendant's wooden shack, while Jaani put the cylinder around the crystal. They both then used the well rope and pulley to lower the crystal with its energy-churning sleeve into the fuel shaft deep underground. The splash in the decomposing fluid was loud. White Dust was expunged, and liquid could be heard churning in the cold air up above. For a few seconds, the fluid rumbled, then churned again, a whirlpool beneath the depths, practical magic in the making. A white cloud began to exit, which, contrary to ordinary Dust, had a distinct smell. Fuel pierced the brain and made nostrils stand on end. Luckily, its smell lasted only two minutes before dissipating. Once it had gone, all three Guides went back to restart their machines, approaching them to the pump beside the well and filling them. With this delivery, fuel would be available for folks in the East for at least three weeks from now.

The wind had died down now that night had fallen. The three Guides rode their machines, now full and humming smoothly and not too loud, back through the settlement. Two of the five cabins had snowmobiles parked beside them, a clear sign of occupation. One other was dark but had ski and snowshoe tracks leaving from it. Perhaps someone had left during the day to go camping. One third of Skrallanders, of course, were still nomads, less sedentary than even the true Mountaineers of Gorrland. Perhaps if one combined these clans, the Mountaineers, and the wild tribes beyond the Outer Rim, North Island had between four and five thousand people who lived entirely with the cycle of the natural world. Kolfinna had said that twice that many lived in and around Torvall. They roamed in the northern plateaux east of the Isaveg, in the forests around the Algystaana Peaks, and around Lake Ayta on both sides of the Jorg frontier. The Greater North—island and mainland —had up to fifteen thousand people preferring Skadi's "wildness" to the "order" Jorgson would propose. Of course Torvall's total population of thirty thousand skewed the balance in favour of the sedentary, but northern common sense in recent years should lead people to seek the remedy that went with nature, rather than against it. Northern Torvall was as cold as the farthest reaches of North Island. It was beyond tameable by Jorgson's devices, his vehicles, his workhouses, and his weapons.

On a hill above the five-shack settlement they reached a dark red wooden cabin. The house was cold and dark, but from that hill came a soul-shaking view. White sea ice gleamed in front of the far mountains that hemmed in this area and gave it its name. Green auroras flickered and swayed on the side opposite the coast. The far mountains were a peninsula that ended well within their sight. In fact, Mikkjal could see the coast continuing beyond to the northeast, where it branched out towards East Tower and the start of the great Isaveg Glacier. Perhaps during the day the Tower, or even the edge of the glacier would be visible. It was still another two hundred kilometres, but Mikkjal was sure that Guides astutely trained and tuned would be able to spot it with the naked eye. He breathed a deep breath, taking in the calm air. It was thirty-five below freezing but the contrast with the afternoon of wind that seared face and fingers made it feel almost warm to the body.

Kunuut and Jaani informed him that Sivkersok had already arrived, and, sure enough, Mikkjal noticed snowmobile tracks, though they came from the inland hills, rather than the settlement. The inside of the cabin was still warm. Embers were still in the stove from a fire set a couple time-lapses ago. It was neat and tidy with windows on all sides, three lower-level bed platforms with thick furs on them, a mezzanine, and ample floor space. Kunuut promptly lit the hanging fuel lanterns with a match while Jaani gathered some neatly stacked wood from the box to stack on the embers.

"People come here a lot?" Mikkjal asked, noticing how neatly kept the cabin was.

"Ask Sivkersok," Jaani answered. "She runs these parts with the eastern Guides. This is her place. We don't usually come here when we pass through to fuel the well."

The fire took on quickly and as the stove had a glass window front, it lit the place up along with the fuel lanterns. On the table beneath the opposite window, the Guides promptly turned the radio on. Its air was mostly dead save for a Hunter or two occasionally making their voices heard. There was nothing coming in from Akinisie's Tower.

Apparently, Sivkersok would be happier if she saw the three cooking when she came back. Fair enough, Mikkjal thought, for she had left them much warmth. Mikkjal set about grabbing a chunk of frozen reindeer meat and hacking at it with an axe near the stove. The thought of meeting this mysterious Guide who ran things in her own way excited and even slightly daunted Mikkjal. He wanted to make a good first impression.

Jaani and Kunuut were both from hunting families, settled in the village for two generations. Both their fathers fished in the summertime. They became Guides because they sought both travel and responsibility. In their attitudes they were free, which is why Mikkjal and Kjartan had enjoyed their company so much last year. Both had heard of Astrid, though they never met her personally. Apparently when she visited Skralland she met with Ungilattaqi for Chieftain-only talk.

Suddenly, the door opened swiftly and before them stood a woman in grey furs beaming with a rare intensity in both her eyes and her body. In one hand she carried three white ptarmigans by the neck, while in the other she carried a wooden bow. "We'll have these. We'll have them plus what Mikkjal's making."

Mikkjal stood and froze, staring at the bow-hunting woman. She didn't have the face of Skadi in his vision, but she had the attire, the bow, and the energy. She came in with a soft but mighty stride, placing the birds next to the stove on the floor and leaning her bow against the table. She removed her mitts and shook herself off while exhaling her energy with loud grunts from her body.

" I'm Sivkersok," the woman spoke in Albrimise, giving him her hand.

"Mikkjal. From Gorrland. I didn't hear you arrive."

"No one ever does," replied Jaani, seated at the head of the table. The woman removed her sash bag of arrows and pulled off her wolfskin parka over her head, going to lay on one of the bed platforms while Mikkjal remained standing by the fire. *She cares not for village life, so I've been told. She trains like a beast on all eastern terrain. If she weren't so friendly, she would be the perfect Great Qivittoq.*

She continued in Albrimese. "We'll ride to the Tower tomorrow. Tonight, I want to think about fun stuff. No one is heavy here tonight." Then she sat back up on the bed and shouted loudly in her tongue, "So, who's cooking my birds?!"

What to say? Mikkjal was already cooking. He'd make another dish if need be. None of the others said anything either, so he looked questionably at her and at them. But before he could think of how to answer this energetic woman, she burst out laughing. "Aww, just kidding. I'll cook the birds!"

And Sivkersok removed her boots and then her thick wolfskin trousers. She kneeled barefoot in sealskin shorts and top that accentuated her well-shaped figure. This woman was in better shape than most Gorrlanders he knew, and her oval face was glowing.

In the heat made by the four hearty land crawlers, they had to remove their heavy trousers. Sivkersok plucked and butchered those birds hard and fast. Soon enough there was a pot full of ptarmigan breast, thigh, and neck boiling beside the reindeer stirfry. It was also the first time Mikkjal had seen Jaani without his parka, and he noticed that the young man was quite muscular. Jaani briefly went outside to chisel up even more slabs of ice for the bathtub cauldron in case anyone wanted to bathe later on. Kunuut was large and chubby but obviously very strong. He tended to the two-way radio, informing Communications that the group had met up and that the crystals had been delivered.

As Mikkjal squatted near enough to the wood stove to tend to the pan, the new woman, one of charm in her rawness, sat on the bed platform opposite him with one bare knee to her chin and one leg outstretched. She removed a thick wooden pipe and lit up a plant wad, adding the odour of pineweed to that of cooking meats and the sweaty flesh of active Guides. The female was distinguishable by the bead patterns on the edges of her shorts and the identical tattoos wrapped halfway around the outside of both her upper legs—three dots across and two lines rising at angles from either end dot. As she gently passed her pipe to him, Mikkjal sat, stunned by her elegant presentation and wild aura.

Exhaling the smoke of concentration, he decided to take the risk and speak to Sivkersok about what was so central in his mind. "Ittoq told me a story about a woman called the Great-One-Who-Left. What he said is very central to one of our own legends—"

"The legend of Skadi. And you think I resemble both of those mythical females because I live on the land and hunt with a bow?" Sivkersok interrupted, immediately foreseeing Mikkjal's thoughts.

He chuckled awkwardly. "Well, yes."

As the pipe went around the circle, she looked him squarely in the eyes. "Those are legends. Whether true or not, I don't care about them. I prefer living on the Land to living in the village and talking on radios. I'm only going into town because of family duty." She lay on the bed and stretched out her arms with a loud sigh.

"Oh, I see. Well, that's understandable," he answered, unsure whether he had offended this woman.

"I'm going to try to help my father," Sivkersok spoke, bringing her knees up to her chin and rocking back and forth in ball pose on the bed platform.

"Important man, her father," called Jaani from beside the fireplace.

"Oh, shut up," she shot out while still rolling back and forth. Her shout sounded serious, though she looked funny and cute in her posture. She rolled to her side and suddenly slammed her feet on the floor as she sat up on the bed. "Mikkjal, Mikkjal, Mikkjal," she jeered. "My father is the person you need to talk to. He should advise you to your quest and your questions. He's the Seer, Storyteller, the Shaman, and leader we had, and could tell you about the Evolver, the Great-One-Who-Left and so on. But now he sits, stares, drools, and sighs. I'm going to try to heal him, for the last time. That's the heaviness of tomorrow, though. Tonight, we're having fun, right?"

That's the man they needed to see, but he's afflicted, Mikkjal realized. Obviously the word had spread far and wide about what he and Kolfinna had said they were after.

"Right," he answered the funny woman's question, again in her language, although she'd chosen to give her previous explanation in Albrimese, no doubt so he would understand it all.

"Those damn birds will be boilin' soon and y'all will be eatin' well." This time her Albrimese was purposefully jolted and Mikkjal couldn't help but raise his cheeks in delight.

Jaani stood up and gave Mikkjal a pat on the shoulder. "He heard lore." He didn't bother trying to speak Albrimese.

"Good, so since you won't be in need of any more lore will you permit me to do fun stuff tonight?" The girl rolled back into her ball position and balanced herself.

"By all means," Mikkjal replied, still awkwardly squinting his eyes and most likely red in his cheeks.

"Yes. Hmm, I'm going to speak our language. Let me know if you don't understand. You'll hear language instead of lore… Mikkjal, one question from a spirit talker's daughter to a spirit talker's partner…" She pushed back with her legs and sat upright while stretching her hands to her toes. "Sometimes don't you want to tell the spirits to fuck off? Seriously, tell the Father of Victory and Mikhail Jorgson to screw each other and leave us alone. Good fishing season's coming!"

That was too much for him to hold back. From the bottom of his belly, from his opening lungs, from his throat that felt itself becoming free, he let loose, bellowing with laughter to the point of falling on the floor. The sight must have made Sivkersok crack up, too, because when he looked back at her she had the biggest smile he'd ever seen and gleeful red cheeks, rolling between Jaani, the wall and the bed's edge. The guys joined in, too, of course, and the laughter was only temporarily paused in order for the group to hear Sivkersok shout to all, "They're too hot for their own good! Somebody give me bird stew before I have to shoot some more!" This girl was a blast.

Everyone cracked up again and Kunuut promptly brought both pots from the stove to the floor. With wooden and metal spoons and knives in hand, the gang sat on the floor between the beds to eat from the pots. "Thank you for your company, dear companions," Sivkersok exclaimed, before proceeding to devour pieces of ptarmigan and reindeer.

What a sight outside! Such a bright night with aurora and full moonlight reflecting off the "lake" below to make an air lit well enough to hunt or trek or to read any runes or Albrimese that one could read by the light of day. This is Life. This is what the Guide was born for. *Why do I have to merely pass through this Land?* he asked himself. *This is me, with a view better than the one I had in my quarters. Kolfinna is my fate. Our travels here are but a small part of a plan far greater than ourselves. But her calling is less and less clear, while, for me, tonight feels like home. This must be what Kjartan, Iafri, Ginnar, and Rikey are living as a household— grounded and at home.*

Starting the multi-male household system was said to be a two-generation necessity following the Nordhemma Tragedy. The effects of the womens' capture waning after nearly four decades, Mikkjal would be under no obligation to live that way. Having one wife for himself, as was custom before, would definitely be allowed for him, like it had been allowed for tradition-oriented Mountaineers even a generation ago. But be it with Kjartan, Iafri, Ginnar, and Rikey or Jaani, Kunuut, and Sivkersok, it wouldn't be a lifestyle that bothered Mikkjal.

He brushed off the thought. He was tied to Kolfinna, regardless of their differences in energetic predisposition. He convinced himself that he was simply experiencing thoughts of nostalgia and longing, two emotions that harsh North Island life taught was best to bury. Perhaps chubby Kunuut and muscular Jaani would enjoy a regular unit of camaraderie, but Sivkersok was probably too wild for it. Mikkjal wouldn't be able to survive her tundra exercises. *Root yourself, but be ready to move, Mikkjal.*

After bird stew and reindeer stirfry, a very large pot of ice was put to boil on the main stove while two oil lamps were lit so that the fuel lanterns could be extinguished. The bathtub was in the far corner, beneath the mezzanine and beside the far bed. It would take this water a long time to boil so no one would be taking a bath right away. During this waiting time Sivkersok revealed the truth of her trying physical nature, as she put the men through a set of trying physical games. From the windowsill above the far bed, she came with a baton about the same size as Mikkjal's birch Sigfather stave, still in his snowmobile's storage box. With her baton she went to the large open floor space in front of the fireplace and sat down.

"A game for Mikkjal. Mikkjal, what is your surname?"

"Aldisson."

"Which means?"

"Son of Aldis, my mother."

"I see. Mikkjal, son of Aldis, sit down in front of me and try to take this stick from my hands." The other Guides sat chuckling while Mr. Aldisson lowered his butt against the pleasantly warm wooden floor. As per her instructions, he pressed his bare feet against hers. His hands grabbed the stick, alternating with hers. *There still might be some sort of trick.*

"One… two… three… go!" And the tugging commenced. Her pull was so much stronger than anticipated that he was immediately yanked against her shoulders and had to brace his feet against hers and lift his bum off the ground. Feeling the man's increasing desperation, the phenomenon named Sivkersok gave another mighty yank, removing the baton from his hands and making him fall flat on his face. Jaani and Kunuut cracked up.

"It's all in the initial pull, good sir Aldisson," laughed Sivkersok. "You use your whole body. But you lose if your ass comes off the ground."

"I see. Let me try again."

"It's Jaani's turn. You'll go against the loser of that match." It turns out Jaani, despite his muscles and tall body, lost to Sivkersok. Though he overpowered her at first, the woman was able to slowly and sneakily use her compact body to yank it away from him.

She's clearly not head Guide of the eastern settlements for nothing. A strong woman with sweet forms! Again noticing her tattooed legs Mikkjal realized that the open triangle of dots and lines must carry a meaning.

She won against the round Kunuut but not nearly as fast as against Mikkjal or Jaani. Mikkjal lost against both. Though he tried to justify the loss in the name of the men's larger body size, he thought of his even quicker defeat to the Girl from the East. *She's something else, that girl. Strong, silent, and elusive.*

That wasn't the only game she had in mind. She had each of the three men engage her in leg wrestles. Surprisingly, after Kunuut's defeat, Mikkjal managed to beat Sivkersok in this. The fight was long and gruelling to the muscle and it brought good entertainment to the two spectators, but victory was sweet. Both groaned and sighed after five long minutes of spasms and tension. Once she conceded and both of their bare legs went limp, the two men applauded raucously.

"I guess Gorrlanders do have strong legs, eh, Siv?" chuckled Jaani.

"Good fight, Siv." Mikkjal offered his hand to his competitor as he stood up.

She laughed and took his hand. "How do you train?"

"Our Chieftain, Astrid, made us run in snow in the mountains."

"I see. That'll do it."

The tension release of the game, as well as Mikkjal and Sivkersok's pain, was the cue for the four to step outside to light another pipe. Sivkersok packed the plant that helped both concentration and relaxation, and everyone stepped into their thick fur trousers.

"Don't worry, Mikkjal. We're in the mountains but the Qivittoq won't approach a cabin." Jaani laughed and ran his hand through Mikkjal's hair, scruffing it up.

"Only wolves," added Kunuut. "But Siv is their friend so we'll be safe."

Siv, putting her parka over her head, smiled and winked, then opened the door.

The night was just as stunning as before and the dancing auroras of pink, purple, and green had not receded. Instead, along with the moonlight, the aurora magnified the bright snow and ice tenfold. Beneath the moon, a quarter way above the southern horizon, was the stunning outline of the planet Boldein. Later tonight, even Ragnik would be visible. In front of that visual magnificence and cold, still air, Jaani went down the cabin steps and lit the pipe. "Do you get nights like this in Gorrland?"

"The aurora yes, but not such reflections on the ice."

"We're training you to become one of us," Sivkersok spoke calmly into the crispness. *Damn. She said it. It wasn't just I who had been feeling it. I would so much want to be one of them but I can't. I have my mission, my Kolfinna, my duty. Duty again… life brakes for duty.* The awkward silence was broken when Sivkersok herself, followed immediately by the two others, burst into laughter. Jaani passed the pipe.

"It's true you are great and well-trained." Mikkjal laughed.

"So are you, Mikkjal. We're each trained on the Land we inhabit," replied Jaani.

"What did you say your Chieftain's name was again?" Sivkersok took the pipe.

"Astrid."

"Astrid. Yes. I remember Ungilattaqi mentioning her. Our Chieftain spoke very highly of yours. I should like to meet her one day."

"She is something else, that woman." Teacher and mentor. *What must she be doing now? She could be as far up as Nordhemma or in the mountains. Perhaps, though, it was more likely that she was preparing the Land defences with Ivaldi in case Jorgson's new type of army invaded.* Still he couldn't shake Sivkersok's joke from his mind. Maybe she was serious. She probably was—at least partly. Skrallanders, he'd learned, often told truths through jokes; the excuse of them "just kidding" was a way to soften the truth. But nothing was clear with Kolfinna and his fate, Sigfather, Skadi and Jorgson. Akinisie was surely correct to be suspicious that Sigfather should call one red-dotted individual from each Land, yet two from Gorrland. Skadi showed herself to him, not through Ansuz Dust messages, not through the pulsating of the dots in the hand, but through a calm vision. Now Mikkjal's Dust-dotted hand felt the warmth of his mitts and nothing more. He turned to Siv to ask one last question that may or may not be pertinent to the mission.

"Ittoq told me that you had a message to carry to Akinisie. I suppose he meant that the message was your plan to attempt to heal your father?"

Sivkersok's brown eyes hardened, and she gave Mikkjal a brief, fiery glance, then cooled. "Yes. She's my aunt. I need no reason to come visit her. But since you ask, I feel I should tell you the truth. I am coming to see my aunt, my father's sister, and together we'll try to revive Ava—my father, Akinisie's brother. However, my aunt also asked for a recording from East Tower that Eqorsuaq, Naujaq's husband, received. I don't know the content of this recording, but I know that it is from Sivulliup Nunaat—Torvall, and sent on mid-range frequency. I know that the message Eqorsuaq received from Torvall is important enough for the Council to call an emergency meeting just a day after their previous

166

meeting. That's it, Mikkjal. I won't say it's not serious, but I will say that there's nothing we can do about it tonight. That's tomorrow's heaviness."

"I see," Mikkjal answered solemnly, breathing into the cold bright night. "You're right. Nothing can be done tonight. Patience seems to help us. I wish Kolfinna had more of it."

Sivkersok's answer was something he'd never foreseen. "Kolfinna is undergoing a lot of change at the moment. This understandably has an effect on her. The person she'll be in a month will bear little resemblance to the person she was when you met her."

Silently shocked, Mikkjal stared widely. Sivkersok understood his unspoken question.

"This I know from a travelling magician from your Land. He passed through the morning before you arrived."

"Eirà? You spoke to him?"

"Briefly. He spoke little but said he's on a journey related to yours. He said you and Kolfinna discovering yourselves, each other, and your differences, was the main part of the journey."

"I see." Mikkjal would never really understand what Eirà encouraged, much less what he was doing on travels to Skralland at the same time as them but separate from them. He had one more question, though. "And since you were at East Tower today, you must have seen the Gorrland Guard ship stationed off the ice floe?"

"It wasn't there today."

"What?! Where did it go?" he asked, startled.

"You tell, me, Mikkjal," spoke Sivkersok, calmly. "It's your ship."

Mikkjal didn't know what to say. He had had no communications with the ship. Such was only partially Akinisie's fault, for at the distance they were at even in the village, Captain Fálgeir and his crew were within reach of two-way radio communication.

"Don't worry, it wasn't destroyed. It was probably called back to your Land—Pigasuallarivik."

"Yes, but we should've gotten news. We haven't communicated with—"

"Mikkjal," Sivkersok sighed. "What can we do about it tonight from here? Anything?"

Mikkjal breathed deeply into the frigid air and watched his breath-steam fade. "No."

"Then that's it. Shit. I wanted only fun tonight and I must have provoked something to making you talk about serious stuff. I'm sorry. Overthinking doesn't suit you as a Guide. You know that, I'm sure. You and Kolfinna are both beautiful souls, but you're different and that's okay. Remember and respect your own roots as a man of the Land."

On the outside, Mikkjal nodded. On the inside, he felt tingles. *My roots are larger and deeper than my body. They are eternal. The Land is me. I'm one to be grounded,* he thought to himself. Sivkersok must be only six or seven years older than him, but she was strong, resilient, and wise like Astrid. She is what a female Guide should be. Land in woman form, rooted but light. And, of course, beautiful. Her almond eyes were intense but didn't push away.

"This is how Guides greet in Gorrland." He firmly put his right arm on her shoulder and brought her arm to his. His brief gaze into those eyes was soulful, and she shook back her long black hair and looked as well. Sense-driven, silly, stealthy Siv. Then the gesture was repeated with Jaani and Kunuut. All three Taqramiut nodded respectfully, then when the gestures were over they leaned in, while Jaani scruffed his hair and Kunuut patted his shoulders.

"I remember you told us how Gorrlanders—or *most* Gorrlanders anyway—live in groups of a few men to a woman," Jaani started with a sly smile. "May I ask, Mikkjal, are we your household now?" He burst out laughing and patted Mikkjal's solid outer parka.

Mikkjal thought a second, then replied. "I guess for tonight you are."

All laughed and Sivkersok then took her turn to rough up his hair. At that moment the night raven called again but didn't allow itself to be seen. Sivkersok motioned for everyone to go back inside.

The fire had been blazing intensely, so the heat upon return made all immediately remove their fur coats, pants, and boots, sitting, lying, and sprawling comfortably in skin shorts and tops. The huge cauldron boiled, so Jaani and Kunuut each took one handle and brought it to the bathtub in the rear, pouring half the water, then returning the half-filled pot to the fire. Sivkersok instructed the two guys to bathe first, which apparently meant that she and Mikkjal would be bathing together with the next batch of water. This made him excited and nervous at the same time. In waiting for their inevitable turn to bathe, she explained more about herself. Her full names were Sivkersok Amaruq Qaqqatalik Napaartutsiaq, and she could be called by any one of those at any time. But since she became an adult she was given the nickname Silent Wolf. The name fit her as well as a snowmobile rides on thick powder.

The Silent Wolf showed Mikkjal another game of hers while the others were bathing. She tied a rope around a stone and hung it from the cabin roof. Then she squatted on the floor. Here, the stone was at eye level. Slowly and patiently, she swayed her arms in concentration, and leaped to kick and bump the stone. Once back on the floor she was shaking with release of tension.

The feat is not of this world! was what Mikkjal thought to himself while watching her collect herself and look him in the eyes with that singular wide smile of hers. He would not try that tonight. Even imagining it with his mind was close to impossible.

Sivkersok smiled and returned to sit in her squat. "I'm twenty-eight years old. I started training with this when I was eight, which was when I knew I wanted to be a Guide."

"All Guides here know how to do this?" In all his years of training, he'd never seen anything resembling such a jump.

"Yes, though not all at the same skill level. I love the feeling of the jump so I practise unrelentingly. But there's a real use for this, Mikkjal." She lay down and stretched her legs over her head. "Sea ice and glacier ice is not as strong in recent years. Often people get stranded on small blocks of ice and have to jump from iceberg to iceberg to get back on the floe. To jump you must be agile, precise, focused, without hesitation. Or else you end up in water that takes your life. Guides feel land and ice but sometimes we can't notice everything, and we make mistakes. The leg jump is the last chance jump. When in small ice floes or when on a snowmobile that breaks through the ice, you have to jump suddenly, quickly, and sometimes far. You need quick reflexes, in addition to the strong legs that you already have." As she finished talking, she sat up and leaned back to stretch her thighs.

"Have you had to use this skill?"

"Several times. On icebergs and on the Great Glacier."

"The Great... Isaveg?! You crossed the Isaveg?"

Sivkersok raised her eyebrows. "Twice."

"I was told no one ever crossed."

"Ooooh!" she sprung up and came straight for his hair again with her hand. "Astrid's protecting you. There are three of us alive today who have done it, either by snowmobile or dogteam. Here, hold my ankle." She had him lift one leg up to his shoulder so that she'd get an intense stretch. Astrid had told him that he would be the first to cross once the expedition left Taqraup Nunaat onward to Torvall. That had put such a pressure on him, unnecessarily it now seemed. But the pressure was probably the reason she hadn't revealed this fact, for fear that he wouldn't take the task seriously.

"Who are the three that have crossed?"

"Switch my leg." She dropped her leg, and he grabbed her other ankle. "Ungilattaqi, my grandfather, and myself."

A voice on the radio was making some sort of announcement. "That's Eqorsuaq in East Tower, saying he's going to bed for the night," said Siv.

The two guys returned from the back room and sat at the table. "All done, tub's emptied out."

"Good. Our turn," said Sivkersok, bringing her leg back to the floor. "Let's take the water over, Mikkjal." Now was the time to share the tub with her. *Beautiful, earthy, flexible, resilient Siv! I wish I didn't have to get so close, but I want to get so close…*

His excitement could be avoided if he thought about it as one more duty. To bathe one at a time would be a waste of time, water, and warmth. The two brought the cauldron, filled the tub, and removed clothing. Sivkersok's eyes reached Mikkjal's chin. Her black hair covered her breasts and reached her navel. She pulled it back then pointed where the soap was and entered. They bathed without words, at peace with the sound of water flowing around their moving bodies. In the midst of it he couldn't keep himself from catching a glance a few times. She had two more tattoos—a wolf's head below her right breast and on her left side was a curving line that wove around her own curves up to a tree on her left shoulder. No, there was one more tattoo, a familiar one. The same three dots and two sets of rising parallel lines from each of her thighs were also on the back of her neck.

What could it mean? He thought of asking but held back. Maybe she didn't need to know he'd been observing her body. Sivkersok was spending her bathing time mostly looking out the large window next to the tub, from which one could enjoy the company of the brilliant land.

ANSUZ

It was unclear in the bathtub if Sivkersok felt any seductive energy. She was definitely moving in a way that, for Mikkjal, was sensual. But that looked to be the general attitude she took towards the world—earthy, fierce, and playful, in a word physical. Regardless, the bath was pleasant for both, and the evening ended shortly thereafter, though not without a new form of continuing sensuousness. Four Guides, they managed not to divide themselves among the different bed platforms. Instead, they placed the fur mattresses together on the floor near the stove and placed four blankets on top of their tightly compacted bodies. Mikkjal lay in front of Jaani and behind Sivkersok, with Kunuut on the other side of the woman. All put an arm over each other, sleeping in comfort and camaraderie. But for Mikkjal there was the added bit of excitement due to the intimate proximity to this remarkable woman. Maybe no one would know about his excitement, maybe everyone would. That night he didn't care. Lying behind her, he wanted to bite at her neck where that tattoo was and take her closer and breathe her in. He wouldn't, of course. The night was already extraordinary without that.

The Guides were in it together that night. This was grounded life with a team. In Sivkersok's house they belonged to her team, and no one was lost or without direction. They extinguished the oil lamps in the Silent Wolf's den and cherished every second of relaxation-until-sleep in the bright and sparkling land near the eastern edge of their shared home of North Island.

Skadi's arrow pierced his eye that evening. He had spent many days and nights in the wild before, but there was a new grounded connection he felt in his body this time. He would not be the same when he returned to the village tomorrow. Skadi's words had been a warning, but they were also a proclamation, a reminder of what Mikkjal needed for himself.

Chapter 10
Air and Land

Akinisie

That *poor girl's Land is about to go to war. She's not well to begin with, but she's here, away from home, and dealing with stuff that dwarfs her understanding! Not to mention that we're hiding information from her…* Akinisie's heart was sinking as she stared out the Tower window. Below, life was as active as one could expect. She could see home on the north end. Rikka was out on a day ice fishing trip and their daughter went to the neighbourhood crafts house for training. Breakfast had been silent. Everyone had business to take care of, and the recent matters of threats of war on the one hand, and Kolfinna magic-seeker, on the other, were not things that could be discussed at mealtimes.

The decision to subordinate Kolfinna and Mikkjal to their own task of trying to heal Ava one last time was not her own but belonged to the whole Council. Only on the night of the ceremony could it be revealed Qaqqariirvik and Sivulliup Nunaat were going to war, and that the North Island neighbours of Pigasuallarivik would come in aid to the ancient territory across the glacier. Such a tactic had its logic, of course. They couldn't risk having the two leave Taqraup Nunaat prematurely, especially given that several Council members, including Elders, were convinced that the foreigners were those who would wake up the Great-One-Who-Left. This was precisely what Eirà said. That hermit had to finish his mission, too. He would return to Taqraup Nunaat and announce the next stage of the journey directly. At least that's what the man said.

Still, withholding valuable information from Kolfinna was manipulation. Yesterday the Shishilm Anavend transmitted on mid-range and again asked Akinisie to transfer to Marja. Iorki-Son arrived at the Uygulaan Pass frontier with his armoured cars and his rifles and said that all these forces would invade if he didn't hand over Lia. He wouldn't hand over Lia, so he asked Marja for an alliance in war. She agreed. Very soon battles would be raging across the glacier, and the whole of North Island would have to act as a rearguard. And because of Eirà's plan, they couldn't let Kolfinna and Mikkjal go on until his return, no matter how many days war would be raging by then. That Mountaineer used dark magic sometimes, but the Elders and Seers here at home trusted him. Brother had met him often and always trusted his knowledge.

Was there no other way? She asked herself as she lit her pipe and stepped out onto the Tower balcony. Facing the town, she wiped a tear from her cheek and blew smoke into the cold, clear air. She couldn't keep this up much longer. She was a good head Communicator as long as her brother was there to handle healing and spiritual matters. Now, with her brother heavy, so many people asked her, on and off the air, for counsel. This was not her vocation. The pressure was too much. To her surprise Kolfinna, in her turbulent madness, appeared at times to see through her veneer of competence and loquaciousness. She felt a strange affection for her despite the girl's paranoia. As such, she felt weight pull at her heart due to the fact that they were burdening her with their need to heal *Angakkoq* Ava. Breathing in smoke, she accepted, then and there, that if she and Sivkersok were unable to revive him, she would resign as Communicator Chieftain and retreat to a simpler, more private life. Maybe Kolfinna would help him after all…

Extinguishing her pipe, Akinisie went back into the Tower operating room and climbed the stairs to the mezzanine. Itassi informed her that Siv radioed while she was out, that they had just passed Etua and Erika's camp, and should arrive in the village by midday. It was another beautifully clear day and without yesterday's wind, so the trip should be quick and swift, unless her wild niece and archer Jaani decided to stop and go bow hunting along the way.

Akinisie smiled and poured herself a mug full of water at the far table. Though they were ten years apart, Akinisie was one year closer in age to Sivkersok than to her brother. Luckily, Siv was very mature for her age, allowing them to become so close in each of their teen and early twenties decades. It had been the unfortunate and tragic death of Akinisie and Ava's parents in a hunting accident that pushed Siv to want to live entirely in the East. She and her grandparents were as close as could be, and when they passed on, Sivkersok the Guide simply told her Chieftain that she would be moving to their traditional homeland, the area between Lake-Like and the Great Glacier. Ungilattaqi, valuing her skills, was not in any position to object. In fact, today, had she expressed any desire whatsoever to take it, the big man would gladly give her his position as Guide Chieftain for the entire Land. Of course, she would never want that. That wasn't like Sivkersok, who was more than happy in the East with her own Guide group. The Silent Wolf's "pack" had just accepted Akinisie's son, Sivkersok's nephew.

Itassi finally asked a question relative to the events of last night. "So, do you still want Kolfinna to come speak on the Tower?" asked Itassi.

"She is most definitely not ready, Itassi, as you witnessed." Akinisie walked toward him with a hand on the metal railing.

"I see. The logic of the Council is that— "

"Itassi, the *hope* of the Council is that in healing Ava, Kolfinna will gain some knowledge that will help her quest, the Elders will gain some knowledge from Ava, Kolfinna, and the Evolver about seeking the Great-One-Who-Left and we can then broadcast our unified public support of our two North Island Folks against Qaqqariirvik."

Itassi nodded, as did his younger female colleague Aaviganguaq. "And—

No, I can't tell them that. Eirà's plan was secretive. The only people that should know are the people that he visited. She stood up tall and shook her head. "No, never mind. Just remember that what's mentioned here doesn't leave this room until after the healing session takes place. We still don't know when that will be." She loosened her gaze upon seeing both acquiesce.

There were no calls this morning. The recorder was playing music for the locals. It was no longer a time for research and experimentation on sparklightness, space communication, or anything else. They would just wait for the midday transmission from other Lands, which were now merely times to discuss with Iorki-Son and his lieutenant Abbott. The latter had fooled her for a few days, for it appeared that Iorki had developed a new way to extract maximum Dust power from the crystals. But whatever they have turns out to be due to the fact that Mikhail is a kind of wizard himself. It signalled perhaps great danger, for resisting wizards wasn't something ordinary folk like Akinisie were capable of doing. Yet it was also strangely reassuring, since it meant that Iorki-Son and Abbott were not smarter than she, or any Communicator Chieftain, was. They had not developed new scientific procedures.

The one thing that Akinisie could work on was her latest project. It was far from being certifiably true or trustworthy, but she thought that she had found a way to magnify crystal wavelengths so that even local-range signals could be captured from far away. Eqorsuaq had actually been the one to alert her to the possibility early this winter. When he experimented with putting a small enhancer on one of his small radio crystals, he was surprised to find replies to his broadcasts from both Pigasuallarivik and Sivulliup Nunaat main Towers. It would seem that, if an enhancer tool big enough were installed on the main crystal, one may be able to intercept transmissions from very far away. Even though Kolfinna refused to answer her question last night, Akinisie refused to believe that continuing to engage in advancing Dust crystal technology would automatically favour oppression, tyranny, and war. After all, Iorki-Son was a wizard, too, just like Kolfinna. She decided to go into the hidden laboratory and work on these devices for the rest of the morning, until the midday Iorki madness began.

***

Attention! Attention!
Midday, on the Sixteenth of Fifteenmonth, 963
On the long-range frequency of one thousand crystal waves per second, I call all-Albrimir Communicators to attention.

I have returned to the Tower, to speak again to you all. I am here to explain what I was doing yesterday, and why you heard from Chieftain Abbott in my stead. But first of all, I would like to thank Chieftains Tia and Ehukai for agreeing to detain your local sorcerers and not hinder my actions. You have made the right choice. Now, as for yesterday. I engaged in negotiations with Shishilm Anavend of Kalyim at the frontier. This was to no avail. He has agreed to side with the sorceress Kolfinna Helensdottir and backwardsness. As such, he has left us with no choice but to intervene militarily. In two days' time, if there is no change in position, we shall commence an operation to seize our deranged citizen. If we meet with any resistance, we will be obliged to engage with fighters of Kalyim, and remove Shishilm Anavend from power. You've left us no choice since you decided to defend the witch. My attention now turns to Chieftain Marja. Will you allow this girl who you have trained to continue to poison the mind of the leader of the Land of all of our ancestors? You can stop this by detaining her, like the other Lands have done.

ANSUZ

My attention turns to Chieftain Akinisie. You are perhaps the smartest Communicator on the planet. Is Taqraup Nunaat to continue to act as vassal to Gorrland? You do not have do side with Gorrland on this.

Greetings from Iorki!

Attention! Attention!
Midday, on the Sixteenth of Fifteenmonth, 963
This is Communicator Chieftain Marja Fjallsdottir.
On behalf of the other Chieftains of our Land, on behalf of our spiritual Seers, our Warriors, and our Guides, I declare that Gorrland shall not obey the dictates of a scheming tyrant. We shall defend our lady Kolfinna by any and all means necessary.
On behalf of the entire Folk of Gorrland, I damn you, Mikhail of Sandrider Clan of Iorki, to the depths of hell. We will meet you on the battlefield.

Marja out!

Attention! Attention!
You have chosen doom.
Chieftain Akinisie Narralik, what shall your position be? We have not heard you in a long time.

Mikhail Iorki-Son out!

***

Akinisie walked uneasily over the hard packed snow between cabins. She reached for her pipe but decided to refrain. It would be wiser to abstain from smoking pineweed until they started thinking together. Two minds simultaneously sharpened by the plant would be more effective than one at addressing the urgent needs of the fast-approaching event. She wouldn't give the madman the type of response he wanted. Maybe she'd give him no response. Of course, she knew how he would interpret a lack of response and knew she would have to prepare the Folk for it, but she wouldn't dignify such a schemer with speech. She changed the subject in her mind. How did Sivkersok and Mikkjal get along? Akinisie wondered as she strolled. The Gorrland boy, like everyone else, would either love her instantly, or desire to run away from her. Maybe her niece, on the other hand, would be one to desire to run away from Kolfinna. Maybe not. People with opposite auras were so interesting to observe. After all, to the surprise of many, she and her niece had always shown the dearest of love.

By the time she made it back to the Tower she made out the two sleds approaching from the bay, one driven by the Gorrland Guide, led by the other, driven by her brother's daughter. She was vibrant as she got off her machine and walked over to embrace her aunt, her forehead reaching up to the Communicator's neck.

"Still working, I see," Akinisie said, before embracing Sivkersok tightly. "I've missed you, niece. I wish our meeting took place under better circumstances but I'm glad to see you."

"As am I, Aunt."

She then walked over and shook hands with Mikkjal, welcoming him back into the village and informing him that Kolfinna was likely at Mikisoq's place finishing her parka. But she was unable to hide her annoyance upon seeing the young woman who had visibly hitched a ride in Mikkjal's sled.

"Nûsa, you followed." Akinisie stood taller and with tenser shoulders.

"Hi, Aki," said Erika's sister, looking at her with an insolent, almost mocking, face before turning to wink at Mikkjal, then running off into town.

"She insisted," said Sivkersok. "Threw herself in the sled when we were at the camp. Maybe we shouldn't have stopped at the camp after all."

"Hmm, it will be okay. She has a role to play, too." Akinisie spent a few seconds pondering over how a girl with such a spirit could help build the necessary tension and contribute to the necessary catharsis tomorrow evening. The answer was that her contribution would be invaluable to the end game, but that Kolfinna and Mikkjal didn't deserve to have to suffer in the meantime.

"I'm going home to rest a bit and then to see Kolfinna," said Mikkjal. "Nice to see you, Akinisie."

Akinisie nodded. "We will contact you soon. For… a… ceremony."

"I told him about Father, Auntie."

Mikkjal then turned to his Guide mate. "Last night was fun, Siv. I hope to see you again."

Sivkersok turned to him and placed her arm on his shoulder. The two performed this Gorrlander Guide salute, then the Silent Wolf laughed and ruffled his hair. "See you around."

Akinisie smiled as she watched the Gorrlander rejoin his snowmobile and head off. She was about to turn and share her intrigue and questions with her niece regarding the nature of this pleasant exchange with Mikkjal when wind of the seriousness of the matter at hand again blew her way.

"I have a pouch full of Greimweiss," said Sivkersok. "It should be enough to turn us posers into something resembling spirit seers or sensitives or sensors… or at the very least talkers." Both cracked up with laughter as they walked towards the entrance to the Tower. "We'll talk in the Tower?"

"In the lounge above the main room. We'll have privacy there. We can just stop by the control room and you can leave Eqorsuaq's recording."

"Yes. I'll salute your protégés."

"Good. Speaking of which, how is my son doing?"

"One of the finest Guides in the pack. Excellent senses and excellent patroller. He never misses a thing."

"That's wonderful. I'm so proud of him."

"You should be."

The two women entered the building and climbed the long staircase in the dark chasm. The hole from the shot she fired was deep in the wooden floor. Sivkersok didn't care to ask about it, though, which was good news. Inside the control room, she flipped the lever to give sparklight power to the entire Tower. They would be up above for a long time, and now would no longer excessively be consuming wood.

The dark branches of the bush known as Greimweiss infused for several minutes before Akinisie poured the mugs. Tea of this kind was in short supply at home, as it grew only in the western mountains near Gorrland, the places Eirà and his lot came from. She was grateful that the Storyteller offered her a pouch of it, for if there were any occasions where its use was warranted, it would be today. She and her niece would try to broaden their spiritual horizons to decide how to deal with the crises the wounded Angakkoq placed on them. While mugs of the dark red tea cooled, both women packed their pipes with pineweed, which they both possessed. Their minds would need concentration and spiritual openness if they were to get to the bottom of anything.

"Aki, I've heard some of the calls you sometimes get on the air," Sivkersok said as she was lighting her pipe and inhaling her first puffs. "I admire you for being able to deal with that kind of stress and sorrow."

"Thank you, Niece. I am doing my best, although I wish I had even half your bravery." The two sat on skin-strung chairs around a table in the upper lounge.

Sivkersok laughed. "I have no such thing when it comes to hearing peoples' emotions."

Akinisie, too, laughed as she exhaled her pineweed smoke. "I guess not. You pick the people up or you leave."

"Damn right." The Guide stepped out of her boots and curled up on her chair.

"Well, we both know who needs to be picked up right now."

Siv simply raised her eyebrows and sipped her tea of connectivity, nudging her father's sister on.

"Siv, Kolfinna does have the gift of sight and communication. Not only was she right about Iorki-Son's aggression, but also about there being people all over the planet with whom she can communicate—people with red dots on their hands. Shishilm Anavend of Sivulliup Nunaat confirmed it on the radio yesterday that he's one of them. That's why he accepts war with Qaqqariirvik and has asked Pigasuallarivik for help."

"And will they?"

"Marja just declared war less than a time-lapse ago."

Siv leaned further back in her chair, her eyes thick with worry. She pulled her parka off. She thought carefully, looking at many spots in the well-lit room. "What an evil man, that Iorki-Son. Kolfinna didn't harm him personally. And so where does that put us?"

"We share an island with Pigasuallarivik. We can't go against them. But we have no connection to this stuff otherwise. No one of our own has those red dots." Akinisie also removed her parka.

"That's what I thought, Auntie," Sivkersok sighed. "That's what I told that hermit Storyteller."

"Eirà came to you, too?"

She raised her eyebrows to affirm. "He told me about her. Who she's called to be, to turn into. I don't see it."

"I know what you mean. She's obsessed, paranoid, and stubborn, not to mention frail. But perhaps there is some way we can make room for his perspective on her." Akinisie leaned back and took a large gulp of Greimweiss tea.

"Were we not here mainly to talk about Father? I don't really have an opinion or a concern about the girl. If she is the one Eirà says, it doesn't change my life out on the land."

Akinisie grinned. "It sounds like your father knew Eirà better than the Gorrlanders know him today. Couldn't it all be connected?" She exhaled, and now a cloud of smoke hung in the room. Both basked in it and in their unravelling minds.

"Maybe. I don't know. Tell me how, Auntie."

"I'm reaching for farfetched stuff, but I'll follow this train of thought. Do you remember the last few visions Ava had before he fell sick?"

"No. I was busy on the land and Father hardly ever shared spiritual matters with me anyway. *You are Air.* You know the whole planet. I'm sure you understand this more than I do."

"Okay, I'll talk. I remember he spoke—rather, your mother told me what he said after an intercession ceremony for hunting at the end of last winter. Your mother said that the following day he shared with her a vision he'd had during the ceremony the night before— the town was besieged by the Qivittut from all sides. As they entered the houses, he heard a cry and saw in the mountains a giant woman who was both bright and also cast a very large shadow. Then, while he was petrified still, there came a strong male voice saying not to be afraid, for this was all part of the plan. He told your mother that the voice was the Evolver."

Sivkersok, wide-eyed, suddenly got up and went to open one of the windows. Within the stimulating smoke, she still needed some fresh air.

Akinisie went on. "That was his last vision. But listen to this. At the Council meeting two days ago—at that time we thought we'd have more time—Taamusi read the girl's aura and saw a vision of the Great-One-Who-Left. The Council was convinced that in these dire times, seeking *her* out is worth the risk. Taamusi's aura-sensing flashes back to Ava's last vision."

Her niece blew smoke out the window then walked barefoot across the floor back to her chair. She'd probably been looking at Itsi's red house below, which now hung seven white fox furs on the balcony. "But honestly, does Kolfinna seem to you like a Mountain Wanderer spirit? Anything closely resembling the Great-One-Who-Left? "

"Not at all. But she keeps talking about '*Skadi.*' The goddess Eirà follows and the Evolver calls, according to them. Now *Skadi* does seem like the Great-One-Who-Left."

"I've heard of Skadi." Sivkersok nodded.

Akinisie got up and poured fresh tea into her mug. Her pipe was now finished but she breathed the smoke-filled air deeply. She would wait until she truly felt her mind altered before refilling the pipe. "Ittoq told Mikkjal the story of the Great-One-Who-Left yesterday. He said the boy was wide-eyed at the thought of Skadi."

"Hmm. It's funny there's so much talk of her now in town, while on the land, the Eastern Guides aren't seeing any new Qivittut," Sivkersok wondered.

"What do you mean?"

"I mean that it's strange that there is talk of the Great-One-Who-Left in relation to Kolfinna and Mikkjal. They both seem nothing like the lore of *her*, Kolfinna especially. Maybe you can ask her about Skadi and how she thinks she can find her next time you see her."

Akinisie sighed. "I won't see her again before the ceremony. I saw her last night and she was paranoid. At the ceremony she'll find out I withheld information from her about the war starting and she'll realize she was right to have been paranoid."

"Oooh, you will have withheld it for two days or so, until that Gorrlander hermit comes back. So what? There's not much she could have done in those two days anyway. Plus, it's for a good cause."

Akinisie laughed. "A good cause. Was that what you were thinking about when you let Erika's sister get in your sled?"

"Poor dears," Sivkersok laughed. "Nûsa will surely mess with them but it will help the *catharsis*. I guess I could have been more insistent with her. I could've tossed her out of the sled... Damn, talk about a test for a couple. Do they have Tricksters in Gorrland?"

"Of course. Every Folk has them. Although maybe not her particular brand. This couple's components are each very different. Air and Land."

"You and me."

"Yes..." Akinisie felt her mind enlarging and so she took the opportunity to refill her pipe. "A fated encounter that requires special trust... which... they don't have yet. I felt it."

"I felt it, too. I don't blame him, though. She's so off-grounded," Sivkersok admitted in stunning honesty.

"Ooooh!" Akinise was surprised to find herself wanting to defend the bizarre Communicator girl. "No, she just needs to trust herself. He needs to trust himself, too."

"True, true."

"Do you know what I think?" Akinisie's mind was now racing with new smoke-infused thoughts, which caused her to stand up. "We started paying attention to the heaviness when your father went completely silent three months ago. But he's been without true vision for almost a year. Yet, I somehow think the problem started years ago. I know how hard you were hit by Mom and Dad's death seven years ago."

"Of course. They were my lifeline."

"You immediately left town and went to the mountains in the East."

"I went to Grandma and Grandpa's hunting grounds to live on the land, to reclaim what they stood for."

"You were the only one, Siv." Her mind sprinted ahead and she paced around, giddily attempting to keep track of her thoughts. "The only one who reacted that way at the time. Everyone reacted, though. Mom and Dad, a traditional couple that tried to avoid town life as much as possible, die in an ice floe accident while hunting. Though you decided to take on the land life legacy, so many took it as a sign of the fear the land brings. They stayed in town. Settlement populations started to dwindle. All fear anything from Out There."

"Maybe you're on to something, Auntie." Sivkersok stood up and stretched. "But don't describe me as some sort of Qivittoq myself. Yeah, I went into the mountains but I chose my own way to help the people."

"Of course you made your own way. You're perhaps more grounded than anyone. You're no Qivittoq but I don't think you're afraid of them either."

"No. There are so many different chances to die out there that I have no special fear of Mountain Wanderers or the woman that commands them."

"Kolfinna said something interesting two nights ago. She said that there are actually *nine* Towers in Albrimir, the ninth being of the nomads. The nomads use a different kind of communication, closer to the older kind. Kolfinna said the nomads use special magic from Skadi to communicate. When she first told me that I dismissed it as superstition. We've heard legends about bizarre clairsentient practices used by Ancient Meniya that some since referred to as Ansuz. I thought it was gibberish. But I recently looked into how Iorki-Son could develop the power to build the tools and weapons he has. He uses the Dust, too. Since modern and ancient forms aren't that different, it's not impossible that there is a ninth Tower of the nomads out there that uses Dust in magic ways. Magic from Dust is not that far removed from what we do. Think about it. A ninth Tower for the nomadic Folks that still live throughout the planet: Glacierfront Mountaineers like you; Gorrland

Mountaineers; Outer Clansmen of the North; Gorrland Beastriders; and Wild Women; Steppe Nomads from outside Qaqqariirvik; Desert Folk of Nuna; Folk of the Great-One-Who-Left. The Evolver calls these people, too. Iorki-Son exiles these people"

"These people?" Sivkersok asked. "You mean Folk who are not afraid of the Great Qivittoq, of Skadi? The ones not afraid of her 'primitive' magic?"

"It's the same thing, Siv," Akinisie shouted with excitement. "She is there. She has been there all along."

Siv was following her thought. "So it's the Evolver who calls to the Great-One-Who-Left, which is what Father saw. And then there's Iorki-Son who… who uses the Flares to *exclude* the Great-One-Who-Left? A false Evolver. That's what we both see as the forces at work?"

"Yes. And our Land has started to take the path of Iorki-Son, excluding *her* and things reminiscent of her. Well, except for you and your pack, niece, and a few others. I would bet there to be little to no heaviness on the land."

"Not for those who truly live on the land and don't just come for the day. But Father, though, why didn't he see this clearly?" Sivkersok asked, as much to herself as to her aunt.

"Perhaps he was afraid to see," Akinisie reasoned. "He made no song from his vision as he usually does."

"Perhaps. But are we sure of the link with events following Grandma and Grandpa's death?"

"I know full well that after they died, no Council ever discussed encouraging full-time nomadic hunting any more. The focus of leadership and the way people communicated shifted. Trade and technology became the priority, as they were in most other Lands. Those who thought otherwise acted on their own accord. They were the isolated wild ones."

The thought sent chills up Akinisie's spine. There had been nothing wild about her own lifestyle of late. In fact, she realized that her words had been about herself as much as they had been about any other person in Taqraup Nunaat. And she was beginning to have her own bouts of sadness, increasing in number. The course she had given herself, and the people, was one that was headed for suppression of the very soul of the Land. It was one that Mikhail would gladly encourage them to adopt before trying to take over.

Sivkersok went to lie down on the floor. Both women's brains burned like bonfires. It was, of course, the Guide from the East, who would still rather be out riding or hunting right now, who asked the question in the back of both of their minds. "How do we know we're right and that it's not just the pineweed and tea talking for us?"

"We don't know," replied Akinisie, full of fire and still standing. "We can't know enough to be positive. But we can use this intuition to set our intentions for the healing ceremony. The Evolver and the Great-One-Who-Left. We must seek *her* out, incorporate tradition in order for the world to evolve to the next stage."

"I can stand by that intention with you." Sivkersok sprung to her feet and went to hug her aunt.

"We'll stand together, Niece. We will bring him back."

Chapter 11
Trickster

Mikkjal

Furs tickled Mikkjal's nostrils as he lay down next to Kolfinna, close but not too close. In the cabin air the sound of radio fuzz mixed with occasional announcements from the receiver below. He breathed deeply and let his feet take in the reindeer fur's pleasant softness. Who was he meant to be? The perspective and life of Sivkersok and the other Taqraup Guides was one he could see himself in. Helping Ittoq on fishing and hunting expeditions on the tundra or the bay gave him purpose. Did he truly have a purpose in Sigfather's Call? Kolfinna did, of course. He knew that, but did he? He was at home as a free Guide, perhaps a Guide leader when needed. That was his destiny, which he'd felt at the cabin.

Sigfather, am I truly called to Meniya? With Astrid's continued training, he would've been able to let his land senses thrive and become a primal, instinctive Guide like Sivkersok. He could have his household, his customs, his free movement—a much more appealing fate than the one he was dealt. Kolfinna was lying on her side, thinking about something far away or nearby, but she became far away again. Two days passed since Mikkjal had come back to the village, and he followed Ittoq for all daylight hours. He met his two mates Jaani and Kunuut, but Sivkersok was up to stuff on her own. His days were filled with activities, but evenings empty with distance. That girl who fate called him to team up with was beautiful and gifted. But the two were not made of the same stuff.

Air and Land are different.

The people here were scared of Skadi and Utgard's magic just as Westfolkers were. *I wish I'd come here under different circumstances*, Mikkjal thought. Perhaps as a Guide training mission wherein the wildest Gorrlanders meet the wildest Skrals-those from the Western and Eastern Mountains, not those from the coast. Then they could ride with their physical senses firmly attuned, and learn from each other without angst.

This evening, though, Kolfinna was somewhat less aloof than the past two days. She was happy to wear her new parka and was happy to give Mikkjal the parka she'd made for him. *She has been doing more than thinking all day!*

Mikkjal stretched out his legs in the bed. From the cabin mezzanine, he looked out the window to gauge the light level outside. Thoroughly dark it was, the growing cloudiness making night come ever sooner. She couldn't shake from sight the idea that Chieftain Akinisie was betraying them. No matter how many times they went over the truth of what Akinisie had actually said and done and no matter how many times Kolfinna would agree that she had been too harsh in her judgment of her, she always went back to it a few time-lapses later. She talked about her so much that Mikkjal even considered that she had a form of jealousy. Such emotion may be understandable, given the technology Kolfinna described the Tower as possessing. The mechanical wing of the Communicator's department must be quite developed, too. The Chieftain had told Kolfinna that they wanted her to be present to try to heal the Seer Ava. That's what they waited for, Kolfinna anxiously, Mikkjal calmly. He was in no hurry to leave this beautiful, though afflicted, Land. He reminded himself of Sivkersok's saying. *Don't burden yourself by thinking about the heaviness of tomorrow.*

His reflection was interrupted by news precisely about the heaviness of tomorrow. A voice spoke loud and clear from the radio transceiver on the table. Akinisie gave news to the whole Folk.

"Good evening. My beloved brother, Ava, has been sick with heaviness for three months. Although healings were tried with other Shamans, they were unsuccessful. Tomorrow evening one last attempt will be made by me and by Ava's only daughter. It will begin at four time-lapses before midnight in Siya and Ava's sod house. As neither myself nor Sivkersok are Shamans, we need all the support we can get. I ask that you keep us in your prayers and offerings. Thank you and good evening."

His partner looked at him thoughtfully. He looked back but had his mind on Ittoq's story. Before her mind could start to wonder, he decided to tell her Ittoq's story, letting the energy flow through him as he spoke of the Qivittoq and the Great-One-Who-Left. She listened intently, becoming more present as he spoke.

In telling the story, memories of loved ones lost came back—of his brother Kieran who explored too far, of Gunnar who guided the Outlands by himself too many times and never came back, of Gjarbid, his friend who was taken by visions. All these people had something in common with the Taqramiut afflicted of today.

"Kolfinna… It's a great shame how we as humans expel the ones we are not able to control, the ones we can't bind to custom so easily. Maybe it's this silly behaviour that's causing our demise. As we banish, we create new enemies that weren't there yesterday—dead or living ghosts that will come back to haunt us. We become scared of the mountains because the mountains are where the Qivittut dwell. Yet they only dwell there because we can't take them as part of our world."

"But sometimes it's impossible not to banish when someone gets too unruly. And sometimes people banish themselves by choice." Kolfinna spoke with surprising calm about the subject of banishment, which touched her quite personally.

"True. But where can they go? They're transported to another realm, another state of mind. It's not like with wolves, where the lone wolf can survive until it gets picked up by a new pack or forges its own. It's still a wolf."

"Maybe they're also still human," said Kolfinna. "Human in a way that's not what we typically consider human. I mean, if we believe Ittoq's story then there is a group of them out there, almost like a *society* of Qivittut formed around the body of the Great-One-Who-Left. Maybe it's a natural occurrence, as natural as wolves that must find a new pack."

"Hmm. It looks like tomorrow we might find some answers," Mikkjal tried to be reassuring, keeping his own words to a bare minimum to avoid provoking her thoughts and leading her astray. She reached over to give him a kiss on the cheek, grazing his chest with her golden mane. A favourable reaction. Conversation was better that way. She enticed him, inspired him, triggered him, and confused him. But she didn't understand him.

He had seen visions of Skadi almost every day. It was always the same place, with the Huntress standing before a cave and shooting an arrow. *Be wild or be dead.* From the way Kolfinna talked, it would seem that she had yet to receive any communication from the goddess. This was strange, but he didn't want to ask her about it so as to not lead her to stressful thoughts at a time when she had appeared to engage him in a relaxed way. He chose a different subject to talk about.

"Mikisoq gave you this idea for the parkas?" he asked, turning to look below, where their beautiful coats lay on the couch. They had enjoyed them so much that they sat indoors with them in silence before climbing to the bed. It was amazing how she was able to sew such a pattern so unlike anything they had back home. In fact, the thought made him sit up and go down the ladder to try his parka on again.

"She showed me patterns and gave me ideas, but the rest came intuitively from my flow." A smile emerged on her face, with her green eyes gleaming, proud she was of her accomplishment.

Just stay like this, Kolfinna! Like this you are active; you are beautiful; you are alive! Don't burden yourself with the rest of things!

The embroidered lines around the sleeve were of masterful stitching, but what was even more impressive was the feel. As Mikkjal wore it he felt somehow more connected, instinctual, primal, somehow himself more *alive*. Her own parka was of similar greyish-white reindeer fur, but the stitching displayed different patterns. Each coat fit its wearer superbly. These coats had spirit.

Tomorrow the women will heal Ava and we will all know. That is as good a plan as any. If it works, we will have an answer to the mystery of the absent New Shishilm of Skralland. If it doesn't work, we might as well go home and forget the whole thing, and prepare for the coming war by conventional means. Mikkjal was resolved to face either outcome. He was sick of spiritual riddles and desired either some clearcut action, or else a return to a grounded life on the land.

That winter night their bed remained cold.
That night the fire died long before last log caught ablaze.
On that cloudy and sparkless night
Trickster showed up,
Forecasting a long winter, spring and summer.
Ever so long it would be for foreign riders…

She Air, he Land, both were put to work.
Hard work, useful work,
They helped the natural exchange;
Catching fish, digging trenches,
Cooking for folk far and wide.
All were happy with these newcomers,
Who had forgotten their cosmic mission,

ANSUZ

Forgotten the call of their foreign gods,
Accepted their hosts' silence as proof
That they'd declined to collaborate in their Quest to Renewal.
That summer the Guests were put to work.

The Communicator Kolfinna was no stranger to the thread,
But a new way she now learned, she made first
coat, dress, mitts, and hood.
She stitched, she built, she taught, and she spoke that year.
Initiated into the airwaves in her native land,
She was even invited to transmit in Skralland,
But in her soul-bound craft, her true skill went unseen:
People heard utterances and whimpers,
cries of her trying to speak their beautiful tongue.
But no one heard the fire behind the voice,
No one heard her drive or her depth.
By midsummer `twas the death of her Foreign Flame.

And the lad endured his own set of trials;
Mikkjal the Guide, rider from a Folk
of warmer climes—though a warrior Folk it was…
He'd tried to ride with host Land's Guides
all through winter and spring.
He'd shot and caught with spear, knife, rod, and lance,
He'd shared his bounty with the ones
who'd become his teachers.
But the man could still be a danger.
He could turn his spear anywhere,
or nowhere—a fate worse even still.
Member of a Foolish Folk to the West,
He could work, he could learn,
But he must be tried before he could be trusted.
So let him walk alone;
There he will learn where his true loyalties lie.
We know all about their Calling and Destiny,
What they were brought here to do,
The Call of Renewal from Sigfather
of the Flares…

There's too much risk in their presence and potential.
Gradually he will forget he's being watched as one apart,
Until he falters,
Until he fails,
And then he learns again that he is Foreign:
An angry member of Us will gladly remind him of that.
What will Mikkjal do then?
Will he understand and submit to his place?
Or will he remember that he was sent here
By some lord of wizardry with a foreign name
of which we want no part?
Tough choices for the would-be rugged man
Who still tries and yearns,
and feels he has to prove.
No trying can ever be enough,
His strong-willed, strong-handed Clan is a foreign Clan.
That summer would be Mikkjal's last attempt to Prove,
As it would be Kolfinna's last attempt to Burn.

And it is there that the veil of sleep is lifted,
Both awakening to a fading voice,
Trickster flying off to slumber,
Winter still so well entrenched.
'Tis but one path I show.
Other summers you still may choose,
Though other lessons you surely may not.

The Guide and the Communicator arose at once, frightened by the dream. A raven's caw could be heard just outside the walls. Perhaps it was on the roof. Faint light was seeping through the darkness and the wind could be heard strongly. Mikkjal put a hand around Kolfinna's neck and sprang for the staircase and made straight for the stove. Still naked, he squatted to pick up logs and place them inside the metal fireplace, giving several blows before the flame picked back up. The ground was cold, as was his body, but the dream had been colder still. Upon blowing the flame, he swore that he would stand tall that day and any other day he spent there.

Just when he was satisfied with the fire he rebuilt he stood up and turned back. "Aaah!" he shouted when he could finally see that there was someone seated at the table. "What?!" His heart nearly left his body.

"Hi, Mikkjal," said a familiar female, smiling and standing. "Your body's even more beautiful than I pictured it." She spoke to him in his own language.

"Nûsa! What are you doing here?" He had to walk uneasily past her to get his fur pants at the porch and clothe his lower half. The girl smiled and brushed back her neck-length black hair, eyeing him.

"Mikkjal who's there?" Kolfinna called from the bed. "Just a girl from the camps that wants to be fucked by your man and who your man wants, too, but doesn't act upon." Nûsa went over to beneath the mezzanine. "Come down, Kolfinna, I'd like to have breakfast with you both.

"We were sleeping, Nûsa. You should leave." Mikkjal walked back with pants on.

"Oh, you don't want some Skrallander company in your bed before you leave? I mean, you guys *are* leaving today!" Erika's sister wore a wool sweater and a loose-fitting black-brimmed cap over her short hair.

"We want to sleep, girl!" Kolfinna shouted. She pulled her shorts and top on and made her way down the stairs with more anger than Mikkjal had ever seen her show.

"Leaving today? What are you talking about?" Mikkjal asked.

"I don't wish you harm but others do. Others want you gone. Make me a cup of tea and I'll explain everything, then leave you alone forever."

"Who wants us gone? Why do you say this and how do you know our language?" Kolfinna asked, now standing in front of the intruder.

"I'll make you tea, if you'll be gone afterwards," Mikkjal accepted. He strode to the kettle by the stove and took it outside to the porch to fill it with ice.

"I'll be gone very swiftly after I share what I share, Aldisson. I learned your language from my sister, Miss Helensdottir. She's visited your Land many times and is very fond of your home, Hrafnshemma."

Mikkjal heard the family reference just as he came back in. He boiled inside. "You freak, if you have something to say or want to threaten us, you come out with it right away. Nothing vague and no riddles, got it?!" The girl's attitude had almost given him the impulse to strike her with the kettle.

"I was just trying to find common ground with her to make conversation. Anyway, now that I see the tea is in the making, I'll sit down and speak." She sat back down at the table and the couple joined her there, he in his fur pants, shirtless, Kolfinna in her tight undershorts and top. "You call me a 'freak,' as if you weren't someone who is himself interested in Qivittut and the like."

Mikkjal took a deep breath. "All right. You just startled me. If you'd come when we were awake, we would have welcomed you gladly."

"I didn't wake you. I came because the matter is urgent. Anyway, here it is. At the healing session tonight, before Siv and Aki deal with Ava, the Council will deal with you. They'll expel you. You see, you've broken our trust."

Each looked at one other. "What? How so?" Mikkjal raised his voice again.

"The ship of warriors you had anchored off the ice edge. It left and then it came back, with no communication about what was going on."

"We have no idea where it went," Mikkjal explained with strong agitation. "I only learned that it left when I asked Sivkersok a few nights ago."

"It doesn't matter. It's a ship from your Land behaving in an untrustworthy way. It's back now. A group of Hunters on kayak spotted the ship there during the night. If you trusted our Folk, why would you not communicate about any exercises you might be involved in?"

The wind was picking up quite a bit outside and it looked like snow was beginning to fall. There was a long silence. They knew not how to answer her. A knot edged at Mikkjal's gut as he thought of words. But the sharp-tongued girl from the sea ice camp continued before he could answer. "A war is starting between your Land and Qaqqariirvik—Jorg, as you both have forseen. It begins as we speak. The presence of your warship in our waters signals that our Land is involved in your conflict, which we want no part of!"

Kolfinna tried to answer. "The ship was meant as backup in case anything happened to us. It wasn't meant against you, mostly against other—"

"Against Qaqqariirvik, yes," Nûsa nodded. She had a most original look in her cap, short hair, sweater and thick fur pants. "Even so, did you ever think of what it might look like to the rest of the world? What it might look like to Iorki-Son of Qaqqariirvik? It looks like we gave you access to our ports and are facilitating your military strategy!"

"Wait, the war hasn't started." Mikkjal crossed his arms.

"Yes, it has. Akinisie knows about it and is keeping it secret from you."

Mikkjal's stomach tightened further. Kolfinna nervously played with her hair. "She's been lying to me? What in the hell is her plan?"

"Akinisie and all the other assholes on the Council don't care in the slightest about your quest to Meniya and whatnot. They don't want to disrupt everyday life here, which is exactly what your presence is doing. They have enough problems with the heaviness here and they don't want you agitating in favour of war among us with

Qaqqariirvik because of your fucking dots. Her plan was to keep silent until Council decides to expel you and your warrior ship, so that Skralland no longer has any implication in your antics. That's what they plan to do tonight before healing Ava."

"Expel our ship?" Kolfinna gasped, fear in her eyes and face. "That means she's essentially allying with Jorgson!"

"Exactly, Miss Helensdottir," Nûsa smirked. "She seeks technology, not whatever it is that you bring from the depths of the darkness. She has been lying to you and stalling for time. She's waiting to expel you until Qaqqariirvik-Son sends his army do defend our Land in case you battle-hardy Pigasuallarivimiut want to attack us."

Mikkjal got up to bring the boiling water over from the fireplace and pour tea. "And why in the world should we trust you? I have no reason to believe that you're telling the truth." He poured mugs for all three and listened to the howling wind as the sly girl took her time in answering. She took one sip, waited for the Guide to regain his seat, then reached over to rub his bare shoulder.

"I see the truth, Mikkjal," she answered, a smirk still clear in her eyes. "I see the truth that is told and the truth that is hidden. I expose the half-truths."

"What are some of these truths," asked a visibly uneasy Kolfinna.

She sipped and grinned. "I know that you both are now questioning the Call of he whom you call Sigfather. I know that you wish your fates were different. I know that you would like to spend more time in our Land, and that you are both extremely attracted to the figure of the Qivittoq: for you this is conscious, Mikkjal Aldisson, and for you this is unconscious, Kolfinna Helensdottir. I know that Kolfinna has no control over her urges and I know that Mikkjal has too much control over his urges. I know that you, Ansuzdottir, have made contact with red-dotted ones in all Lands but this one. I know that you're worried about how the red-dotted ones from the South will make it to you. I know that your fear of Skadi is growing equally to your attraction to her, of which you've yet to become conscious. I know that you both dreamt of a trickster raven last night. I know that your motivations are pure and noble but that outsiders don't see it that way.

"I see that you both need to get back into your own element. I know that Mikkjal has been fed up with Kolfinna's absences and her visions and feels he is *serving* her. I know that you are both attracted to other people but never speak about it. I know that Akinisie and the rest of the Council don't have a personal problem with you, but they would rather peace with all peoples, including Iorki, than friendship with you two. I know that they will give you two options: leave immediately or abandon your warriors, your ways, and your beliefs and live like us."

Mikkjal's guts were tied, his chest barricaded, and the air was thick. Only the storm wind spoke. Everything that girl confirmed concerning himself was true, meaning that the things he didn't know of were most likely true as well. What did any of it matter, anyway? Either there was a red-dotted one in Taqraup Nunaat and they would go on with the journey or there was not one, and Sigfather was a trickster spirit and they could go home and fight, or not fight, the war in best the way they saw fit, believing anything and nothing they chose.

Kolfinna's voice pierced the rising winds over the steam-filled tea. "You have spoken all truths in saying the things you know. Now tell me, what do you know about Ava?"

Núsa looked deeply into her eyes. Her energy was soul-piercing but Kolfinna stared back into hers. "I know that Ava knew your Storyteller Eirà very well. I know that Eirà came looking for him but was unable to speak to him, so he met with three people: Akinisie, Sivkersok, and myself. I am the only one heeding the advice he gave. Concerning the man himself, I know that Ava will be healed. I know that his powers will be stronger than ever before. His descendants will be mighty and known to every corner of North Island and Sivulliup Nunaat."

"Very well," said Kolfinna.

"But neither of you will leave here with what you thought you'd find. If you go to that healing session, you will forfeit who you thought you were. You will be bound to our ways and without protection. So I'll give you a last chance to believe me when I say they've been lying to you. Look at my hand."

The girl showed her right hand, upon which was a very large red mark on one side and the other. "I am the one you need and have been looking for. If you stay here, you'll be holding our Land back and killing yourselves in the process. Take me instead. Take me to Meniya to make your Sigfather happy—one from each Land. I will ride with you there. And I will keep you company, making love to both of you when you need. I'm not a bad person. I am who you need!"

She held her hand out into the centre of the table. Kolfinna eyed it then reached out to touch it. Mikkjal followed. Nûsa rubbed both of their hands and grazed their forearms with her fingers. Both closed their eyes and stroked her smooth skin. Her touch was sensual and she was oozing with attraction. But nothing was similar about her hand mark at all. Mikkjal felt nothing when he touched her, and judging from his partner's expression, neither did she. Coming to, he removed Nûsa's hand from theirs.

"Anyway, you'll soon find out about the war with Qaqqariirvik, but I've taken enough of your time." Nûsa grinned. "If you decide to take me to Meniya rather than let your fate be decided by Akinisie and her alliance with Mikhail Iorki-Son, you can meet me on the rock deposit on the point above the bay at noon. A strong

Guide like you, Mikkjal, will find the place even in the storm. Remember? It's the place you went to curse out Kolfinna's name after you found out about her... *attitude towards fulfilling her urges...*"

Nûsa cackled and got up. She ruffled Mikkjal's hair, then Kolfinna's, placing a kiss on each of their cheeks. "Both of your urges won't be lost on me. As long as there's truth!" And Erika's little sister winked and got her coat from the porch, stepped into her boots, and walked out into the coming storm.

Mikkjal slammed the door behind her. "Don't listen. She said herself that she exposes half-truths," he shouted. "She said many lies in that tirade!"

"Surely, yes," said Kolfinna, retreating to sit on the couch. "Yet I know she also told many truths."

Chapter 12
Visions and Storms

Kolfinna

The wind howled like a wolf gone mad outside, but Kolfinna was none the lighter. She felt as if a rock was crushing her chest as she opened the stone door from the blizzard night. Blowing snow entered the sod house Mikisoq led them to on the far outskirts of the village—the zone they'd passed five nights ago when they arrived from the West. So much had changed since then. Only uncertainty had come to pass, and with the sole exception of her parka, she wasn't sure she'd actually accomplished anything in Skralland. She had made no more contact with the New Shishilms from the South and didn't know if they were even able to make the journey. Perhaps they had been detained by their own leaders, and Jorgson had already won. With every step forward into clarity, Kolfinna's swamp fog of doubt returned. Both her mind and its visions, and the differing priorities of the host Land were beginning to take their toll. Akinisie thought of healing her brother, Mikisoq and Naujaq of sewing, Ittoq of hunting, and Mikkjal of riding and shooting arrows with his new Guide friends.

Their intimate partnership was not working out, she had to realize. He was strong, honourable, and brave, but they didn't have the same attitude faced with the world. For, though she'd always seen things that others missed, Kolfinna had a great many fears. Stories of the outer world terrified her, whether they be told by Father Siraz at home, by Ivaldi or Astrid when they came for special lessons at school, or by Kjartan or other Guides she'd known in bed during the Testing Period and after. It was unclear if Mikkjal knew about their affair. Now, however, in the throes of uncertainty, war, and demise of purpose, she would not talk to him about such matters of the past. The thrills had taught her some. But her sight was obstructed of late.

The couple had ridden separate machines in the blowing snow, following Ittoq and Mikisoq's trail and taillights, and they entered a packed hut where thirty people or so sat huddled around the edges. Both wore their new parkas. For Kolfinna, it was in an attempt both to show their hosts that she was indeed interested in what they had to teach her and to prove to herself that she at least produced something during this five-day period of inner turmoil in a foreign Land.

Of course they'd turned down Nûsa's bizarre offer of departure and decided to stay. She had to have known that they would. Departure in a storm would've been too risky, even if they had wanted to leave. But the girl must have known of Gorrlanders' reputation as a proud Folk and couldn't have honestly thought they'd take such drastic action because of her words. As these thoughts ran through her head, Kolfinna saw that very girl, crouched over near the wall on the far edge of the hut. She, too, would be watching Ava's last chance. *Not a word shall I say to her this evening. She is a mischief-maker and there's a good chance that what she said isn't even true. My Folk couldn't have gone to war already! But Akinisie… it is true that I cannot trust her. She may well hide even this from me! And the girl spoke the truth about what's been happening between Mikkjal and myself.*

In the precise centre of the crowded hut, the afflicted man was propped up in a wooden chair. Frail, his eyes staring out into nothing and his mouth gaping open, Ava sat. Akinisie sat next to him, and on the other side was a young woman of particular vigour. This must be his daughter, the Guide from the East. They sat on both sides. Both had special ink designs painted on their faces for the ceremony: Akinisie on her chin and the Guide on her chin, cheeks, and forehead. Akinisie nodded coldly, and Kolfinna returned the salutation. *Conniver! You and Eirà and so many others!*

The sod house was lit by half a dozen torches on the walls and a large oil lamp in the centre, near where the ill Shaman and the would-be healers sat. People nodded. Some shook the outsiders' hands. Kolfinna wanted to be somewhere else, light-years away.

No... perhaps she wanted to be back home, at Westfolk, in the company of her family, before Sigfather, the red dots and the Spell of Ansuz; before there was Mikkjal, who was but another man she saw herself pushing away after having bedded him; before the Curse of the Visions and the Quest. Perhaps she would redo the past eight years differently if given the chance. She'd already proven that the Curse of the Visions wasn't a death sentence. Maybe she would go back and heed Father Bjorn's lessons more carefully. Alas, none of this was possible, of course. She was far gone on her new path. The old Kolfinna was being the old Kolfinna in new places and in contexts where the world was at stake. Blasted old Kolfinna. She couldn't even die to her old self.

Though people nodded and shook hands, very few smiled. Akinisie was especially serious, not speaking to her brother but looking out at everyone present. She, Ava, and Sivkersok were seated in the exact centre of the house and could be aware of the entirety of the audience gathered along the edges. All Council members were present, including Elder Taamusi who had questioned her about Sigfather's message and her own aura that other night. Tonight, all eyes would be on Ava, but the travellers would probably receive eyes that night as well. In addition, at the foot of Akinisie's chair was a radio transmitter. They may well be transmitting this event for all the Land to hear.

Then suddenly, without anyone making any announcement, the quiet talk subsided, freeing up ear space for the mighty gale to be heard loud and clear. The storm signalled that the events were to begin without delay. The Communicator Chieftain arose and stood before all, at which point those who were still standing sat down on the furs used as blankets. Akinisie addressed the crowd with a dramatically exaggerated expression on her face. For reasons Kolfinna could not grasp, she addressed this crowd in the language of the Albrimese Communicators rather than in the tongue of the Taqramiut Folk.

"We are here tonight to bear witness to the final attempt to retrieve the soul of my brother, Ava Inngiq. I ask you all to let go of all of your worrisome thoughts so that we may create an air suitable for travel. Release your stresses into the hut and let the wind carry them out."

Easier said than done, woman, but I'll give it a shot.

Sivkersok said something quick and short in their language, then the house was bereft of human noise. There remained only howling wind and the light hissing of seal oil and fuel that burned in lamp and torch. But Akinisie had more Albrimese opening remarks to give.

"Those of you in attendance are here because you were chosen, though the event is being broadcast live by radio so that all may listen. For my niece and I are aware that this is to be a determining moment for all of our Folk. Its outcome shall herald either an era of fear and hiding or an era of healing and reclaiming ourselves. Among those in attendance are two travellers from Gorrland, who seek to the ancient temple of Meniya.

"They receive communication from the Evolver, who Communicators call *the Flares*. This communication manifests as two red dots. Kolfinna and Mikkjal claim the Evolver has told them that one such Dust-sensitive person exists in every Land, plus a ninth, who roams the mountains and has done so since the previous Age, since the Destruction of Meniya herself. The Folk of Pigasuallarivik, or *Gorrland* as they say, refer to the person whom the Evolver identifies as the Ninth, as *Skadi*, a goddess of the realm beyond orderly human society. *Utgard* is this realm's name in the Gorrlander tongue."

No one in the audience said a word. Kolfinna's heart skipped a beat. Despite her objection, her deviation from direct talk on the matter, Akinisie understood her and Mikkjal's quests perfectly! She explained it in more precise words than Kolfinna herself had used. How did she know all this?

"Neither of you know why there are two of you from Gorrland with this sensitivity but not even one from Taqraup Nunaat with it."

No, neither you nor me nor Mikkjal know that, Kolfinna shouted within. And as soon as she thought those thoughts, she noticed Nûsa smile and wink at her before stroking her bare forearm seductively. *Spooky phantom girl!*

"I give news to you, Kolfinna and Mikkjal, as I give to everyone in attendance." Akinisie spoke with an exaggeratedly grave, theatrical, and jolting voice that Kolfinna had never heard before. It bore no resemblance to the professionally elegant voice she normally displayed.

"This will not be easy to hear." She placed both hands on her high cheeks and rubbed her skin down to her chin below. "In the Land of Iorki, or Qaqqariirvik as we say, the leader Mikhail, who has threatened war with Kalyim —Sivulliup Nunaat—and has amassed on the border an arsenal of highly destructive war machinery of a technology no Land has seen before. He threatened to attack unless Kalyim's leader, Shishilm Anavend, releases the Dust-sensitive Lia Jackrabbit into his custody. Anavend refused three days ago, ready to risk war, admitting that he is one of the people with the red dots of the Evolver. He has received communication from the girl Kolfinna Helensdottir by way of the ancient practice we know as Ansuz. Anyway, this Anavend has asked for protection from the Land of the fiercest warriors of the planet, your Land of Gorrland, my Guide and Communicator guests.

"Three days ago, your Communicator Chieftain Marja Fjallsdottir declared hostilities against Iorki. Two days ago, I spoke with Marja myself. Arrangements have been made to sail the Gorrland fleet to the shores of Kalyim and disembark to engage Iorki's army on land in the snowy forests of Kalyim. Ivaldi has sailed with his host. Your people are now at war. It is in a state of war that this ceremony shall take place. For a war in which our North Island neighbours participate shall not be without consequence for Taqraup Nunaat."

"How can I believe you?!" Kolfinna shouted. "You're tricking us now, Akinisie!" But in her heart she knew that Akinisie was not lying about the matter. She was someone who would strategically withhold information, but she was not an outright liar.

"I can answer your question with solid proof, which we can provide thanks to our recording technology. This, Kolfinna, along with our sparklightness, was something I was prepared to share with your people this winter, before this hellish chain of events was unleashed. Stand by."

Hushed comments fluttered here and there throughout the room. Most people appeared as unaware of this as Kolfinna was. She looked to Mikkjal, who appeared to be questioning Ittoq.

This was why they had an emergency Council meeting the other night.

Across the room, Nûsa, almost directly behind Akinisie, was smiling. *She was right.* Her smile got bigger and bigger until it permitted itself to emit a shrill cackle. A lump grew and tightened in Kolfinna's throat. War would affect Skralland, too, and they hadn't asked for anything. Nûsa gave a shrill shriek for all to hear, whose tone may well have set fire to the heaviness of the hut.

ANSUZ

Damn her. Damn them. They want us gone! Maybe the strange, laughing girl was to be our only ally indeed. She did offer, after all, offer to leave with us so as to spare us this moment.

Akinisie walked over to the radio transmitter on the sod ground behind her. From the pocket of her white parka, she pulled out a capsule, which she attached to the device, then pressed a switch to activate. Crackling radio fuzz came over, then, rapidly, a clear voice could be made out.

Attention! Attention!

Seven time-lapses past midday, on the Fifteenth of Fifteenmonth, 963

On the mid-range frequency of 1800 cw/s

This is Shishim Anavend of Kalyim, speaking to Akinisie Narralik of Taqraup Nunaat. I ask you once again to transmit a message for Marja and the Communicators of Gorrland. I am at the Algystaana Peaks Tower, broadcasting to Taqraup Nunaat's East Tower, glacierside. Eqorsuaq, please transmit to Akinisie. Akinisie. Please transmit to Marja.

Chieftain Marja. On this day, as Chieftain Abbott of Iorki broadcast to the planet, squads of Iorkian warriors were deployed near our frontier at Uygulaan Pass. They had ridden upon wheeled vehicles, including several the size of a dozen bears and with walls and a roof of the most solid metal. Iorki-son himself stood there, having summoned me to the frontier. There, he told me that he would forgo his wish to see the refugee farmers returned to Iorki, but he only required apprehension of Lia of Jackrabbit Clan. He said Jackrabbit was a woman of evil actions and seditious intent. Through magic she communicated with a malicious young woman from Gorrland. He said that for their own protection, Kalyim should distance themselves from this demon from North Island and detain anyone capable of receiving messages from her via her magic, as the Southern Lands had done. None should make Lia Jackrabbit's mistake of following this foolish witch, who admitted on all-Albrimir communications that she had been into the Gap. Iorki-son said that if its one citizen in league with Helensdottir wasn't handed over, the troops that I was looking at, with all the weapons I could see, would invade Kalyim. I've never seen this kind of weapon before.

As you know, Iorki-son claims to be the leader Albrimir needs, capable of unifying the peoples of the planet and protecting them from demonic forces and the challenges we face as we enter an era of space exploration. He reiterated these claims and stated that the greatest threat to the new era came from that wretched girl that you, Marja Fjallsdottir, should have never allowed to become a Communicator.

Marja, I speak honestly. We are afraid. We've never seen this kind of weapons technology before, though several of the Iorki farmer refugees have described it accurately. Many, many Kalyimians are ready to appease Iorki-son and hand over Ms. Jackrabbit. I would be, too, if it weren't that... if I didn't feel the Call myself. You see, I have been contacted by your Communicator, light-haired and glowing, moving the Dust across air and land, and flowing with my hand upon which I now have two red dots! She has called me to Meniya. She relays the Flares. And because her energy appeared pure, oh so different from what Mikhail described, I shall greet her, and other followers in Ancient Meniya. I believe in the Council of New Shishilms.

However, as a Land with little warring experience in recent years, we will not be able to defend against Iorki-son's invasion. My refusal to hand Lia over will look like I've condemned my Land to destruction in the name of a strange, demonic, magic. Unless we have protection... I regret this message, but I have no choice. If you stand by your young Communicator's will and mission to reach those who receive the call to Meniya, as I do, we ask for your protection in a military alliance to stave off Iorki-son's threat. I wish I didn't have to make this request, but I know in my heart that this is the right decision.

"That was four days ago, Kolfinna," Akinisie spoke. "Now, hear Mikhail's announcement to all Communicators of Albrimir the day after:

Attention! Attention!

ANSUZ

Midday, on the Sixteenth of Fifteenmonth, 963

On the long-range frequency of one thousand crystal waves per second, I call all-Albrimir Communicators to attention.

I have returned to the Tower to speak again to you all. I am here to explain what I was doing yesterday, and why you heard from Chieftain Abbott in my stead. But first of all, I would like to thank Chieftains Tia and Ehukai for agreeing to detain your local sorcerers and not hinder my actions. You have made the right choice.

Now, as for yesterday. I engaged in negotiations with Shishilm Anavend of Kalyim at the frontier. This was to no avail. He has agreed to side with the sorceress Kolfinna Helensdottir and backwardness. As such, he has left us with no choice but to intervene militarily. In two days' time, if there is no change in position, we shall commence an operation to seize our deranged citizen. If we meet with any resistance, we will be obliged to engage with fighters of Kalyim and remove Shishilm Anavend from power. You've left us no choice since you decided to defend the witch.

My attention now turns to Chieftain Marja. Will you allow this girl who you have trained to continue to poison the mind of the leader of the Land of all of our ancestors? You can stop this by detaining her, like the other Lands have done.

My attention turns to Chieftain Akinisie. You are perhaps the smartest Communicator on the planet. Is Taqraup Nunaat to continue to act as vassal to Gorrland? You do not have do side with Gorrland on this.

Greetings from Iorki!

"And your Chieftain's response:"

Attention! Attention!

Midday, on the Sixteenth of Fifteenmonth, 963

This is Communicator Chieftain Marja Fjallsdottir.

On behalf of the other Chieftains of our Land, on behalf of our spiritual Seers, our Warriors, and our Guides, I declare that Gorrland shall not obey the dictates of a scheming tyrant. We shall defend our lady Kolfinna by any and all means necessary.

VISIONS AND STORMS

"And now we come to the events of today, Kolfinna," Akinisie spoke, a theatrical grin covering her face. "For we are now not two, but three days past Iorki-Son's warning, and Marja's declaration of war."

change our course of action. I am now ordering the occupation of Kalyim with the brunt of our land forces. We do this so as to be in a position to engage the hordes of wild beasts of men unleashed by Gorrland's bellicism. Kalyim, Albrimir… whatever destruction is unleashed, the blame can be squarely laid upon Chieftains Marja and Ivaldi of Gorrland.

Which brings me to Chieftain Akinisie. Southern Lands have moved to not oppose my actions. Marja has declared war. You are the last to remain undecided. I bring you the question that requires answering, given that you share an island with them. Yet we can protect you from the war that they bring. Will you side with Marja, Ivaldi, Kolfinna, and never-ending war and tribalism, or will you side with me and the unified world I bring? You, with Abbott, can be a pillar in this new world's technology!

Greetings from Iorki!

Kolfinna couldn't contain herself anymore. As Akinisie unclipped the recording device from the radio, she stood up and stormed forward at the deceitful woman. Her neck taught and her teeth biting her lip, she shouted, "*Go with him, then! Put your skills to work for Jorgson, you lost, wavering bitch!*" Then she shouted from her gut and reached her hand back to strike her, but before her hand could touch Akinisie's bright cheeks it was stopped by Sivkersok, who grabbed her wrist, pushing it back.

"I would think more clearly if I were you," the intense Guide said in strongly accented Albrimese.

She stepped back. It was true. She raised a hand to a Chieftain. They would definitely expel them now. Nûsa was right about everything. She knew all along what would happen and that Akinisie was using trickery. Mikkjal came and put his hands around her shoulders. "Kolfinna, come here," he spoke quietly. "We'll leave now."

As despair breached the borders of Kolfinna's heart, and she began to cry, Mikkjal turned to Akinisie. "Chieftain, this is a grave matter that should've been discussed sooner. Seeing as we can't force a decision on you, we will leave now. We will go and prepare for war." Mikkjal backed Kolfinna away back to the spot they were sitting before. The only sounds was the howling wind of the nighttime storm.

"You'll leave in the blizzard?!" Sivkersok came forward in her dirty-white wolf-skin, a strange smile peering from her vibrant marked face. "Having Sigfather's Gorrland Chosen lost and frozen to death in the mountains of Skralland won't help anyone find Skadi and it sure won't help in the fight against Iorki." She heard the breathing and moving of several people in the crowd. Some may have even laughed, because Sivkersok employed a mock Gorrland accent and a quirky and intentionally stilted manner in the delivery of her words.

"No matter what you call me or what you think of me, we will not let you go," Akinisie spoke, reverting to her calm normal voice. "Kolfinna's fate is now tied to ours, as is Mikkjal's." She returned to her theatrical voice to continue. "Your actions will affect us and ours will affect you. Everything is revealed at the right time. I'm sure Sigfather would tell you the same thing. We need you here at Ava's healing, and we need your emotions." And with those words said, Kolfinna suddenly felt her hand pulsate and heard Sigfather's familiar voice in the wind, but coming from the direction of the distraught Shaman.

"I have not forgotten you. Fear not the Wolf."

He hadn't spoken in several days, so his voice soothed her somewhat, though she had no idea what wolf he may be referring to. She knew only Wolfman, the head of the Beastriders, but couldn't figure that he was the one the voice meant.

"Tonight all is revealed and we join fates and paths. Whether we like each other or not, we must accept each other." Akinisie gave Kolfinna a nod, signalling seemingly that everything was back to normal. Sivkersok gave her a look that was both an intense stare and a slight comforting smile. With their looks

Kolfinna sat back down alongside Mikkjal, though not without looking over at Nûsa, unable to avoid the impluse. That girl was, of course, looking back at her, grinning up to her nose.

Then, from either side of the besieged Shaman, the two ladies removed their thick outer clothing and looked to one another. Both were barefoot. Sivkersok stood with only tight shorts and a thin skin shirt, while Akinisie wore thin reindeer pants and a red shawl covering her shoulders. The younger of the two, the Guide, picked up a drum and beat it intensely while swaying back and forth. Her rhythm was powerful, and Kolfinna breathed to it. She planted her feet firmly on the ground and swayed with beast-like flow, letting her intense black hair dangle and undulate with her movement.

This Guide had many ink marks, including matching marks on her thighs. Ava's daughter must be some sort of a Shaman herself. Her arms and legs were visibly very strong, and her drumming was almost powerful enough to block out the howling of the wind on the other side of the sod wall. Given the might of the blizzard outside it was very likely that they would be in this sod house all night. After the Guide set the tone with long drumming, the Communicator Chieftain came in with a song.

What a voice she has. What a high-pitched, beautiful, resonating, and piercing voice. Akinisie was singing off of Sivkersok's drumming, and the energy was all entering Kolfinna, unprepared for the feeling it provoked. She resisted at first but couldn't avoid it, so she had to move with it, letting her body flow to the tune it made inside and outside her body. She was flowing and floating, with her feet feeling the warmth of the blanket fur.

Sivkersok drummed, looking here and there, moving freely across the space of floor around the three of them, sometimes while bending knees and squatting, sometimes while standing and spinning. She walked to Akinisie, then past Ava, then back again. She did several circles while Akinisie stood still and sang.

VISIONS AND STORMS

In the deepness of the drum Kolfinna's legs were frozen, though her body flowed. The awesome powerful sounds were pleasant but also unsettling. As such, it took a rather long time before she noticed that she couldn't escape, even if she'd wanted to. The sounds planted her in the ground, freezing her crossed legs. Her eyes surveyed the room, going from Mikkjal on her left to Mikisoq on her right, then going across the house to Ungilattaqi and Taamusi, and in the far left corner, the spiteful girl full of trickery was there, smiling through it all. *Trickery was happening. She was right. My Land was going to war. It was going to protect Torvall. But you Skrallanders didn't tell me right away! You kept the news. You don't see how our Quests fit into your needs. Wretched Akinisie!*

The air was like stone and the sounds were like rumbles. Sivkersok's drumming was an earthquake and Akinisie's voice was the piercing lava of Astrirbjärnir Peak when it erupted over the bellowing land north of Nordhemma.

There she was, alone, in a place she'd only dreamt of before. Alone in a building used for a higher purpose than herself. In its centre she stood, light shining next to her. A flame shone from the torch and on the outside the wind was blowing. But the wind didn't pierce her, for she was alone in air heavy as lead. A heap of heavy air she was in. The light shone beside her but did not touch her. She was alone in a dark house of ceremony, a dark temple. None could reach her, not even the brightest of lights. She looked closer. She was the source of darkness. Then her eyes removed themselves from the place. *The wind is trying to get me. Light's trying to get me. It can't. I am the darkness. Light is trying to reach me.* Then she panned back and saw many lights flicker here and there at each other.

Where am I? This is strange. She saw a vision. She looked down at her red dots. They were not brightening but they were becoming warm. They pulsated to the rhythm of Sivkersok's drumming, and then looking in the space above Avasdottir she was brought to a vision of herself with her father in Hrafnshemma. He was drumming around the fire. He was preparing his next story for Kolfinna and Heidi. Siraz and Haral would listen, too. Maybe Mother if she wasn't busy. Light shone from Bjorn's drum. Light and Dust emerged from his mouth. And from his throat echoed a yell that shook the earth below. He disappeared before Kolfinna's bewildered eyes.

Now she was in the cold, snowy mountains. She was near the top of a peak that was very tall but very broad. Below her descended a long, gently sloping plain that was almost flat before it dropped like a cliff. Below that cliff were trees, even thick forests.

The thick forest descended into a valley below, where there was light. The light was slowly advancing, step by step through the forest, but it would never make it up the cliff. There she was, alone. In the snow she walked, one step at a time, sinking ever deeper. Akinisie's song, on the world outside the vision, was soothing, even if troubling.

Damn her!

She sank deeper. Behind her, Gjarbid appeared on the top of the mountain peak—her first lover, cursed by the Visions. He fell off the peak, falling down in an avalanche that pummelled an unsuspecting village below, destroying all the houses.

Damn him!

Many others appeared there, many partners she wanted but could not keep. They fell off the broad peak, too, while she was still there, standing, besieged by visions and thoughts she could not control.

Damn you all, and damn you too, Mikkjal! I wasn't meant to be understood by humans so I'll go to my own beings now!

She could not prevent herself from being driven out, far from the light, far from people attempting to climb the mountain. From afar she saw a ship arriving from the South, anchoring at the foot of the Great Glacier. Beside East Tower it anchored, and a man stepped off onto the ice. A hooded, cloaked man in black. He was her teacher,

Eirà of the mountains, returning to Skralland shores. He took his leave from the Southerners who were passengers on the Gorrlander ship and the warriors that had rowed it.

She flew above Jorg. There was a large settlement there of many thousands of people with bright lights and highly decorated streets that were well organized. People dressed impeccably. But underneath this magnificent city were bones and ashes and ruins.

The drumming intensified. Sivkersok let out a series of throaty grunts as she pressed on with her visceral and intense music, walking around her father. *I don't know what I'm seeing, but I am sure Ava is seeing something.* For her hands were again pulsating and the source of the energy was the Seer, now slouched back in his seat in total listless receptivity. *Whatever he is receiving I am receiving through secondary transmission. Ava is the principal antenna, I am the backup. The heavy Shaman moves. Whether he can speak remains to be seen.* But by sight, sound and breath Kolfinna could tell that he was receiving. He could see and she could feel that he saw.

I am there, back in the mountains. The light is getting closer but it still can't mount the cliff to reach me. I sink deeper into the snow. I try to walk forward but with every step my upper body falls more and I get ever more stuck. Mikhail Jorgson faces off against my Folk's warriors in forest battle. He even faces off against the Beastriders. Jorgson is especially ruthless to beasts of the planet. The Beastriders fight him severely but he vanquishes them through the use of his new machinery. This is what he's doing now!

Kolfinna sank deeper into the snow, but as she sank she turned her head and saw a new threat. A giant wolf glared down at her, growling, its snout the size of her skull, and barely a metre away it bore its teeth. Its white fur darted out in her direction, piercing her just as much as its teeth threatened to do. She could not move. Around the sod hut where her body was, the air's howling continued. Around the snowy mountain where her soul was, the wolf's growling lasted. The beast's eyes stared into her being. She couldn't fight it, and she couldn't escape the snow. There was nothing else for her. *This is it.* The mountains would be her end. She sank through the snow as quicksand, her legs dangling through the other side on the bottom.

Her eyes saw the world beneath the snow. A sanctuary of a room with nine seats, in a circle, all forsaken, all forgotten. This room was being destroyed as she watched. There was no quarter for her in this lair, so she struggled to climb back up to the snow and saw that the wolf was still there. But though it stared intently and growled, now it offered her its paw.

"Fear not the Wolf," Sigfather had said. Since she could not move and could not flee, Kolfinna gave in and opened herself up to the wolf. This beast's paw grabbed her hand and pulled her body up to the surface of the snow. It pointed its snout in the direction of the climbing light.

With wolf's company she descended the long, sloping plain. As a team, she and the wolf ran to the cliff, to get a good view of the lights gathering below. The drop was not quite a cliff, but it was sharp and rocky, not one for ordinary folk. And below were people holding torches, which they waved at her and the wolf with frowning faces and condemning glances. Some even bore lances and daggers. *It's a friendly wolf, after all, good folk. Do not be afraid!*

But the wolf was only part of what frightened them. It was she who stood next to it that incited their hateful ire. For no reason, they feared her, for no reason they poked at her. In the group below were people she'd known—Communicators, Teachers, Westfolkers. There also stood people she'd never seen, faces with the traits of the Folks of all Eight Lands. Familiar and less familiar they were, but none of them knew her on the *inside*. Wretched condemnation they give... *Jorgson's ilk they all are,* she scathed inwardly.

Let the wolf bare its teeth, she thought, and the wolf did as her mind instructed. It growled and it howled at the hate crowd yelled right back, torches and fists at the ready.

Kolfinna looked over at the wolf, but, to her surprise, she saw that it was now much smaller than her. Its face reached above her knees, but that was all. The fearsome beast was her companion now.

"Fear not the Wolf," Sigfather had spoken. She heeded, and the wolf stayed, seeing her and believing in her. Like Sigfather, who she'd once thought a foe, she transformed the white wolf into her companion. She wanted to attack the vile crowd below but saw a small group of them scaling the steep rocky climb. These had torches to see but no weapons, no frowns, and no scowls. Like her, they wanted to climb. So she turned around and walked upward on the peak, holding the wolf's fur when she started to sink into the snow. One step after another, they advanced, woman and wolf together, with people following behind.

She fell as she neared the peak, hands swimming in powder snow. But the black sky echoed with a voice she'd once heard before.

"Shadow for light," resonated the powerful and eerie female spirit voice. Surely she felt the darkness of the night creep into her. The Shadow resounded in and around her, yet the light creeped closer from behind, also seeking the same destiny. Back to her feet she sprung, grabbing the wolf's fur and letting it pull her all the way up. And at the top, on the peak that was a plateau before many peaks and valleys below, her wolf howled, and Kolfinna released everything with a shout. In her scream and her wolf's howl, the small crowd at her feet cheered. But the small crowd was larger. The whole distance covered from the cliff to the summit was full of folks, all cheering, all smiling, and some even howled back.

With cheers the mountain peak opened up, and she floated back down into the room of thrones. This time the room was bright with light, decorated finely, and flowing with the energy of eight other beings. Energy Dust in the air, she breathed and connected, her heart joining the light of the Shishilms. There was Lia of Jorg, Anavend of Torvall, Ashkii of Steigsonland, Lowanna of Kaltland, Filemu of Solicia, Hunapo of Lackjell, Mikkjal of Gorrland, and… *Ava* of Skralland. Each sat in his or her throne, and each looked at her, sitting, comfortably for once, in the tallest throne in the room.

"*Skadi*" they all called out, together. With that name came a surge of energy that barrelled into Kolfinna at every turn of her body; Dust seized her, penetrated her, but she remained at home in the room of the ancient temple, with the people she had called. Dust seized her. Shadows bound her, but she was at the one place where she belonged. Here all was true. Here all was wild.

"*Be wild or be dead*," Kolfinna Helendottir's mouth moved the words, but it was the deep and strong voice that emerged. From the hole in the roof from which she had fallen, she saw the crowd of cheering humans and one nodding wolf. *This is Sigfather's new Council, but she will carry out my legacy*, the woman spoke to herself. Yet everyone seated, and the wolf above, all understood. There was balance. There was peace outside. The world was wild as it should be.

Just then, Ava, radiating Dust on all sides of him, stepped forward and walked to the Ninth Throne. "This is where things are to be taken. But there is a trial, even for the Great-One-Who-Left."

And then the room went black, the cave took form around her, with a far stone door slowly opening. *Who will come?* asked the deep female voice, that was now Kolfinna's, one and the same. Sensing danger from the door, the Huntress gathered her spear, ready to growl with all her fury. It slowly opened, white Dust slowly entered, and a shrouded man stood in from the snowy forest. From him, all Dust protruded, and Skadi engaged him with his spear. He wouldn't kill her, but he wouldn't get closer to her either, with her hands and spear engaging his Dust all the way.

This is the trial, she knew. One of two men were trying to awaken her, *Skadi,* as she was. She had to face with both.

Chapter 13
Purposeful Sensings

S he flowed off of what her aunt was singing, dancing to the pulse of the land below. Father wasn't moving. She could only move in her body, nothing more. She was unable to go searching the realms for his soul, so feeling was all she had. The earth came up into her feet, through her legs and out the banging drum. Aki's song so perfectly in tune, she dug deeper into the earth to get her primal force that let her feel from a perspective wilder than normal. *Feeling heals all. With a loose body, we can loosen the mind.* But although she tried her best to make energy contact with Father, she kept bumping into Kolfinna instead.

"You always feel what everything and everyone's purpose is. You're not so different from me after all." Father told her those words when Grandma and Grandpa died, and even then she knew that their death would serve a higher purpose. They were reminders of a lifestyle lost. Many times she'd thought back on Ava's teachings and his last visions of the *Qivittut* besieging the houses led by a bright woman who cast a large shadow. The Evolver told him not to fear, for this is the way things must pass.

Come to from this vision, Father. Bring its meaning forward. You know it more than me, Angakkoq!

But Sivkersok's *Purposeful Sensings* were bringing her back to this strange, lonely girl of much-talked-about potential named Kolfinna. She has a mental ailment. While Mikkjal had strong potential, though unrealized in its wildness and in need of true purpose, Kolfinna's potential was less readable. Visions were striking her as her spirit bumped into the drummer. *Father, come to! Tell me who this girl really is! Is she the one who the hermit of Pigasuallarivik said she was?*

Everything had gone according to the script for release-making. A tense and volatile emotional setting had been created. Akinisie told the disturbing news of war and oppression, showing Mikkjal and Kolfinna how the Skrallanders were subordinating their quests to their own needs. By her grins and cackles it was clear that the Trickster had visited the guests and mumbled slyness into their ears. And then the contagious heaviness of Ava and the disoriented stoicism of the Elders of the Council combined to make this house an explosive ball of energy that only wanted to be released into the howling blizzard. Everyone contributed to put pieces at play.

That girl is in the mountains somewhere, far from here. Those faraway mountains have a familiar quality to them. Their rocks are ancient. They provide shelter to those who without need of roofs, tales, and lies to live. She sits below troublesome Truth Peak, shrouded and heavy by what she refuses to see. She is frail, but that is because she chooses to be. That is all she knows how to show. But all around her from the rocks and the air of this Truth Peak comes a strength I've never seen before. I don't know what I'm drumming anymore or even that I am still drumming, but I see the strength around this girl. If she chooses to use it, she will rise into something terrifying—terrifying, that is, to those who are instinctively afraid of mountains and the wild. This is the fear that consumed most people after the Accident. But the mountains are a source of Life, and so what I see is a rapidly transforming woman, if a mortal human she even is.

Rapidly, she looks down below to the villages, which look with disdain at the settlements, which look with disdain at the Peak from beyond and with terror at the Peak's mistress. Mountain Wanderer. That is Kolfinna's Purposeful Sensing, indeed! Visions torment her and she is to become the one good folk dread.

She leaves and may or may not visit society again. She may approach the civilized with comforting guidance rather than vengeful fury, if she chooses to. But she may not choose to live for good among the civilized and fearful, with their reassuring attempts to not see. That path would bring her death and demise. And it would bring a resistance to the Evolver's call and a collapse of Albrimir. Something else would then take over in the spirits' stead...

Yet, despite all her fear and trepidation, she is starting to seek me out for anchoring. She wants me to guide her. She seeks a Wolf.

Once Sivkersok fully realized that feeling in her body, she experienced it in vision—the night sky in the mountains above Kolfinna was bright with aurora, and then white with a shooting star just above the atmosphere. The sky was brightened and the light from the star crashed into the earth. There was Dust among the light, and Kolfinna was lost among that. But the woman who came from her ruins regained her footing and began to walk firmly across the snow toward the villages. She was now joined by folk who appeared lost, but who were simply those living differently than what village dwellers had deemed correct. These folk, led by the transformed Kolfinna whom Sivkersok guided, shook hands with the villagers, and the world was bright. It was at that very moment that she felt Father looking at her, his eyes wide open and his body standing up from his chair. Siv was consumed by chills and her drumming came to a stop.

He shouted with joy with glee. "Eeeeeeeeeh! I'm back!"

I never have visions, Siv thought, trembling and gasping as Father was coming to. But that wasn't all. As he took his first free steps, Ava raised his right hand to the sky and held it out before all. There, very large and very visible, were two red dots on either side. The gasp in the audience could be felt, though Father responded to it with a great cackle as only he knew how to do.

Aki began to laugh too. Soon laughter erupted in the whole house, granted all a well-deserved release.

Even Mikkjal appeared lighter, though Kolfinna, sprawled out on the ground, may well be in shock. For her as well as her father, this was a moment unlike any other in her life, Siv understood. Could she actually have his gift? She was twenty-eight years old, though. Why would it come to her so late?

"Good folk of Storm Shelter, I give you Ava Inngiq who has returned among us!" Aki shouted in her silly exaggerated voice. A hearty round of applause erupted in the hut, but Sivkersok could only squat and collect her senses.

"Hello, my people!" said the Angakkoq. "My daughter! My sister! What a beautiful family I have. Now where is my dear wife?"

Mother stepped forward. She had been sitting near the wall of the house and now walked over, boots dragging on sod ground and fur carpets, to put her hand on her life-filled husband. Her deep eyes smiled, something she hadn't been able to show her daughter in so long.

Father cackled some more. "What a storm we're having out there! A beautiful storm it is! Now I have thoughts. I am to go to the Council of Meniya, following the Evolver. All the Nine Dust Shishilms are in motion and on their way to Meniya. It seems like I'm the last one to be woken out of my stupor. It's not without meaning, though, my delay."

Father went up to Mikkjal and shook his hand. It must be said that he was speaking in our tongue, and as he made his presentation, Auntie began translating his words into the Albrimir language.

Mikkjal was puzzled, as one would expect him to be. "We're *welcome*?! I thought you were displeased because we brought North Island into war. I thought you cared little for our journeys and spirit matters." He implored to Aki, then to his hosts Mikisoq and Ittoq.

Auntie, Mikisoq, and the Elders laughed. Aki would, of course, be the one to explain this one. "And just *who* told you such things?" she asked in Albrimese with an exaggerated grin.

"You yourself did!" Mikkjal protested, before adding, "And so did she," gesturing in the Trickster's direction.

"Catharsis is necessary for healing. For catharsis, we need tension—as much tension as possible. We both did our jobs. Mine was to instill anger, hers was to tell half-truths. Hers is the path of bringing about necessary change. Truths can be the catalyst for such change. Half-truths sometimes even more so. She prepared tonight, that young lady with many names. Healing partly belongs to her."

And with that our frightening but beloved Trickster, who this time carried the name Nûsa, walked from the far wall, past the healers, placing her hand in the lamp oil without flinching, then placed a warm hand on Mikkjal's forehead.

"I act this way, yes, but I didn't act entirely alone. I was encouraged to do so by a man you Gorrlanders know well." And with that, the Trickster pointed to the entryway, where Eirà stood in white reindeer parka, holding a set of skis and wooden poles.

Mikkjal's eyes went a bulging blue. His throat emitted a quick and loud croak at seeing the Mountaineer man. It was at this moment, though, that they all noticed that Kolfinna was still lying on the ground. She had not yet returned to the physical realm. Eirà stepped forward, into the seated assembly, and walked straight to the oil lamp. He put his hand in the flames for a second, then kneeled to touch Kolfinna's forehead. With it there, he breathed several times in silence, pushing Kolfinna from her side onto her back. Her eyes were blank, turned upwards and looking at nothing that was in the room. So Eirà stood back up, and moved to shake Father's hand, then embrace his old friend around the shoulder.

The hermit spoke to Mikkjal in their Pigasuallarivik tongue, and seeing from his reactions, the young Guide didn't suspect a thing. He had no idea how much of an active part the Storyteller was playing in bringing about the things they saw and feared in visions. He had Auntie promise to reveal nothing, and not let them radio home. He had Siv lie to Mikkjal about her not knowing where the ship sailed off to and why. He had indeed informed her of who this girl was to become but warned that she was not ready for the news. Given that she was lying on the floor in prolonged absence, she still might not be ready.

The Trickster came to place a kiss on Mikkjal's cheek and bid him farewell, walking over to the exit.

"Wait, Nus." A look of confused relief crossed Mikkjal Aldisson's eyes.

"She returns when she is needed. Do not worry about her fate," performed Auntie Aki, still in the over-the-top voice that made it clear that she was Father's sister.

Now it was Father's turn to perform. Daughter, wife and sister all expected a song, as was usually his custom, but instead Ava simply spoke with a soothing and gentle voice.

"We've been living a tragic lifestyle in our Land of late. Accidents sometimes happened in our lifestyle of the past. Helas, one took away my parents. But the biggest accident was when we became scared to live that way, for out of fear came something far worse than accidents or even Death.

"From there comes Numbness to Life. We've been afraid of the ones who dwell in the Mountains, and their leader, the greatest of all Qivittut. But I just saw that the Great-One-Who-Left has returned. She's coming to greet us if she'll just be awakened. She seeks to enter and live through this girl here. There are eight towers of Albrimir, and one person from each of the eight Lands receives the Call to Meniya. I am blessed to be the one from Taqraup Nunaat. Eight receive the call plus the Great-One-Who-Left, who will soon meet village folk in fellowship for the first time since she was removed one thousand years ago.

Kolfinna has a trial that she must undertake, now, before becoming who she was meant to be. She is called to Meniya, as she said herself. But she is not called as Kolfinna. She saw herself, but she has to claim herself. For that to happen she must be awakened. That is the task the Evolver now gives this Guide Mikkjal. Old friend,"—he turned to look at Eirà—"where did you arrive from?"

The thin man spoke in the Taqramiut language. "I have returned from the Lands of the South, where I have picked up the Shishilms of Siqinnisiarvik, Nuna, Unatalik, and Solicia. They are safe on our ship anchored again by the Glacier. I have political news, too." He looked to Akinisie. "The leaders do not all support Iorki-Son, contrary to what was announced on the radio. They announced that to keep him at bay. However, the man *does* have supporters and agitators in the South and probably in Kalyim as well. Mikkjal, all that has happened to Kolfinna was foreseen. I told Akinisie, Sivkersok, and the Trickster. I had them keep secret until now."

Mikkjal, bewildered, stood up and faced his Storyteller. He asked him a question in his own language.

Eirà, though, insisted on answering for the benefit of all, therefore using Taqraup Nunaat's language. "Skadi, the Great-One-Who-Left, lives in the mountains. However, for her magic to be accepted and understood by the world, she needs to fully return to a human form and incarnate in a human's body. It is Kolfinna who she chose for that. Kolfinna was partially ready but not quite. She was too eager to flee her former life for her to see the life she was called to take on—a mighty life indeed. But now, she must be awakened."

"So, I am supposed to awaken her to bring her back to consciousness?" Mikkjal asked in the Taqramiut tongue.

"Yes," answered the thin old Gorrlander. "But it cannot happen just anywhere."

Father took over. "Kolfinna will cross with me by boat into Sivulliup Nunaat. Mikkjal, however, will cross the glacier and enter the deep Albrimir Mountains of northern Sivulliup Nunaat, where Truth Peak lies. There he will 'confront' the Great Qivittoq in friendship. To go there, he will need passage from a Guide who knows the glacier. He will ride with you, Sivkersok, my daughter. Siv, you will ride across the glacier once more. Kolfinna and I shall cross by kayak with the aid of Ungilattaqi. Eirà will ferry the others on his Pigasuallarivik battle boat. This is what I've foreseen. Whether anyone else goes with you is their choice to make. We must make haste. As soon as the storm clears in the morning, we shall leave. We are to ride to East Tower, then split up, Glacier riders and kayakers. But for now we shall feast, for the heaviness is behind us. We've taken a step away from it, and we know which direction the light is in."

Mikkjal looked at Father, his body held in visible deference but his eyes seeking. "Why must I go somewhere else to awaken her if she is crossing directly into Meniya, which is where everyone's supposed to be."

"Because the Great-One-Who-Left is to be awakened at Truth Peak," Father answered with such a calm smile. "Don't worry, she'll be there."

The room lightened somewhat. Of course, Mikkjal wouldn't understand right away. He would grapple with the fact that his partner stopped being his familiar woman right before his eyes. She would become a fearsome Qivittoq. It would take time for him to understand further. But what Sivkersok saw, *where* she saw, and the fact that she *saw* was unmistakeable. She knew what it was —Kolfinna as the great Skadi and herself as the Wolf to guide her—but didn't know if she could trust herself. After all, she wasn't a Shaman, so she would need to ascertain the prophetic nature of it from Father. This she would ask after the tension faded and a nightly calm settled in.

ANSUZ

Auntie kneeled and put her hand on Kolfinna's forehead and hands. She called Mikkjal to bring her to lie in rest on the outside of the circle, wrapped in a blanket. Assuming Siv's visions, Father's prophecy of awakening the Great Qivittoq, and Eirà's prophecy of Skadi taking root in this girl's body all matched, Kolfinna would struggle with her new identity until she was awakened in full. Lucid moments would be few and far between. Mikkjal did not expect this. But if her visions were true, he was not the only one she would have to guide her; the Great-One-Who-Left—Skadi—sought out the guidance of her, the Wolf. They would both share the task of seeing her come into her new form. Siv felt for Mikkjal and hoped that he hadn't developed too much of an attachment to Kolfinna's old form.

Amid bright torches, Aki went to her recording radio device and changed the frequency. "Itassi, Itassi in the Tower, do you read?" she called out, her voice loud enough to cut above the low chatter.

The Tower worker replied amidst raido fuzz.

"My brother has been healed. Tomorrow I am riding to East Tower to transmit directly to Sivulliup Nunaat. Since I'll be away at midday, please record me so we can send a message on the midday air to him... You're recording now? ... All right, I'm beginning...

Attention, attention!
On the twentieth of Fifteenmonth, 963, on the long-range frequency of 1000 cw/s
This is Chieftain Akinisie Narralik of Taqraup Nunaat. This is a declaration of war against the rule of Mikhail of the Land of Iorki. Along with our neighbours from Gorrland, North Island shall defend the great northern Land of Kalyim from your incursion.
Akinisie out!

The sod house entered into muffled cheers here and there. War was a necessity but not a celebration. Hunters, archers, and fighters would be called into action very soon.

It was now midnight. A late supper was slowly beginning and some among the crowd was beginning to laugh, albeit reservedly. Kolfinna was asleep, fur blankets keeping her warm. There was no telling whether she was in a peaceful place or a tumultuous one. In the sod house, Eirà sat with Mikkjal, Mikisoq, and Itttoq, talking seriously. Siv sat on her knees with her family, occasionally eating chunks of frozen fish. Aki put an arm around her niece, while Father and Mother quietly ate and said a few words to one another.

"Well done, Siv," said Auntie Aki.

"Same to you. We gave it our all."

"Indeed. You still seem unsettled, though," Aki said with a hand on her shoulder.

"It's about what I saw. I need to ask him." Father heard what she was saying, and slowly turned away from his conversation with Mother.

"You *saw*?" Aki still spoke. "Visions are new for you, are they not?"

"They are. I saw what Father saw. I saw who she is."

"Speak softly, my Siv," Father replied as he came over. "You and I both saw it, yes." While Mother faded into the back to let her husband and daughter speak quietly, Auntie remained close by.

"Why didn't you confirm it to everyone? You saw that we were both seeing?"

"You *did* see, my daughter. You take my skills when I cannot use them. You are more than just a Land one. All the energy of the Great-One-Who-Left… you showed it to her. You will continue to drive it into her, forming her, teaching her. You've always felt energy, even if you say seeing is something new for you. While you've always felt, you will now see. Your body is your tool, Land girl, but even the Land can sometimes carry visions. I am proud of you. I'm proud of all your gifts, and how you handled the ceremony tonight. I'm also happy with my sister, even if she really made that girl mad."

Auntie breathed a quiet laugh.

Father continued, "The girl needs to go to Meniya. Along the way, she'll be guided by the Evolver. She is finally validated in her Quest by seeing me with the red dots. I saw it. She will go to where she needs to be to fill her mission. Sending her directly to Truth Peak would only delay things. But you must be sure to guide that Mikkjal to the Peak, as quickly as you can. You and he are both her Guides."

"You're right," Siv said. "You see things as they will happen. They must both learn to be who they were meant to be and they must learn it now. I don't have *Purposeful Sensing* for nothing. They must learn and accept who they are, and so must I."

"Indeed, they will," spoke Father as he placed a kiss on his daughter and his sister's cheek. "Now you and I will enjoy a family night together before we're called off to new Lands and war, and before you have to admit too loudly that you are a little bit like me." Ava Inngiq, Angakkoq, and now the Evolver's Chosen shared a laugh with his family for the first time in many months.

Chapter 14
Intercepted Transmission

Mikkjal

Eirà's consistent reassurances forced him to show a human side. He felt sadness at Kolfinna's state, though he maintained that it was truly her destiny. He also showed some regret at hiding his dealings over the seas. The Council of Chieftains would never have allowed his departure to the South, though, at a time of uncertainty for the planet. He even set anchor on Läckjell, a Land that had not made any peace overtures since their raids on Gorrland three decades ago.

Yet he was correct in every assessment.

Mikkjal's body was subdued as he rode across the sea ice and hills, eastward beyond the Lake-Like cabin. He rode with Ittoq, Ungilattaqi, Eirà, Ava, and Akinisie, who carried Kolfinna under furs in her attached sled. Sivkersok had left earlier, alone, to tend to her own business before departure. Kolfinna's snowmobile would be taken to Naujaq's place. It was unclear if she would ever return to ride it.

Of course, Mikkjal felt guilt at seeing his partner's extended trance. He wasn't there to support her, and he didn't piece together the riddles fast enough to be able to tell that she wasn't called merely to convene with Skadi, but to *become* her. To this, Eirà was at his highest receptive and healing nature. The austere man actually placed his hand on Mikkjal's, back in the sod house, and told him that there was nothing that he could've done differently. He also read the thoughts that Mikkjal didn't dare admit to anyone, not even to himself—that he wasn't at ease in a relationship with Kolfinna. He grabbed his throat and squinted when he said it, holding back tears, but the Mountaineer Storyteller held his back and said that he needn't worry, for he was not called to partner with the girl she had been, but with the being that she was to become. He was to awaken Skadi in new form.

"Will she come back and talk?" he asked.

"She'll show up here and there, but she won't be a wife to you, if that's what you want to know," and Eirà had himself a good laugh. "Think of how things worked out with your ancestor Njord in his marriage to her all those ages ago!"

Mikkjal breathed both sadness and relief. There would be no partnership with Kolfinna Helensdottir. Perhaps it was true that that type of marriage to her was doomed from the start, yet he wished he could have helped that frail and frightened Communicator at least be at ease with herself in the world.

Now, she was going to be at ease with her new self, with Kolfinna-as-Skadi. If it worked, the change would be unrecognizable; the blond girl of Westfolk was as unlike how he thought Skadi to be as anyone he could imagine. Mikkjal pulled to a quick stop to light his pipe, continuing the rest of the ride to East Tower with the improved concentration of pineweed. With motor humming again, he remembered Eirà's words before they parted for bed in the hut:

"Everyone is in the place they need to be. Everyone must know what they need to do by remembering. Skadi's Time is Wildness Time. Wildness Time is Remembering."

Mikkjal had to remember his instinctual drive.

East Tower was but a simple shack with an antenna, but the Glacier behind it dwarfed its height. At four time-lapses past midday, the sun shone between partial cloud cover, radiating back from pure white and blue ice. Here, the sea ice offshore was broken, and the warrior ship from Gorrland was brought very near to the land. In front of the antenna shack the group disembarked. Ava, who was now a very dynamic and humorous man, helped lift up Kolfinna, along with his sister. Kolfinna's eyes were elsewhere but she was mouthing sounds, talking somewhere and to something. Mikkjal opened the door for them, placing his hand on her cheek. Threshold girl she now was. He had to awaken her all the way.

Inside he saw a host of familiar and unfamiliar faces. Captain Fálgeir strode forward to greet him. "Greetings to you. We've had a long trip. Eirà's taken us to the edge of the southern tip and back in six days."

"I suppose you're ready for a rest in a sod house," laughed Mikkjal, putting his hand on the Westfolker Guard's shoulder. The man, in deerskin jacket and hat, laughed and presented his crew, mostly Westfolkers descended from Nordhemma clans.

"The Guards sent the entire fleet. It's anchored just beyond the pass. Ivaldi's leading the charge." Fálgeir gave very welcome news to Gorrlanders who had had no news of their own Land's preparation for this ensuing war, other than the recording of Marja damning Jorgson to hell. Mikkjal felt some strength knowing that Ivaldi took that damnation seriously as well.

Fálgeir greeted Akinisie and Ungilattaqi and then saw a propped-up Kolfinna. "She is alive. Just in transformation," Akinisie told him in Albrimese. The captain gasped but being a silent type, he left them to go on to his other business. Eirà came in and spoke to the group, again in the Skrallander tongue, which he knew Mikkjal was learning.

"Here is Ashkii of Nuna," he said, coming to a young and thin man. "Lowanna of Siqinnisiarvik." He introduced a young woman from the desert dry Land of Kaltland. "Filemu of Solicia, and Hunapo of Unatalik." The two Shishilms from the island Folks were older, closer to Akinisie's age. Filemu was a stout woman and Hunapo a muscular man, and each of them bore the tattoos symbolic of the South Island cultures. Hunapo showed a friendly face, no sign visible of the old hostility between their warrior Folks. "All have the marks of Kolfinna Helensdottir. All received the Dust communication from her," Eirà finished.

"Kolfinna!" the young woman from Kaltland shrieked, her hand going to her mouth.

"Kolfinna spoke to you all?" Akinisie asked, removing her fur hat to reveal her long hair.

"Not spoke but sent images and visions," answered the Steigsonland boy Ashkii. "We had no choice but to come this way. Looking for her and fleeing Mikhail."

"Fleeing Iorki-Son?" Akinisie asked, raising an eyebrow. "Didn't your Lands' leaders agree to side with him? Was it not *they* who tried to detain you?"

Ashkii looked down and spoke in a low voice. "He sent agents. They arrived five days ago and intimidated our Communicators. Thugs came and they went to Shá, too. Our leaders wouldn't have declared for Iorki otherwise. They threatened what would happen to our Land if they didn't support him."

"I see," Akinisie replied. She began to pace around to another table nearby, where she put down her hat and removed her parka.

"People even went looking for us. We fled to the islands, and good Eirà found us on Solicia. Other people chased us, not our leaders. Iorki-Son sent people… assassins."

Akinisie looked on with her breath increasingly heavy for a good while before she could think of a reply to such treacherous news. "Well, we have decided to support Gorrland and go to war with Iorki."

"We heard your announcement, Chieftain," said Hunapo, a tall man, whose large muscular build could not be hidden even beneath the thick furs he was given to wrap around himself. *These Southerners must all be freezing,* Mikkjal thought.

A new Skrallander, without a parka and touting a small black beard, came forward from his seat beside a set of monitors, receivers and microphones. "I transmitted the message at midday, like you asked, Chieftain. His response was the same he gave Marja. 'You have chosen doom.'"

Eqorsuaq, Naujaq's husband, accentuated his imitation of a thick Jorgian accent in reciting Jorgson's words.

"*He* has chosen doom!" Akinisie raised her voice in the Albrimese language. "The heaviness is broken and we are back to ourselves. Here is my brother, recently healed, and confirmed as the New Shishilm, red dots and all."

Ava presented his hand to the group, and the other Shishilms nodded in respect. At fifty-one years old, Ava was definitely the oldest in the group of Dust-called Seers.

"We shall talk about it all later, though," she shouted, her shoulders extended back, well visible in her tight deerhide sweater. "War is an urgent matter. Let us get on with our transmission to Kalyim. Eqorsuaq, get me on the 1800 cw/s transmitter."

"Right away," the man answered. "Welcome, everyone, to East Tower," Eqorsuaq continued in Taqraup language. He left his chair for Akinisie and went to the gentle-faced Ava to shake his hand and bid him welcome more personally. Inside, the place was very basic, with a few tables used to hold receivers and microphones for Eqorsuaq to monitor. His living space must be on the floor above, where a small wooden staircase led.

"Sivkersok didn't come with you?" Eqorsuaq asked, looking at Ava, then Akinisie, who was now sitting in front of the transmitter. Kolfinna was able to stand on her own, swaying back and forth but not interacting with anyone. "I thought she planned to come back east with you after the session," the solitary operator continued.

"She came with us but went to meditate at Sikutsiaq," replied Akinisie from the chair.

"And my daughter is going further East than here, that's for sure," cackled Ava, bobbing his head and shaking his long hair. "She's gathering riding companions to make the trip across the Glacier to Truth Peak. She will take Mikkjal there."

"The wolfpack advances. So it is true about the girl, then," Eqorsuaq whispered. "She is the Great Qivittoq to be?"

"She is. She will become her." Ava answered his whispers wide-eyed and emphatically.

Eqorsuaq then glanced at Ungilattaqi the giant. "Won't it be enough for you and Siv to go? After all you are the only two living ones who previously crossed."

"I am not taking the Glacier," Ungilattaqi stepped forward. "I am kayaking with Kolfinna and Ava to Sivulliup Nunaat."

In Eqorsuaq's glazed eyes could be seen the same confusion Mikkjal felt when he had heard Ava's instructions last night. *Why in the world would she not ride to Truth Peak if she is to be awakened at… Truth Peak?!* But the East Tower Guardian just breathed deeply without a word, then went over to greet Ittoq and Mikisoq, who were here to see their guests off beyond the threshold of North Island, before returning to his boss.

"Let's start!" Eqorsuaq announced.

"No. Wait." Akinisie stood up abruptly. "Kolfinna should transmit." She walked to where the girl stood, back against the wall, and looked into her distant eyes. "Are you able to speak, Kolfinna? The war has started, and *he* has decried you, but you are here to be the one whom the world needs. Try to be her now!"

Mikkjal felt like walking over and shaking Akinisie out of her foolish plan. He squinted and frowned, but Eirà was the first to speak. "Akinisie, we can't expect her to be already awakened in this state," the Storyteller objected. "She's not—"

"She is breathing. She is even speaking. She's very much alive," the Chieftain stared him down. "I would like people to hear her voice."

To the surprise of several, Kolfinna's eyes flashed present, and she looked back into Akinisie's. "I see you're no longer afraid, Tower Woman," spoke Kolfinna, her voice more grounded and deeper than it had been before. "I will let Torvall know I'm coming."

Akinisie touched her two forearms, leaning in so close their noses almost touched. "We'll speak together," she said, fixing Kolfinna's eye before pulling her hand to follow her over to the seat and microphone.

Kolfinna appeared to respond to Akinisie's encroaching, almost sensual, physicality with her. She sat beside her at the transmitter, in silence but with powerful eyes, looking at the Chieftain, the machines, and the microphone, but no other human. Mikkjal remained standing between Ittoq and Ungilattaqi while each put on a headset. "Kalyim North Tower. Algystaana Peak Tower, this is Akinisie from Taqraup Nunaat. I'm here personally at East Tower, Glacier's edge, to relay a message from our Land and from Gorrland. It is Kolfinna Helensdottir, Communicator, Chosen one of the Flares, and heir to the mysterious Ansuz practice, that will speak."

Akinisie let it out there. She passed the microphone over, leaning back in her chair, where she placed her hands on the sides of her face and breathed heavily. Kolfinna, slowly, steadily, presently, leaned forward and took the microphone.

"Understood, Akinisie," came the reply, punctuated by a great deal of radio fuzz. "Kolfinna, you may transmit when ready. You're on 1800 cw/s frequency. No one south of the Algystaanas or west of Taqraup Lake-Like Settlement will be able to hear you."

"I shall commence," she began, strength piercing her voice. "I am a disciple of Marja Fjällsdottir. Recently, when the Flares came to Gorrland, our Folk went to confront them. At the Gap, I and my partner, Guide Mikkjal Aldisson, had been receiving a pulsating call from the Flares, accompanied by two red dots on opposite hands. We fell into the Gap, through time and space, where we consulted with the Flares, as well as the spirits of our bygone leaders. The Flares—Sigfather to us, Ulgan to you—spoke to us. He gave us counsel. He said we must unite the Nine Towers."

Kolfinna's words were clear, though she spoke faster and faster. Though her voice was strong, she gulped and her lips quivered. Sweat was beginning to emerge from her pores.

"We have come to understand that 'uniting the Nine' has to do with communicating in the style of ancient Meniya, through the use of the Dust. Ansuz. We are instructed to go to the old Temple of Meniya. We were told that there was a person from each Land that received the Flares' Dust Call, like the Shishilms of old. One from…"

Now her voice was beginning to shake and even crack at times. It hadn't been wise to ask her to speak. She still wasn't ready to speak as Skadi…

"One from every Land, and a ninth person, issued from the Folk Without a Tower, the world's nomads…"

"Kolfinna you're speaking fast," came the Torvallian transmission.

But she didn't hear him. She barrelled onwards with intense and jolted words. "One who we in Gorrland call Skadi, but who seems to have an equivalent in every Land's lore. One who never died but still communicates in the ancient way… who Taqramiut call the Great-One-Who-Left, whose magic must be taught to the other eight Dust Communicators!"

Her words turned into a frenzied fit of shouting as she got them out and pulled her hand off the transmit button. But before she could meet the eyes of anyone else in the room, the door burst open and Sivkersok walked in, brown eyes filled with fire, her face bright in the wolf parka.

"Do you still have any doubt as to what you and your purpose are, Kolfinna?" asked the Silent Wolf. Two unfamiliar young men followed behind her, shutting the door. Sivkersok strode beside her seated father and put a hand on the man's shoulder.

Kolfinna's expression bore terror, but Siv walked over to her and put her nose to her cheek, gently sniffing it. She then stood in front of her and watched with a gentle smile.

Kolfinna stared Siv in the eyes silently, then shed a tear.

"It is scary. But only because people are scared of you —of she who you're called to become. But I'm not scared of her."

Sivkersok grabbed her wrist, never letting go of the eyelock she held with the transforming Kolfinna.

And with that, Helensdottir stepped forward and embraced the Girl from the East.

Amidst the Torvallian Communicator's confused questions, Akinisie took the microphone to request he stay on the line for a couple minutes while Kolfinna regrouped.

"My daughter is right," spoke Ava. "She—the Great-One-Who-Left, so you—has always been a reflection of humans' own fears. As a Shaman, even I was afraid of her, because we are afraid of what lies beyond... in *Utgard*, I believe is the word you use that I learned from my old vagabond friend." He winked at Eirà. "Now I see that that fear was what caused my heaviness. You, child, were called to incarnate her. You must not be afraid of her!"

All others stood in silence, eyes on the trio of Ava, Kolfinna and Sivkersok. Akinisie softened her wide eyes and breathed. "Brother, you've been able to see and sense animals over the horizon and spirits in other realms. But what you see you communicate only when prompted. Whenever you do communicate, it is exact and we've known how to act. So, now that you have said things as clearly as you have, last night and now, I can say I relinquish my fear of Kolfinna and of who she is fated to become. Your daughter has never feared the Great Qivittoq, and I trust your guidance and prophesies as much as I trust that the sun will continue to rise."

"In that case, tend to the radios, Auntie, the Sivulliup Nunaat guy's still waiting," Sivkersok cut in.

Akinisie, on the air, made room for Kolfinna to return to her transmission chair beside the microphone. Sivkersok stood next to her with a hand on her shoulder. Her presence and words seemed to have helped Kolfinna. Though she said no words to Siv, she now sat calmly and securely in her body, beginning once again to transmit with a strong and reassured voice.

"This force must be reawakened to teach the ancient magic to the Flares' Dust-sensitives, and the Nine must reconvene in Meniya to stave off the plan by Mikhail, Son of Iorki, to take over the world's Communications. The Flares—Sigfather—Ulgan—told us about being slaves to a force far worse than himself. It is clear, given Son of Iorki's act of war against your Land, that he is this force."

Kolfinna finished her words firmly. After that, Sivkersok stood by and comforted her, and Ava came next to Mikkjal and spoke.

"You've realized she won't come out of this the same," spoke the Seer calmly, soothingly and quietly close to his ear in his language. His face was experienced but gentle, his eyes relaxed. "Accept transformation. The Evolver told us this. We learn from our fears. A Qivittoq will rule us all." The dynamic man laughed wildly and placed a hand around the back of Mikkjal's neck.

Kolfinna's transmission continued. "I have received visions of all people who feel the Flares' Call. This includes a man from Taqraup Nunaat, a man, your

Anavend, from Kalyim, a lady from Iorki, a man from Khairtai, a woman from Shá, a woman from Solicia, a man from Wanautipun, a man, my partner Mikkjal from Gorrland, and… myself… I say who I am to be and it is not Kolfinna. I use the Gorrland name for her, but all the others have seen her in their visions. I am the *Ninth Tower*… I am… *Skadi*. We shall travel from this Land by sea to Kalyim to meet in Meniya. We are on our way."

Her clear description of the plan, the discussion of which took place during her trance state, meant that she was always present, even if she didn't speak.

"If you arrive by kayak, I imagine you'll be at the South Algystaana area when you reach our shores," came the echoing Torvallian voice.

"My Guide won't arrive with the others. He takes a different route… he must… ensure the prophecies are fulfilled, so he will arrive from the north. Expect Eight for now. When Mikkjal's business is done, we shall be Nine." Kolfinna accepted the plan to "awaken" her at a place she wasn't even travelling to. She understood it even more than Mikkjal did, and he was supposed to be the one to awaken her there. *She has a strong trust in Ava. Could it be something that she and he both saw in vision?*

"Will he need help navigating down from the north?"

"I do not think so," Kolfinna answered. "He will be riding with an expert Guide. My Wolf Guide takes him."

"Very well. I don't quite understand but if you know the route that's good—

"I understand," said Kolfinna, making deep use of her voice and gut.

"Now, for the more urgent matter… Iorki-Son's armoured car army has breeched at Uygalaan Pass. The thick forests slow their progress, but these machines have been reported to be able to shoot down trees. Our first battalion is at Radlik Clearing, a hundred kilometres northwest. Our weapons supply is low. We're dividing the crystal to make more Dust-throwing swords, snow throwers, and javelins, but we have to keep our radio capability. Is the Guard from Gorrland on its way?"

Eirà sprung forward and took the microphone to answer. "It's here, too. It will arrive on your shores tonight."

"Understood. They will be welcome with open arms. Is there anything else any of you would like to announce?"

Akinisie went back to the microphone. "All has been said that needs saying," she replied after a brief pause. The silence among everyone else in the control room lent itself to approval of the Chieftain's words. But just as the Torvallian man sounded ready to speak, a static of a different sound came on the air and there spoke the most sinister voice ever heard.

"*I* have something to announce, Akinisie," came a piercing male voice in Albrimese with a thick accent. The voice shook Mikkjal's spine and brought on many a worried look to break the contemplation in Eqorsuaq's shack. "It is time we got acquainted, my lady of Taqraup Nunaat, and especially with you, Kolfinna of Gorrland. I have heard word of your foolish siding with Gorrland, Ms. Narralik."

"Mikhail of Iorki," Kolfinna said, her eyes blank.

"Surprised, are you? You seek me out and I seek you out. You plot to destroy me with devious witchcraft, I outsmart you."

Commotion and chatting ensued in the control room. *This was a medium-range frequency. How could Jorg's towers intercept it?*

Jorgson answered those very reflections himself. "*I have a special knowledge and power over the crystals, and I now exert control over all Albrimir's radio towers. Dearest Akinisie, if you had any regard for your own people's lives you would rescind your declaration of war and expel that treacherous sorceress from your Land at once. I can forgive the rudeness you displayed to me in your recorded message. She, though, must be stopped. She is not the frail thing you think she is. But I know you have a soft spot for her, therefore, Taqraup Nunaat won't be spared after we take Kalyim. Thank you for revealing the Gorrlanders' attack plans, I will instruct my warrior divisions to meet you at the shores. And don't think of trying to change course now. I will hear everything."*

In the room, the Southern Shishims gestured frantically to whoever was on the microphone so that they would avoid any mention of their presence on North Island.

Akinisie waved them away with recognition. "Mikhail Iorki-Son," she started. "What makes you think Kolfinna should be resisted and that you will have the support of other Lands in taking over the Towers? You claim Kolfinna's magic is evil, yet you are willing to wage war."

"Sweet woman," chucked Jorgson's voice over the air. *"If you knew why ancient Meniya fell in the first place, you would not ask me this question. I fell into the Gap once, too. I also learned the secrets of the Flares about the Tragedy of Meniya. That wretched woman left back then, leaving the world unable to withstand the Dust of the Flares. That was her choice, the dishonest schemer who used Ansuz to spirit-speak through Dust and vision. But the old world fell. We evolved. We have Towers now. And now, in Iorki, we have developed such technology as to not only communicate with other planets but to visit them. The Flares—Sigfather—the Evovler learned to make communication and travel happen, in spite of that savage woman abandoning the Council. You see, I also was initiated by Sigfather... The ninth Shishilm was cast out then, and she shan't ever return, no matter what guise she comes in! Not even in the form of a charming twenty-three-year-old blonde Communicator from Westfolk!"*

Akinisie stood pale-faced. Mikkjal was just as taken aback as she was. Jorgson spoke of Meniya in a way similar to how Sigfather had. He told the same story of the woman who left and began to wander. He told of Skadi. And he knew about Kolfinna. His story of Gap initiation bore an aura of truthfulness.

But Kolfinna appeared without fright as she took the microphone from Akinisie. "Sigfather warned us of a force far worse than himself that would take over if we did not unite the Nine Towers. It is clear that this force is you, Mikhail. If you are a war-maker and oppressor, you are not the Evolver. False Sigfather, we will complete our mission—all of us! You who want war, do you not know who you are messing with?!" Her voice resonated in the small shack, and its timbre sent chills. It was the strongest she had ever spoken. It was the strongest voice Mikkjal had heard from anywhere. The depth she had came from *somewhere else.* No one dared make a sound inside that shack.

"I see the wild woman has awakened," chuckled the sinister voice of Jorgson. *"But you are not her yet. When faced with true fear you'll only be that lonesome, flighty, crazy girl from the sea. Come at me and you'll meet your doom. Speak to anyone more using the Dust and I will destroy your fleet and your port. Remember who you are, cursed girl. Don't try to be anyone else. Go home! Her energy—she who you call Skadi—will rip you apart. Stay tuned to your radios, all. I will soon announce my intentions to provide protection to the planet. Protection and a new way. New connections on our world and to other planets too. Space is the future! All will flock to me and you will be—*

Sivkersok came and flipped the sound switch off. "We continue with the travel plans. I'm sick of radio shit, and that man has a bad voice." The Silent Wolf cut away at the war angst present in the room, while Akinisie, Mikkjal, Ungilattaqi, and everyone else looked around in apprehension. Sivkersok and Kolfinna shared a nod and a glance at the Shaman Ava. They knew something that others did not, or they at least felt something.

"I trust your Land's fleet to take on Qaqqariirvik," Siv spoke to the Captain Fálgeir and his crew. "Ungilattaqi can take my father and Kolfinna directly to Meniya. I will take Mikkjal on the longer route via Truth Peak, accompanied by Piitarjuaq and Aksaq." She nodded to the two young men by the door who had followed her to the Tower. "All other eastern Guides will be activated to conduct operations wherever they are needed. We have declared alliance with Pigasuallarivik, too. Our battle-ready Hunters should go by kayak when they're ready, with lance and bow. Ittoq, you and Singataaq should gather javelins and lances and go by large boat as soon as you can. I will make sure my pack is ready on the Glacier and into Northern Sivulliup Nunaat." She walked over to place a hand on Aksaq and Piitarjuaq's shoulders.

Cheers errupted from the Skrallanders and Gorrlanders present, and the foreign Sishilms understood the energy enough to know what was going on.

"Siv is right," spoke the giant Ungilattaqi. "We will take the Shishilms to shore by kayak and boat. Then we will veer off to join the Pigasuallarivik fleet. Any kayaker from our Folk may be free to join the fleet."

The war plan was set. Again, I set myself in place to follow my duty. My partner is no more, but she shall return even stronger. Duty has always been my theme, along with Land. I must accept. "Everyone is in the place they need to be. Everyone must know what they need to do by remembering. Skadi's Time is Wildness Time, Wildness Time is Remembering." You're right, old hermit, but it still hurts.

Mikkjal walked towards Kolfinna and spoke. "So, it's goodbye, then? We have no choice but to follow this plan I do not fully understand?" He was unsure if she would reply to him, since the only speaking she'd done was for her messages on the air.

The girl looked Mikkjal in the eye, eyes deeper and full of fire. She did bring herself to speak, again showing her new power and groundedness. "It's goodbye for now. If we succeed, we shall meet again in another era. But it shall no longer be Kolfinna who you shall meet. I will leave you now, but remember I am fated to you and to the Wolf. You both guide me, and you shall awaken me. You are the truest Skadisfolk of the time. Remember. Thank you." And with that, she gave him a kiss on the cheek and put a warm hand on Siv's shoulder. The understanding she had developed with the wild wolf-woman was such that words were not even necessary. So Kolfinna's eyes returned inward, and she wobbled on her feet, returning to her trance, and returning to the trance of the waiting place in which she was now dwelling. She was rising. She could sometimes be here, but the new time was intense for her still. Skadi's energy had yet to awaken every cell in her body and her aura.

All of this trouble only to separate? That wasn't how it had happened. He had misunderstood the person to whom he was fated. It was not Kolfinna, daughter of Helen, Siraz, Haral, and Bjorn, who he was called to serve. It was Skadi of Utgard, the Great-One-Who-Left, guardian of the wilderness and the world beyond. Utgard needed to be let in to this new world. And in a fight between Jorgson's great new modern order, and the savagery of the wild, it was the savagery that had to be supported more than a hundred times over.

The answer in the air was clear. This was where fate was calling them. Kolfinna will take form on her kayak crossing and ride to Meniya; taking form and taking root, the Great Qivittoq will enter the foundation of Truth Peak, as Ava had long prophesized. He would ride with Sivkersok and those in her pack, to awaken the unbridled force that She is to become, cherishing, nurturing, and freeing her in unbridled presence and Life in the Albrimir Mountains. Wildness to stop the war.

"So let us make haste," spoke Skadi's co-Guide, the Silent Wolf. "There is no time to lose."

Chapter 15
Dead Air

Ivaldi and the Gorrland Guards

Ivaldi joined in the rowing, eager to make it to shore before nightfall. That bastard Jorgson would get a taste of what was coming for him, a proper Gorrlander greeting. The sea was smooth, and the icebergs easy to navigate, so the captains and their thirteen other ships could easily follow the Chieftain's path.

Marja loved her Kolfinna so much that he was sure she would prefer sailing with the fleet and stabbing Jorgson herself than staying to man the Tower. For a brief while she worried about the welcome Kolfinna and Mikkjal got in Skralland, since it was never them who radioed, but always their Communicators speaking for them, saying they were all right. Now she must be so pleased to hear Akinisie tell that whining king off. They needn't worry about an honourable Folk like the Skrallanders. Their culture was different, but they shared so much of the same Land as Gorrland that taking positions on a war such as this was a matter of *instinct*, and not of politics. North Islanders all shared the same instinct. Perhaps even Torvallians shared this, and the Northern Soul was what was calling the three Lands to oppose Mikhail's vile onslaught.

Or maybe it was because Northerners were closer to Skadi.

The bald and strong Guard rowed hard at the back of his ship, but he saw a vessel coming from behind at even greater speed. It approached, southward bound from the glacier. Ivaldi immediately recognized it as Fálgeir's vessel, its red dragon sail visible from fifty kilometres away. They must have something to say, Eirà back from his foolish mission that somehow succeeded. The dark hermit was lucky Fálgeir was the captain and not Ivaldi, for he would've never allowed them to embark on a six-day journey at sea, around the Gap, to all the southern Lands, including Läckjell, of all places. Lucky for Eirà, lucky for Gorrland, lucky for Albrimir Fálgeir was the captain on that ship. Because he'd actually succeeded in gathering the Shishilms from the South, Ivaldi would stop rowing and hear what Eirà had to say.

Eirà wasn't on the ship, though. Neither were Kolfinna nor Mikkjal. Only the foreign Dust-readers were there, shivering in frigid air they never thought in their lives they would have to breathe.

"Chieftain, there's an announcement!" shouted Fálgeir once his ship was within hearing range. "Kolfinna and the Skralland Shishilm are kayaking close to our course to make landfall further north closer to Tiumen Village. Mikkjal is going by Land."

"By Land? You mean by *ice!*" Ivaldi shouted back. "He's taking the Isaveg?"
"Yes. With Sivkersok, the Girl From the East."

The Girl From the East. That was a name Astrid had heard so much about that she'd even made mention of her to him. Ungilattaqi talked about her so much it would look like he was ready to retire from his Chieftain role and leave it to her. *But why would Mikkjal take the Isaveg with her, when Kolfinna and the others were going directly to Meniya?*

The ship came beside Ivaldi's, and by now the other ships in the fleet had stopped rowing, with some even lowering their sails. "Kolfinna... she's not Kolfinna anymore," said the captain. "She's becoming Skadi. Chieftain, your goddess is taking physical form among us. And it is Kolfinna."

Ivaldi's Skadi amulet vibrated with those words —words which, on their own, made little sense.

But it seemed, somehow, that it might be true. He felt his goddess's energy in him. He would ask no more about this matter, for feeling Skadi was all he needed to know the path was the right one. Spirit stuff was not his domain. He would keep his mind to war.

"Another thing, sir," Fálgeir added. "Somehow Jorgson was able to intercept the mid-range transmission from Skralland East Tower. He says he has special control over the crystals."

Ivaldi cared nothing for those crystals in the first place and would gladly use one to shove up Jorgson's rear end to destroy him. "All right, Captain. Our fleet's all together anyway, so we don't need a radio."

The captain continued, his face long and his voice quick. "Jorgson has found a way to tap into all communications on the planet. This may even include short-range local Land frequencies. He knows some sort of superhuman ability to manipulate the crystals."

"All right! So, communication is down!" scoffed the Guard, placing a hand on his exposed bald head. "Where's Eirà?"

"He stayed, sir. Chieftain Akinisie had a matter she wanted to discuss with him."

"Right." Ivaldi was at least relieved that the Storyteller would no longer be around to suggest any new extra trips out of their way. He could at least concentrate all his energy on the battle plans.

"Ivaldi, look!" Captain Fálgeir cried out, pointing to far out at sea.

Ivaldi swivelled around. Seeing nothing in plain view, he removed his telescope and looked to the southwest. There it was. One of the ships he hadn't seen in thirty-two years, when he led the campaign that ensured they'd never visited North Island since. Its long, narrow hull, short single sail, and two dozen oarsmen. *Could they be after their man? Blasted hermit Storyteller should've never set foot on Läckjell!* And to make matters more urgent, he noticed that the ship was sailing in his direction, and beyond it were several other similar ships.

"Battle ready!" he shouted out to his crew and all the ships in earshot.

They allied with Jorgson, I bet! And Eirà just stole their Dust man. We'll have battle before we set foot on Torvallian soil!

As he heard the swords, spears, and bows readying and the shouts multiply, Ivaldi looked through the telescope again. The one ship was coming, making quite good speed, but the others stayed behind. But no… was it? Squinting his eyes, Ivaldi managed to see something moving. It was what he thought it was; a man was actively and enthusiastically waving a white flag at the ship's bow.

Ivaldi wouldn't have them lower their arms just yet. Läckjellians were tricky and deceitful people.

"Chieftain, on the radio," Captain Fálgeir interrupted his thoughts.

"Damn the radio! Those are Läckjellians coming! They show the white flag but I need to make sure it's not an ambush."

"It's Jorgson, though!" screeched the man on the ship with the many folks from foreign shores.

"Play it!" Ivaldi shouted, keeping his glance through his telescope.

And the captain turned up the volume on his portable crystal radio, so that the people on both ships could hear the broadcast.

"Greetings to all Folks of the planet Albrimir. My name is Mikhail, the leader and son of the Great Folk of Iorki."

The foreigners on Fálgeir's ship started to become agitated. Ivaldi's Communications Albrimese was rather rusty, but he could understand the gist of what was said on broadcasts if need be.

"I have an important announcement for everyone on this beautiful planet of ours," continued Jorgson's voice, laden with mock gentleness.

"He's even on local frequencies, Chieftain!" Fálgeir cried, standing unsteady on the ship's deck. *If he's right, that Westfolker captain has good reason to be scared…*

"*Yes, your Communicators right now must be realizing that I am not transmitting on the inter-Land frequency, but on all frequencies. You see, I control the airwaves now.*" A hint of laughter could be heard from the corner of the man's lips in his Tower across the sea. "*Rest assured, you will know why. Rest assured, you will regain your radio power back.*

"*Please do not see me as a conqueror but as a man who is here to herald a new era. For years, Communicators have been in contact with beings of other planets, both within our solar system and outside of it. Our chief Communicator Fraick Abbott is regularly in touch with Boldein and Ragnik. Yet, though we've been able to contact them, we've not had the means to travel to them.*

"*That is until now.*

"*Iorki has completed Albrimir's first ever ship for space travel. We will be launching a mission in one month, just in time to greet the spring!*"

"What? How long has Jorg been working on that?" Ivaldi shouted to no one in particular. Jorgson's enthusiasm over the air, in addition to the approaching vessel from the South, only made his heart beat even faster.

"What shall we do about the ship?" asked one of his warriors.

"Wait!" the Chieftain cried, listening to the radio.

"*Rest assured that our space mission is to be in the name of Albrimir as a whole. Our technology, which we've developed in space travel, weaponry, ground transport vehicles, and, most importantly, work and industry, is to be your technology. Albrimir will be united. But before then, I have the obligation to purge certain disruptive elements, and others who are downright evil.*

"*Kolfinna Helensdottir of Gorrland has discovered a form of witchcraft employed by the wretched savage woman responsible for the fall of Meniya a thousand years ago. This magic can bring about only madness and destruction. Savagery in its purest form.*

ANSUZ

She has made contact with various people from across Albrimir, who now have red dots on their hands. So as to ensure Albrimir's welfare, I am asking that any person with such marks be detained until the witch herself can be dealt with.

"And I will deal with her.

"The beast that she is will be cast out once more!

"Unfortunately, the good Shishilm Anavend of Kalyim has decided to side with sorceress Kolfinna, refusing to hand over Lia Jackrabbit, a girl from Iorki who Kolfinna communicated with. As such, we have commenced our military campaign in Kalyim. Our armies are marching steadily over the snow toward the villages of Tomsk, Ralmov, and the capital Tiumen. We shall also take the main Tower in the Algystaana Peaks. We shall occupy the Land and render it worthy of the heirs of Ancient Meniyan Civilization. We only intended to collect what was ours, but since Anavend refused, we will occupy his Land and overturn his rule. In its place we will build a worthy Kalyim, a worthy, dignified North.

"Do not interfere with our operation. Any Folk that does shall see the wrath of our army.

"Our army shall soon be the army of all Albrimir!

"Our spaceships shall be the spaceships of all Albrimir!

"Our Towers shall be the Towers of all Albrimir!

"Hand over the red-dotted devil's spawn. Until the day that they are no longer a threat, I shall control the airwaves, as a reminder of the power that exists in Iorki's technology. The choice is clear—Iorki and progress or Kolfinna and backwards beastliness.

"So, as Albrimir will be acquainted with Iorki's power, Albrimir shall see first-hand the technology we have built. As if our crystal radio control wasn't enough for you to recognize our formidable power, our new flagship of space will make a flight around the planet the day after tomorrow.

"Please wave as it flies overhead..."

Jorgson cackled and ended the transmission.

Ivaldi wanted to break his telescope, but wisely put it in his pocket and kicked the ship instead. "I'm going to lead our fleet to Torvall and drown every last Jorgian soldier. We'll see our glorious battle deaths rather than live in Jorgson's new world!"

But the warriors were more worried about the approaching ship. It still sailed alone and still waved the white flag.

"They won't attack. Some of their fighters probably still remember you." Ivaldi knew that voice to have come from old Haral Vindursson.

"I hope so. Pathetic raiders who mistook our peace for our weakness. An opportunistic Folk who still could easily ally with Jorgson. They could've timed it out perfectly to coincide with the message."

"We'll soon find out," the old man answered. Ivaldi took his Skadi amulet necklace into his hand. The goddess had always provided for him, and if she was appearing in Kolfinna's form, all the more beautiful and powerful is she.

"We'll let them approach to talk!" he shouted to his men.

Even as the foreign oarsmen passed the closest iceberg to the Gorrlanders, their bowman was still frantically waving the white flag. With the sea being calm, the crew's oars stirring the water was the only sound anyone could hear. All the crewmen had stopped what they were doing and stared out at the approaching ship. It was of fine quality, on par with those the Gorrlanders readily made. Ivaldi didn't recognize any of the oarsmen or the young flag-waving skipper but then again all the Läckjellians he faced off against were dead. Killed by Gorrlanders or Skrallanders they had been.

That campaign wouldn't be forgotten today. If they truly waved a white flag, times must be dire for them.

The ship approached and they dropped anchor. Oars were put aside. The crew had the familiar South Islander facial traits, watching the Gorrlander host in intense trepidation. A man tightly wrapped in wool stood up. He was of medium height, shoulder-length hair dishevelled, and thin. His age was hard to tell. With a neutral expression on his face, he inclined his head slightly as he stood before the Chieftain and his crew.

"Ivaldi," the man said.

"That is me," the Guard replied in his native language.

"You are known and heard in our Land," the man continued, in Albrimese. "Yet we now have someone we fear even more. So we do not seek war against Gorrland, but seek fraternity with you against him."

"Mikhail, Son of Iorki?" Ivaldi asked in the shared Albrimese tongue, taking one step closer.

"Yes." The man bowed before him. "My name is Rangi. I am a captain and warrior from Wanautipun or Läckjell as you call it. My crew are here to seek an alliance against Iorki."

"Why?" Ivaldi demanded. "Jorg threatens Torvall, not the South. We prepare for battle because he's threatened our lady Kolfinna. But what reason have you to go against this new world he proposes? Your Communicators announced that they wouldn't interfere with Mikhail Jorgson."

Rangi sighed and looked down. "Ivaldi, Son-Iorki's actions don't match his words." The captain did not hasten his speech but softened his gaze. "He announced his plan to attack Kalyim. But he has already attacked the South by different means."

"What do you mean?" Ivaldi shouted.

"The Shishilms, who I see on the ship, are safe, thanks to your Storyteller, Eirà. Hunapo is our own. He still lives thanks to Eirà. Son-Iorki sent agents to intimidate Communicators in Khairtai and Shá into submission. Later these agents learned the Shishilms fled to the islands. They came to our Land, looking for Hunapo. They killed one of our Communicators and intimidated our Chieftain into declaring for Iorki. Those with red dots are not plotting against any Land. They are the ones who carry the soul of the traditions of each Land. They are to be protected. And the lady who speaks to them is to be protected above all. Mikhail tries to gain support among our people. But in plotting against people who are dear to us, like Hunapo is for Wanautipun, he turns us against him." Rangi answered so that Ivaldi and Fálgeir's ships could be addressed. He then proceeded to speak to the elder of the islander men in Fálgeir's ship. In their discussion they mentioned the names of Kolfinna and Mikkjal.

"So Jorg—Iorki—has soldiers in the South?" Ivaldi asked when their exchange was done.

"Not soldiers but spies. Agitators. And now with his communications control we have no way of getting news."

"By Skadi and all the gods he must be stopped. Tell me, Rangi, or anyone else. Does Mikhail have enough equipment and men to fight in the South and in Torvall —Kalyim—at the same time?" Ivaldi turned around to ask any of the foreign Shishilms if they had any possible answers.

The young man from Steigsonland replied. "Being on the border, our Guides go to Iorki often, as do our Communicators. When they visit they always report that Iorki's authorities are secretive. They have noticed their technology. But the Iorkians always minimized their armed forces. Maybe they can fight on two fronts, but most likely not against serious resistance."

"Not against Gorrland's fighters, good Ivaldi," spoke Captain Rangi. "But if they are defeated in the North, it is entirely possible for them to go invade and occupy the South. We have sent half our fleet here to fight alongside you, Taqraup Nunaat, and Kalyim. Our other half defends the South. I ask that we seek alliance. We fight together in the North, in victory and defeat. But if, at some point, our Lands to the South are also threatened, will you, Gorrlanders, fight with us?"

Ivaldi thought of his Quest's words. *You shall partake in a battle across the sea that the entire planet would remember.* His heart tingled, as did his spine. This was what he was initiated for, as a Guard, thirty-five years ago.

"I want to fight with you, Rangi. I want us to help each other. But you know that our two peoples have a long history of mistrust. Please, I need you to give me some guarantee that we can trust you this time."

"I understand. And for that reason, we have brought Epa, our princess, on our journey." Rangi motioned to the ship and a young woman stood up. She walked to the ship's edge, vibrant and glowing, from her beautiful brown eyes and face. Her body was entirely wrapped in thick furs, and a rabbit fur hat covered her hair, no doubt long, dark, and graceful. She waved to Ivaldi, then to Fálgeir, and to the Shishilms. "She is the daughter of our leader. She is here to stay in Gorrland for the duration of this war as a symbol of good faith between our peoples."

Ivaldi was beside himself. This gesture was the closest they could come to a display of total trust. Offering their princess as a hostage could only mean that Captain Rangi was telling the truth about the events in the South. The two ships were joined, and the young princess stepped off, onto the deck of the Gorrland vessel.

"My lady," Ivaldi started, then kissed her hand when she removed her glove. "Your father was a young man when he sent attackers to our coasts after we had ceased raiding. He has admitted defeat. If he has sent you here as a peace offering, I gladly accept his display of humility. You will be treated with the utmost hospitality here for the duration of our campaign. Fálgeir, you ferry her quickly back to East Tower and ask Eirà to take her back to Gorrland Central Village."

"Thank you, Ivaldi," spoke Epa, bowing before the large warrior. "My father mentioned your name. He says that you always fight fiercely but with honour. He also admits that he fought dishonourably against your Folk in his youth."

"I was a young man then, too. The world has since changed a lot." He looked at Ragni, then the other four.

"Now, my question is for you, Captain, and for you all. How many ships and fighters do you have?"

"Eight ships this size here. Seven remain in Wanautipun. More are being built as we speak."

"I see. And you, miss, on your Land?" he turned to the Shishilm from Solicia, Filemu.

"Ten ships. Around seven or eight hundred warriors," the sturdy woman replied.

"Understood. In that case I shall extend my word. If you help us in our fight in the North—in Kalyim—we will help defend both South Islands, and the two Southern mainlands, if need be afterwards."

The men on Rangi's ship cheered. They were a rugged lot, but still could never pass themselves off as folks prepared to deal with the cold of the northern Lands.

"Princess Epa, you shall stay at a home in Westfolk, near the sea," Ivaldi spoke strongly but with kind eyes, then called Fálgeir over to take her on his ship.

"We will go as fast as possible back. I hope we meet Eirà."

"If not, ask one of the Skrallander Guides of the East to take her back. They can make the journey west in no time.

With the agreements made, Ivaldi nodded to the princess and saluted Captain Rangi, who raised anchor. Their ships sailed together, with the rest of the Gorrland fleet behind them. They would set off, former enemies united to defend those who spoke from the souls of their Lands. For although Skadi was a northern goddess, those who remained true to the wild, to their true selves as individuals and peoples, were those whom she held dear. Ivaldi, Warrior Chieftain of a fighting Folk in the North, found peace in the present course and its goals. He also found assurance in his plan, in case anything happened to the fleet, and they didn't return home to Gorrland from the Battle of Torvall.

ANSUZ

I will leave the avenging rearguard to the Beastriders. They will summon the beasts, like the Wild Men and Wild Women of the island once could. Only the Wild Ones can truly defend us now.